Searching
for the
Postmark

*Enjoy the journey to
Door County --- and beyond*

[signature]

a novel by

Jeff Donovan

Editor: Scott Renschler
Proofreader: Dick Londo
Cover and book designer: Fiona Raven
Lighthouse photograph: John Donovan

National Library of Canada Cataloguing in Publication

Donovan, Jeff, 1960-
      Searching for the postmark / Jeff Donovan.
ISBN 1-4120-0025-4
      I. Title.
PS3604.O56S42 2003   813'.6   C2003-901353-7

 *Printed in Victoria, Canada*

This book was published *on-demand* in cooperation with Trafford Publishing.
On-demand publishing is a unique process and service of making a book available for retail sale to the public taking advantage of on-demand manufacturing and Internet marketing.
On-demand publishing includes promotions, retail sales, manufacturing, order fulfilment, accounting and collecting royalties on behalf of the author.

Suite 6E, 2333 Government St., Victoria, B.C. V8T 4P4, CANADA
Phone   250-383-6864   Toll-free   1-888-232-4444 (Canada & US)
Fax   250-383-6804   E-mail   sales@trafford.com
Web site   www.trafford.com   TRAFFORD PUBLISHING IS A DIVISION OF TRAFFORD HOLDINGS LTD.
Trafford Catalogue #03-0387   www.trafford.com/robots/03-0387.html

10   9   8   7   6   5   4   3   2   1

Acknowledgements

~

My opinion of acknowledgement pages has changed considerably now that I've written a book. For, while there were many lonely nights spent staring at a blank page, this book was not a solitary achievement, and acknowledgement pages just became much more meaningful to me now that I have so many people to thank. So, just in case this turns out to be the only book I write, I'd like to take this opportunity to thank all those who helped me along the way.

On the personal side I'd like to thank my wife, who put up with my insecurities over the years I kept saying I should finish the book; my three girls, for their patience when I was preoccupied and said 'just one more sentence' one too many times; my father, who prodded me to finish, sometimes when I didn't want him to, sometimes when I needed him to; my brother and his wife, who lent me the use of their cabin in the woods as a writer's retreat; my sister and her husband, who raced each other to finish first, and gave me hope that the book held interest; and finally my little sister, who called me after the first chapter to say that she was hooked, and that she could picture my mother reading the book at the cottage.

On the literary side I'd like to thank Nan R and Jenny W, who fought through first readings of a less than good book; Dick Londo, for his expertease in prufe reeding; Fiona Raven, for her assistance, guidance, and patience with page layout and cover design; the people at Trafford Publishing, who helped turn a dream into a reality; and finally, my very sincere thanks to my editor, Scott Renschler, who helped me turn a manuscript into a novel. I sure did hate editing, though I sure did need an editor. The book is better for his efforts. Thanks, Scott.

For my mother,

Mary Marcia Donovan,

whose death, and life,

provided the inspiration

for this book,

and whose spirit was with me

during its writing.

Searching
for the
Postmark

a novel by

Jeff Donovan

Chapter 1

⁓

*I*nching her way along the desolate country lane, wipers beating on high in complement with the slashing rain, Colleen O'Connell knew she was lost. The map spread across her lap was of little use, due to a broken dome light, except when a flash of lightning illuminated the sky. When she did manage to sneak a peek at the crumpled map, the tiny gravel road she was on was nowhere to be found. As she wound aimlessly along the deserted lane it struck Colleen that she had never felt so lost and alone in all her life.

She had been driving since early that morning, and the long trip was beginning to take its toll. Two and a half days from Arizona, she had driven 1700 miles, arriving in Chicago in time to be greeted by the rush-hour traffic. Winding her way through the maze of freeways, barely moving out of first gear, she had thought about pulling off and getting some much needed rest rather than driving the remaining five hours to Door County. But she had come this far already, and feeling so close, she couldn't wait to make the final leg of her journey to Brenden's beloved Door. If she pushed on, she would be there by midnight.

Almost as soon as she crossed the border into Wisconsin the

weather began to change. It was hot and humid in Chicago, unusually so for this early in the year, though by the time she was through Milwaukee the air had turned decidedly cooler, and held the faint smell of rain. As the city wound down behind her, the landscape changed from cold concrete to lush green rolling hills. Rows of newly sprouting corn were just becoming visible in the fields she passed, mesmerizing her with their patterns. Lake Michigan was intermittently visible on her right, its deep blue waters a stark contrast to the fields of green. Long gravel driveways led to old wooden farmhouses perched atop each rolling hill; black and white cows lay scattered in the fields beyond, melting into the black roofs that sheltered proud red barns. Colleen rolled down her window to take in the setting and began to drift off, thinking about Brenden and the land he so loved, this place that was so foreign to her.

Brenden had been the one person she had truly loved. The only time they were apart was summers, when he would come, alone, to his special place in the northeast corner of Wisconsin. Brenden had always pleaded with Colleen to come with him for a summer, or part of one. "Just come with me once," he had said, "and you'll know why I go back every year." But Colleen never had come with him, not once in eleven summers, and now she wondered why.

Brenden had always flown into Chicago at the start of each summer, driving the extra five hours to The Door "to better appreciate where I'm going, and what I'm leaving behind." Colleen was beginning to understand why. Only two hours out of the bustle of Chicago, she was comfortably north of Milwaukee, in the middle of beautiful farm country, a cool breeze blowing in her window. Though tired from her long trip, she felt relaxed. She was finally on her way to see the place that Brenden loved, so she could be with him again.

Brenden O'Connell, Colleen's brother, had been dead for six months.

A loud clap of thunder jolted Colleen from her memories. In

the distance she saw a thick line of dark clouds drowning out the remaining daylight on the horizon. The air coming in through her open window had become noticeably crisp, and she found herself suddenly shivering in her cutoffs and tank top. She knew that Brenden was welcoming her with one of those brooding black storms he so loved.

As she rolled up her window, Colleen saw she was approaching Manitowoc, where Brenden had always gotten off the freeway to take the back roads the rest of the way. "Ten miles shorter, ten minutes longer, ten times prettier," he used to say. She decided to pull over for a quick rest stop.

Chilled by the cold as she filled up with gas, Colleen reached into the back seat of her car, grabbed a baggy old sweater, and headed into the station. Warming her hands around a steaming cup of coffee, she studied the map on the wall. Though Brenden had preferred to take the scenic route along the lakeshore, it was nearly dark, and soon she would have no view, no matter which route she took. Colleen felt suddenly sad that she wouldn't arrive in Door County in the daylight, as Brenden had loved to. "You just come over this one hill and – bam! – it's cherry blossoms as far as you can see." A single tear slipped out of the corner of her eye. She wiped it away, looked out at the dark storm clouds looming on the horizon, and decided the prudent thing to do would be to stay on the freeway as long as she could.

By the time she reached Green Bay she was in the middle of the storm, crawling along at half speed, inching her way more slowly thereafter, on the two-lane highway that cut up the peninsula – the last leg of her journey. Wipers on high, radio off, defroster blasting, she drove on, eyes unblinking, darting across the road from side to side. The deer her little car had almost kissed a while back still had her heart racing. Brenden may have enjoyed going out with binoculars at twilight to look for deer, but Colleen would be happy if she didn't see another one the rest of the night.

Making her way northward, searching for the road under the beam of her headlights, she almost missed the lighted wooden sign welcoming visitors to Door County. *I finally made it, Brenden,* she thought to herself as she crossed the big bridge in Sturgeon Bay that separated the peninsula from the mainland. She knew she was nearly there. "Half an hour over the bridge, on the quiet side," Brenden used to say. She knew the way by heart, Brenden had said it so often. "Institute, Valmy, then Jacksonport – the golf course and causeway lead right to my fort."

But the first town she came to was Carlsville, not really a town, and she knew she had missed the fork in the road. Trying to cut back across the peninsula on the tiny back roads, she had gotten herself twisted and hopelessly lost, and now hadn't the faintest idea where she was, or in which direction she was heading. She could barely see the road for the storm, she was tired, cold and hungry, and she was becoming a bit scared.

To her surprise and relief she came to an intersection with a wooden signpost pointing towards Jacksonport and soon found herself driving past Vi's grocery, then north out of town, back on course – over Hibbard's Creek, past the wayside, then over Hein's Creek. Taking a sweeping right turn near the sign for Kangaroo Lake, she split the fairways as she drove through the break in the trees that was the old golf course, her little car shaken by the winds blowing over the open expanse. If she hadn't appreciated the storm before, she surely did now.

At the end of the golf course she turned left, onto the road that would lead her to Brenden's. Approaching the causeway that divided Kangaroo Lake in two, she heard the sound of the waves crashing over the road just before they came into view. By the time she could come to a stop on the wet pavement she was halfway across the causeway, her little car being pushed sideways by each wave that hit it. Barely able to see the low road drowning beneath her, she could only sense how near she was coming to the lake, and that there were no guardrails between her and the water.

Gripping the wheel firmly with both hands, she aimed for the centerline, pointed herself toward the far shore, and stepped on the gas. The water poured across the causeway, momentarily halting her progress as each wave hit her, the tiny car shifting closer and closer toward the edge. A few feet forward, a few inches sideways, a few hundred yards to go.

Struggling to keep her car on the low road, and out of the lake, Colleen willed her way across the causeway, somehow managing to reach the far shore safely. Relieved, she pulled over to the side of the road to collect herself. Shaken emotionally, and shaking physically, she put the car back in gear and drove on, thankful to have only the rain to contend with for the last few miles. Coming up the hill that led away from the lake, her damp car began to sputter, coughed a few times, then backfired, the headlights flickering off as the engine gave out.

~

The din of the rain on the metal porch roof had long ago drowned out the song that rose softly from the tape deck beside him, though Brian Bailey neither heard, nor cared. Nor did he notice the headlights that flickered off at the bottom of the hill below him.

Brian hadn't slept well in the year since he'd moved into this house, nor had he in the year or so prior to that. It was his habit, on nights he couldn't sleep, to walk through the darkened rooms of the house, then sit on the porch, playing his tape as he drifted off with the night.

As he heard the Clancy Brothers finish the same song for the eighth time in a row, Brian silently sang along:

And we'll all go together
To pluck wild mountain thyme
All around the blooming heather
Will you go, Lassie, go?

∾

Colleen O'Connell surveyed her circumstances. The usually sound advice to stay put and wait for help didn't seem to make much sense. Already soaking wet from looking under the hood of her car, she was becoming more than a bit chilled, quickly realizing her Arizona wardrobe was wholly inappropriate for a Wisconsin spring. She had rarely seen another car since crossing the big bridge in Sturgeon Bay, the good people of Door County having more sense than to be out on a night like this, and thought it unlikely anyone might venture down this empty lane the rest of the night. Colleen decided to walk a few hundred yards in either direction, in search of a house with a light on.

Leaving the car behind, she headed up the lane, away from the causeway. Ascending the steep hill, she began to make out the scattered shapes of her surroundings as her eyes adjusted to the color of night. Rounding a slight curve in the road, she paused, focusing on the light that shone from a window in the farmhouse atop the hill. Glancing back at her stalled car, she headed toward the light.

As she made her way toward the house, Colleen could, during flashes of lightning, catch a glimpse of the setting. A long, tree-lined driveway angled up the hill toward the house. To the left of the driveway stood a barn and some outbuildings; to the right, set off from the rest, an old wood-framed farmhouse drew her toward it. Jutted with dormers and bay windows, the roof crowned by three chimneys, the place was charmingly old, yet well kept. A huge porch wrapped its way around two sides of the house, across the front and down one side, back toward the barnyard and outbuildings. The light still glowed from a window off the front porch. As she approached, she was hopeful someone might still be awake.

Rounding the last tree that lined the drive, Colleen was shocked and surprised to find someone sitting on the porch, staring out into the darkness. She paused. The figure on the porch did not move.

He sat on the top step in baggy shorts and an oxford shirt, apparently unaware of the cold, or the rain, or her. Through the din of raindrops on the metal porch roof she could hear the soft lilting of an Irish folk song rising in the background. She studied him for a moment, then sneezed as a chill ran through her.

~

Brian Bailey was startled by the sudden sound. His first thought was that one of his girls was catching a cold and was in need of some medicine, or a glass of water, or a hug and a story. Turning to see which child needed him, he froze as he stared at the unexpected visitor.

She stood near the corner of the porch, the prettiest, most pathetic-looking woman he had ever seen. Drenched beyond soaking, her wet hair was matted flat against her head and face, her sweater dripping faster than the pouring rain. The long, tanned legs shivered between a pair of frayed cutoff shorts and flat brown leather sandals. He sat there a moment, focusing.

Packing away his memories, he rose. "Can I get you an umbrella?" he joked as he motioned her onto the porch. "Come on, let's get you in out of the rain." He led her down the side porch toward the back of the house, grabbing an armful of firewood from the bin under the bay window. Opening the screen door, he invited her in.

Colleen hesitated, then entered.

Jackets and sweaters hung on pegs along the wall of the narrow hallway, shoes and boots lined on the mat below. A tiny powder room sat on her right, the slanting ceiling barely allowing space to stand before the sink. To her left, a staircase, which curved as it rose. At the far end of the hall the stairway continued, angling down toward the basement, the steps steeper, the headroom shorter.

The hallway opened into a vast old kitchen, built to accommodate a large family of farm children. As he turned on the light, Colleen thought she'd taken a step back in time, to another century.

The large room was filled with antiques, and the smell of dark coffee. Pots and utensils hung from the rafters above, alongside bunches of spices and dried wildflowers. A brass-handled ice chest and screened pie safe stood against one wall, on either side of a metal-lined dry sink, an ivy winding its way through the earthen crocks and copper bowls that rested on top. The oven and chopping block sat opposite these, next to an old Hoosier cabinet with white porcelain knobs, a tin scoop dangling between the flour and sugar bins. In the far corner of the room, near two swinging doors set against opposite walls, the long kitchen table was pushed back against the wall, half the chair space unused. Beside the table an old Franklin stove stood against the back wall, its dying embers still visible. Colleen was drawn towards the remnants of warmth they offered.

Brian followed, setting the firewood on the floor by the Franklin. Making his way back across the wide pine floorboards to the sink, he filled the teakettle, lighting a burner as he opened the oven door and flipped some switches. Colleen heard the sound of the pilot lighting, saw the blue flame rise from below.

"This will heat up faster than the old Franklin," he said.

She sneezed.

"Stand over here while I get you a towel," he continued as he disappeared down the narrow hallway.

Returning from the powder room, he handed her the towel. "So," he inquired as he grabbed a ladle and saucepan from overhead, "what has you out on a night like this?"

"I was on my way to my brother's place. I've never been there before, and I got lost in the storm," she explained as she dried her face. "Then the waves came up over the causeway and soaked my car. It stalled down the road a bit. I saw a light on in your window, and, well, here I am."

"And your car is stranded out there?" he asked, nodding toward the window as he grabbed a jar from the pantry.

"Yes, and it won't start, and all my clothes are in it, and my brother's address, and everything." The events of the past hour were beginning to catch up with Colleen, as were her concerns.

"We'll get it sorted out," Brian assured her, reading the look on her face. "Everything looks different in the morning."

"But my car?"

"I can get it for you."

"But it doesn't start."

"If the waves came up over the causeway it's probably just wet," he explained. "I'll tow it up to the shed, let it dry out. By morning it should be running just fine."

"But I can't ask you to go out in that storm."

"Well, your car will never dry off out there in the rain," he answered. "Besides, you'll need your things."

"Thank you," she smiled, then sneezed once again.

"But first," Brian instructed, "you need to get dried off and warmed up before we worry about your car."

Colleen turned and held her hands out toward the warmth that rose from the oven. One concern taken care of.

Brian loaded a few logs into the old Franklin. "Something warm to take the chill off?" he asked. He scurried about the room, gathering some items out of the Hoosier cabinet, heating a jar of homemade soup, slicing some bread, the efficiency of his movements showing his familiarity in the kitchen.

"Something warm sounds nice," she answered, "if it's not too much trouble."

"No trouble," he said. "You look like you could use it."

"I'm sure I must look quite the mess."

"I'm sorry," he began to apologize, "I didn't mean to…"

"That's all right," she laughed. "I must look about how I feel right now."

Brian leaned back against the sink and studied her for a moment. She stood in front of the open oven door, the towel hung loosely over her shoulders, her hands stretched out toward the warmth that rose from within. Her pose reminded him of his mother, standing in front of the stove in her bathrobe on a cool fall morning at the cottage. Her features, vaguely familiar, reminded him of another. On a cold, wet night Brian thought back to a warm sunny day, long ago. "You look fine," he said as he began to drift away, "just fine."

A sudden chill ran through Colleen as she watched the blank look come over his face. She knew the position she found herself in, alone in a strange house in the middle of the night, in the middle of nowhere, and she began to grow apprehensive about the hollow eyes that seemed to stare past her. Hearing the crackle of logs starting up in the Franklin, she made her way toward the flames, distancing herself from his empty look.

The teakettle began to whistle. He removed it from the stove, taking a cup down from overhead, mixing together the items he'd set on the chopping block. "My mother used to make these," he said as he offered the steaming mug to her. "A hot toddy, she called it."

Colleen took a sip, instantly feeling the warmth spread through her. "It's wonderful," she said. "What is it?"

"Hot water, brandy, a drop or two of honey. My mom used to make them at night every now and then," he remembered, "to warm you up, help you relax."

"I think it's working already," Colleen said as she took another sip. "Thanks."

"Not at all. Have a seat," he offered, motioning her toward the table. He returned to the stove, taking a taste of the soup from the tip of the wooden spoon, then grabbing a few spices from overhead and crumbling them into the pot. "Soup's almost ready," he called over his shoulder. "I'll head out for your car once it's done." Crossing the room, he set the bread on the table. "Would you like a hot bath, after you eat," he asked, "to help take the chill off?"

Colleen hesitated. "That's very nice, thank you," she replied tentatively as she reached for the pendant on her necklace. "But I'm not sure if I'd be completely comfortable with that. I mean, I appreciate the offer, and I don't intend any disrespect, but ... I don't know...I don't know you, and I'm ..."

"I understand," Brian said, raising his hand to stop her as he returned to the stove. "I've got daughters."

"I don't mean to offend," Colleen tried to explain, "with the help you've already given me. But, well..." she trailed off.

Brian stirred the soup, staring out the window into the darkness for a moment before turning to face her. Her look of uncertainty reminded him of the frightened little bunny the girls had taken in earlier that spring and nursed back to health. "I guess I never thought about it from your position," Brian said. "My mistake. A woman's perspective is sometimes missed around here," he explained. "I just thought, with your clothes soaked through and all, a bath might help take the chill out."

"Well, I won't say that getting out of these wet clothes and into a warm bath wouldn't be nice," Colleen confided, "but..."

Brian turned down the soup and leaned back against the chopping block. "Look, I understand your concerns," he offered. "I know you don't know me from Adam, but you can trust me when I say you've got nothing to worry about. I'd like to think I'm a little further along on the food chain than someone who would prey on a stranger in need. Besides, I'm guessing you're here because you didn't have a whole lot of other options. Lights are usually out at all the neighbors by the time I finally roll off to bed."

"Well, yes, yours was the first light I saw," Colleen acknowledged.

"So," he said, "sometimes we have to play the cards we're dealt. If you're worried about being alone with me, you're not. The girls are asleep upstairs. Of course," he added, "if they can sleep through this storm they just might sleep through your screams."

Brian paused, waiting for the smile that never came. "You do understand," he continued, "that this will go a lot more smoothly if you laugh at my jokes."

"How about I laugh at the funny ones?" Colleen smiled back.

"Ouch," Brian chuckled. "And to think I was actually a little worried about leaving you alone in the house with my girls while I go get your car."

"Now that one was funny," Colleen laughed as she sat back in her chair, relaxing for the first time.

"So," Brian asked as he brought the soup to the table, "do we have a deal?"

"I'm sorry?"

"You don't chainsaw the girls while I'm out getting your car and I'll refrain from doing the same to you after I get back. Fair is fair, don't you think?"

"Was I that bad?"

"No, not really," he replied. "You had legitimate concerns. Hell, sometimes I worry about being alone with myself. But we all need a friend now and then, and for better or worse, tonight you're stuck with me."

"I'm beginning to realize I could have done worse."

"So, how about that bath, then?" he asked again. "Everything else around here may be broken, but the lock on the bathroom door still works."

"Well, a bath does sound nice," Colleen conceded. "Thanks."

"Great. I'll get it ready while you eat, then go get your car when you're in the tub. Phone's over there if you'd like to call your brother," Brian pointed out as he headed down the narrow hallway and up the curving back stairs.

~

Colleen sat alone in the empty room, staring up at the antique wooden phone that hung on the wall, the receiver resting silently alongside the mouthpiece, no one to call. She remembered how Brenden used to call her at all hours of the night when he just couldn't wait to tell her some news. Colleen took a sip of the warm drink, then turned her attention to the meal.

A hearty barley soup steamed up at her, the thick broth pulling the barley down to the bottom of the bowl. Only the thinnest pieces of carrot floated on top, along with some minced garlic. The soup was warm and soothing as she took her first few spoonfuls, though it offered a hint of the freshly crumbled spices that hung overhead. The homemade bread was served warm, with soft real butter, the air holes that bubbled throughout the slices holding the light flavor of cheese.

Looking up from her meal, Colleen peered across the large open room, then down the narrow hall he had left by. Had he really made the soup and bread himself, she wondered? Why had he been sitting alone on the porch so late at night, she thought, in the middle of a storm? And why had he drifted off when he stared at her before?

She was startled when he appeared behind her, entering the kitchen through one of the swinging doors in the corner beyond the table. He stood there, a childish look of confusion on his face.

"Is something wrong?" Colleen asked.

"Well, I, um...I don't have much in the way of clothes to

offer you," he apologized, "for after your bath. I mean...well, you see...the thing is...."

"Oh, don't worry about me," she offered, "anything's fine. It'll just be for a little while anyways, until I get my things."

"Right. Your things. The car," he said, as if the thought had just come to him. "Well, I left something on the back of the bathroom door, for now. Tub's filled, towel and hair dryer laid out. First door on your right, at the top of the stairs," he said, pointing up as he headed down the back hall. "More soup on the stove if you like," he called back as he grabbed a jacket off the rack and went outside, the screen door slamming shut behind him as he jumped down the porch steps and crossed the barnyard toward the shed.

Colleen stared down the empty hall, puzzled by his sudden unease over the clothes, then picked up her spoon. Having been more cold and hungry than she realized, she quickly finished her soup, and the bread.

Standing between the stove and sink, debating another small bowl of the delicious soup, Colleen heard the sound of the tractor as he backed out of the shed. Peering out the window, she watched his silhouette, illuminated in the barnyard light, his head bent into the driving rain. She rinsed her bowl, leaving the remaining soup simmering on low, then headed up the curling back hall stairs.

A child's nightlight softly lit the upper hallway, guiding her to the bathroom door, left slightly ajar. Tastefully done in the period of the kitchen, the bathroom looked like a picture from a magazine. Two braided porcelain sinks sat below matching medicine cabinets that hung on the wall above them, their mirrors reflecting the antique commode on the opposite wall, its exposed brass pipes running up to the hanging water closet, a brass pull chain dangling from its side. Against the far wall, set on a rise in the corner, an old claw-foot tub sat perched on four enormous brass feet. The tub was filled with steaming water and soothing bubbles, inviting her to join them. Colleen locked the door, slipped out of her wet clothes, and climbed in.

~

Reaching Colleen's car, Brian was already completely soaked through, his clothes clinging to his skin – cold, wet, and heavy. The car had been farther down the road than she'd led him to believe, a good walk downhill in fair weather. He thought of her trudging up the hill against the cold wind and rain. She shouldn't have been out driving this late at night in such a storm, alone. Many a driver had trouble on that causeway in just this kind of weather. Most ended up seeking refuge at one of the houses at the bottom of the hill. Few ever climbed the hill to his house. Why had she? Why hadn't she just pulled over, called her brother, and waited out the storm? Why did she end up at his house, and on this of all nights?

~

Colleen climbed out of the tub and wrapped herself in the soft red towel he had left out for her. Everything would be fine, she thought to herself. She could feel it. The bath had warmed her body, the soup satisfied her hunger, the hot toddy eased her fears. She felt relaxed and at home in the period room, so different from her modern condo back home. Looking at her reflection in the beveled mirror, she wondered how it was that she found herself in this room. Then she wondered what she was going to do with her hair.

On top of the dry sink sat a man's electric razor and a hair dryer, plugged in, along with an assortment of brushes and hair clips. Colleen remembered the brightly colored children's coats hanging in the back hall, underneath his jackets. Had she seen a woman's coat, she wondered? She turned the hairbrushes over. Hand painted on the back handle of each was a name. *Shannon. Kerry. Mom.* Two of the brushes were full of hair. She grabbed the one with little trace of recent use, switched the hair dryer on, and began to brush out her long hair.

Hair dried, she noticed the clothes he had left out. On the back of the door hung a man's white cotton dress shirt and a pair of Green Bay Packer sweatpants. Colleen recalled how he had been uneasy and unsure of himself when he said he had nothing for her to wear, then looked back at the unused hairbrush. She slipped into the clothes he had left and opened the bathroom door.

The nightlight on the landing faintly lit the long hallway, and the three closed doors that lined the way. At the far end of the hall sat a stained glass window, backlit by the light in the barnyard. Colleen walked down the hall toward the window and peered out. Visible in the distance, at the bottom of the hill, was her car, and the tractor, and him.

Leaning back from the window, she looked at the two sets of steps on either side of her. To her left the attic stairs curved their way up, past the push-button light switch, into the darkness. The other stairway curved away from her, back downstairs. A faint blue light rose from the darkness below. Drawn toward the light, Colleen descended the stairs.

Reaching the bottom step, Colleen could feel the layout of the old farmhouse, as if she'd always lived there. To her left was a swinging door, certain to be one of the two in the corner of the kitchen. To the right, tucked under the slanted ceiling, a tiny desk was built into the crook of the alcove under the stairs. A blue light rose from the computer that sat on the desk. Colleen drifted toward the monitor, and the unfinished letter on the screen.

∼

June 15
My Dear Christine,

It's twenty years today that we first met. Happy Anniversary, Honey. I love you.

Who would have thought when we met in the bookstore that day that a chance meeting would so alter and entwine two lives. I'll never forget how I felt, or how you looked, as we walked down that street, your books under my arm, then stopped at the sidewalk café for coffee and iced tea. You wore a bright yellow sundress. Your golden-brown hair was long and straight and shiny, with a few light streaks the color of the summer sun. Your eyes, deep brown, twinkled back at me, your smile raising your full cheeks. I remember how I thought I'd never seen anyone so beautiful, and I still haven't to this day. I knew right then I'd be carrying your books for the rest of my life.

I know you've been watching me today. Some days I need you to more than others. Certain days, special days like today, are the worst. I can't seem to function at all on these days, and I'm afraid I'm not much good to the girls either. I can handle the days I'm supposed to be strong for them, like birthdays and holidays, put on my game face and give them a happy memory. But it's days like today, special days with memories only you and I share, that seem the longest. Oh Honey, I miss you so much, sometimes I just feel like I'll never be able to....

Colleen heard the tractor coming up the drive. Feeling suddenly intrusive for having read the letter, she pushed her way through the swinging door into the kitchen, where she stirred the soup and put the tea kettle on to boil.

∾

Car in tow, Brian Bailey pulled the tractor into the shed and shut off the engine. He was cold and tired, and wanted nothing more than to get out of his wet clothes, take a hot shower, and climb into bed before the girls woke up. Hanging his jacket on a hook in the hallway, he sat on the bottom step, removed his soaked boots, and remembered he had left her suitcase in the car.

Walking down the narrow hall in his wet socks, he entered the kitchen. She stood at the stove, lazily stirring the soup, the teakettle whistling softly beside her. His long white shirt hung down over the sweatpants, the top two buttons left open, revealing the gold cross and chain that lay flat against her chest. The sleeves of the shirt were rolled back a few times, like Christine used to wear it.

"How about a hot toddy," she greeted him as she took the kettle from the stove. "I'd be happy to make it if you tell me how."

"Make it a double," he answered, shaking off the comparison. "Brandy, two fingers, hot water, and a spoonful of honey."

"I'll have it right up."

"Not much of a host, am I?" he said as he went and stood in front of the warm Franklin. "How was your bath?"

"Oh, wonderful, thank you. Warmed me up, calmed me down. Did you have much trouble with my car?"

"Not really, just took a little longer than I thought. One of the wheels had slid into the ditch," he explained. "I doubt there's anything much wrong with your car, just wet, I'd guess. I pulled it into the shed to let it dry out. Should be fine in the morning."

"Thank you, again," she said as she brought him the drink.

"No problem," he answered as he cradled the warm mug in his hands and took a sip, remembering his mother doing the same in her rocking chair.

"No, really," she continued, "I mean it. I can't thank you enough for all the help you've given me, um…."

"Brian," he filled in. "I'm sorry, I guess we never introduced ourselves. I'm Brian. Brian Bailey," he informed her. "And you're welcome."

"Well, thanks again, Brian," she smiled. "And my name's Colleen, Colleen O'Connell. Well, Colleen's really my middle name, but that's what everyone calls me. My first name is Mary. Mary Colleen O'Connell." As she spoke her full name Colleen noticed his grip tighten around the mug, his knuckles whitening. "Is something wrong?" she asked.

"No," he said softly, "nothing's wrong. Bit of a coincidence, that's all. You see," he explained, "my mother's name was Mary, Mary Margaret, but she called herself Maggie. And my wife's name was Mary," he continued, his speech slowing as he thought of the computer screen in the alcove, "Mary Christine, but she went by Christine."

She watched him as he drifted off. He stood across from her, not seeing her. His brown hair, darkened by the rain, lay in curls down the back of his collar. His rough, weathered face looked as if it hadn't seen a razor in days, yet it was soft just the same. His lips were full, his nose thick but not unpleasant, turning up slightly at the end.

His eyes. His eyes were what drew her in. Blue. Not bright, like the sky, nor deep, like the ocean, but troubled, like the blues. And distant. They were staring at her, not seeing her, but looking through her, past her, or into her. There was a certain gentleness to them as well, a troubled tenderness. She wondered what he saw with them at that moment, and what she could see in them.

He blinked.

"So," he asked, nodding toward the phone. "Get a hold of your brother?"

Colleen shook her head.

"Was he expecting you? Will he be worried?" Brian asked. "Should you try and call again?"

Colleen looked over at the phone. "No need to call again," she said after a moment.

"Where does he live?"

"On Dried Marsh Lane."

"Why, that's just a few miles up the road from here," he told her. "I can drive you up there now, if you'd like."

"Thanks, but no," she replied. "It's late. The morning will be fine," she said, "if that's all right."

"No problem," he answered. "To be honest, I wasn't really looking forward to going back out in that storm anyways. Sofa bed in the living room," he offered, "if you like."

"That would be great," she thanked him, "if it's not too much trouble."

"Not at all, if you don't mind making it up yourself," he said as he spread his arms out to dry in front of the Franklin. "I'd drip all over it in these wet clothes."

Brian led Colleen through one of the swinging doors and down the front hall, alongside the stairway, and the alcove with the computer. Entering the living room he pushed aside an old washstand that had been made into a coffee table, plates of glass laid where the washtubs used to sit, the wringer rising between.

"Pillows and blankets in the trunk," he pointed out to her. "Fresh sheets on the bed, line dried."

"Thanks."

"I'm sorry," he apologized, "but I'm afraid I forgot to grab your suitcase when I ran in from the rain. Anything else you need right now?" he asked.

"No, thanks," she said, "I'll be fine. Go ahead and get out of those wet clothes."

"I think I'll do that," he said as he headed toward the door. "Leave a light on if you want."

"Thanks."

"That's about it, then, I guess," he said as he turned to leave. "Except," he added, "that I should warn you the girls will probably be down fairly early in the morning, though hopefully they won't bother you too soon. Sleep well."

"I believe I will," Colleen replied. "Good night, and thank you again."

～

Colleen pulled out the hide-a-bed, the fresh scent of the sheets unfolding with the mattress. Retrieving the blankets and pillows from the trunk, she could hear his footsteps as he walked through the house – turning off the lights, and computer, rinsing the mugs out in the kitchen sink, then slowly climbing the back stairs and making his way across the floorboards that creaked overhead. As the sound of his footsteps faded she sat down on the edge of the bed and surveyed the room.

Decorated in the same antique theme as the rest of the house, the living room had the comfortable feel of a place that hadn't changed much since it was built. A commanding two-piece butternut hutch stood in one corner, the glass-faced doors on the top half revealing a collection of old medical textbooks and antique pill bottles. On the wall behind the sofa hung a 1906 bicycle road map of Wisconsin, framed by an array of ancient cobbler's tools and a wooden hay rake. Near the front door stood an old school desk, complete with inkwells, the black metal legs that had once been screwed into the floor of a one-room schoolhouse supporting a walnut writing top, which lifted open, offering a home for books and slate. A spinning wheel sat in the opposite corner, old daguerreotypes displayed in handmade barn-board frames hanging on the wall behind it.

Sitting on the corner of the bed as she took in the décor of the room, Colleen found herself wondering which of the closed doors in the upstairs hallway led to his room. Was it also decorated to period, with a fine oak dresser and matching wardrobe? Was there a big brass bed that sank down in the middle, engulfing him under thick, soft quilts? Did he sleep alone?

The sudden click of the pump kicking on in the basement startled her from her thoughts. She finished making the bed, then climbed in under the covers, drawing in the sweet smell of the line-dried sheets. Laying her head on the pillow, she began to think of Brenden.

She had waited so long to come here – six months since his death, but eleven summers of his life. Why had she not come before, just once in all the times he'd asked, to be here with him, to see him in life in this place he loved, not remember him in death in a place he would come to no more? She knew she was finally so close, "just a few miles up the road," Brian had said. Yet, for as far as she had come, for as long as it had taken her to get here, for as close as she now was, Colleen no longer felt in any great hurry to get to Brenden's, and she wondered why. Replacing the longing, nervous desire she'd felt over the past six months was a calming, soothing feeling of comfort, of belonging. Pulling the covers tightly around herself, she drifted off to sleep.

Stepping from the shower, Brian Bailey stood facing himself in one of the twin medicine cabinet mirrors. His stubble – three, maybe four, or was it five days old? – was beginning to show the hint of gray that told him it had been too long between shaves. His wet hair, long and straight before the curls of dryness would set in, hung over the tops of his shoulders. He thought maybe it was time he had a haircut, though he thought this more often than he acted upon it. Studying himself, he saw the large bags under his eyes, the result of too many sleepless nights. Through the mirror he noticed the neatly folded towel resting in the corner beside the tub, her wet clothes laid across the top.

Turning, he surveyed the items. A baggy yellow sweater, large wooden buttons down the front, elbow patches sewn on the worn sleeves. A small white tank top, embroidered around the neck. And a pair of cutoffs, frayed legs below a tiny waistband that seemed meant for a child.

Gathering the items, placing them atop his own stack of wet clothes, he descended the back stairs toward the basement, and the dryer that sat next to the abandoned cistern. Holding her clothes in front of him as he made his way through the darkness, he could smell her scent rising from the damp cloth. He remembered how he used to smell Christine arising from her clothes when he did her wash, and how he cried when her clothes no longer smelled like her, but only like the closet.

Placing the clothes in the machine, he climbed the steps to the first floor and made his way toward the living room. She lay snuggled under the covers, her long hair fanning out across the pillow. He stared at her for just a moment too long before turning off the light and quietly tip-toeing out of the room and up the stairs, closing the bedroom door behind him. Another night in solitary confinement in his private prison, chained to his memories.

Being alone he could accept. Loneliness he could not escape. In the darkness of the night, alone in his bed, he often found himself unable to hide from his own thoughts. Lying awake for hours, he would get out of bed and silently walk the darkened rooms of the house, or sit on the porch and stare off aimlessly, empty headed, free from his racing mind.

He tried, some nights, to gather the girls in bed with him, to read a children's book that would go unfinished as they drifted asleep, one by one. On the nights this worked he slept well, snuggled safely between his two girls. More often, though, trying to recreate the good times he so cherished was too painful, the memories too dear. The laughing, the tickle fights, the stories; the warmth they all felt for each other when the family had been whole, four across the pillows. On those nights he slept poorly, if at all. Most nights he lay flat on his back, alone, staring up at the cracked plaster on the ceiling.

He lay there again tonight and thought back to the day he'd first seen Christine. Her eyes. Her hair. Her smile. He thought of how he knew that first day that he'd met his wife, and would spend the rest of his life with her. Then he thought of the girl downstairs, curled up under the covers, asleep on the couch. He thought of her eyes. Of her hair. Of her smile. As the first traces of dawn slipped in through the window, Brian Bailey drifted off to sleep.

Chapter 2

~

Colleen rolled over and pulled the soft quilts tightly around her, nestling deep into the covers. She had always been a morning person, waking quickly and completely. This morning she lay in that gray void between darkness and daylight, wanting to stay as she was and prolong the feeling of comfort.

Drifting off, she heard a sound, a soft whisper coming toward her. Rolling over, she slowly opened her eyes. Staring back at her were two pairs of eyes set in nearly identical faces, of slightly different ages. Startled, Colleen shot upright, the covers falling onto her lap. The girls made no move, nor uttered a sound. They sat there for a moment, the three of them, eyeing each other.

"Hello," Colleen offered as she pulled the covers around her.

"Hello," they answered in unison.

"You must be 'the girls,'" Colleen said, picturing the two of them standing side by side in front of the twin medicine cabinets, brushing their hair.

"I'm Shannon," said the older of the two, who looked about eight.

"I'm Kerry," said the other one, a few years younger.

"Well, it's nice to meet you, Shannon, Kerry," Colleen said, nodding and smiling at each as she said their names. "I'm Colleen, Colleen O'Connell."

"That's a pretty name," said Kerry, repeating it to herself.

"We're sorry if we woke you," Shannon said to Colleen before turning to her sister. "I told you we'd wake her if we sat here any longer," she reprimanded.

"Well, you wanted to know who she was too," Kerry snapped back.

"And now we know," Colleen stepped in. "And you didn't wake me, not that much anyway. I was just starting to get up."

"What are you doing here?" Kerry asked.

"My car stalled in the storm last night," Colleen explained, "and your father rescued me."

"I suppose he was sitting out on the steps," Shannon said, glancing over her shoulder towards the porch.

"Why, yes – yes he was, as a matter of fact," Colleen confirmed. "Sitting on the steps staring off into the darkness with some Irish folk song playing in the background. I'm afraid I startled him. I don't think he saw me coming up the driveway." Shannon simply nodded and lowered her head as Kerry began to bite her nails.

Watching the look of concern come across the girls' faces, Colleen allowed them a moment while she straightened the blankets. Studying the girls, she noticed their eyes were brown, like hers, and not the stormy blue of their father's.

"Does your dad sit out there late at night a lot?" Colleen asked.

"Only when he's not walking around the house in the dark, or standing out by the barn looking down toward the creek," Shannon answered.

Kerry shifted in her seat, then resumed nibbling at the tips of her fingers.

"Dad doesn't sleep very good," Shannon explained.

"Yeah," Kerry offered, "when I get up at night to go to the

bathroom his bed's usually empty, and I have no one to snuggle with. We usually find him on the couch in the morning," she continued, "curled up under the Afghan my grandma made."

Colleen shifted under the covers, turning to face the girls. "And why doesn't your father sleep well at night?" she asked.

"I think he misses my mom," Kerry answered with a shrug.

"And where is your mom?"

"In heaven."

Colleen looked from one girl to the other. They stared back at her, their young faces so similar, their expressions so lost. Colleen grew uneasy with their stares, uncomfortable with the silence.

"I'm sorry," she offered, reaching for the chain that hung around her neck.

"Yeah," said Shannon.

"Yeah," said Kerry.

Colleen rose and busied herself tidying up the bedding. The girls watched her as she neatly folded the quilts and closed up the hide-a-bed. She was slightly taller than their mom, and a bit thinner, but her hair was just as long, and when she fluffed the pillows the way she did she reminded them of her, dressed as she was in their dad's white shirt.

"Well, the bedding's all put away," Colleen stated as she set the last pillow in place. "What shall we do now?"

"I think we should wait for my dad to wake up," Shannon replied.

"But that could be hours!" Kerry complained.

"We can wait," Shannon snapped back.

"But we're not gonna just sit here, are we?" Kerry asked.

"You know what Dad says," Shannon lectured under her breath. "You know, about strangers."

"Oh, yeah," Kerry whispered back, chewing on a new nail.

Colleen overheard the private exchange. "Oh, I'm no stranger than most people," she joked, hoping to calm their concerns.

"You know," Kerry thought as she turned toward her sister, "Dad knows she's here, so she must not be too much of a stranger."

"Well, I guess since Dad knows you're here it's all right," Shannon conceded.

"Great," Colleen said. "So, what shall we do?"

"I'm kinda hungry," Kerry told her.

"And I could use a cup of coffee," Colleen replied. "Shall we head for the kitchen, then?" she asked as the girls rose and led the way.

As they entered the kitchen Colleen grabbed the kettle off the stove, lit the burner, and ran the water in the sink. Looking out the window, she paused, taking in the view across the barnyard. Last night's storm had blown over, and a beautiful spring day greeted her. The lush green grass, still matted by the rain, rolled down the hill away from the house. At the bottom of the hill sat a marsh, tall cattails billowing in the breeze, a lake in the distance beyond, the morning sun shimmering across its lightly rolling waves. Across the road stood a cherry orchard, the clean white blossoms reaching out toward her against a backdrop of short brown trunks. Thinking of Brenden, Colleen drew in the scene, setting it to memory.

"What should we have for breakfast?" Kerry wondered.

"What would you like?" Colleen asked as she turned to face the girls.

"Neuske bacon!" Kerry shouted. "With syrup!"

"And you, Shannon," Colleen continued. "Any requests?"

Shannon hesitated. "Maybe we should just wait for my dad to get up," she suggested.

"We can do that, if you prefer," Colleen replied, not wanting to push the child.

"Aw, man," Kerry cut in. "Do we have to wait?"

"Well, your sister seems to think so," Colleen answered. "Although your dad did make me a much-appreciated little meal last night," she reasoned, trying to balance the girls' concerns. "It might be nice to repay the favor and make breakfast for him, don't you think?"

"Well, I guess it would be all right," Shannon agreed. "Anyways, I am kind of hungry too."

"Then it's settled," Colleen stated, to Kerry's delight. "And what would you like with your bacon?" she asked Shannon once again.

"Can you make Swedish pancakes?" Shannon asked. "Dad likes Swedish pancakes."

"I don't know. I've never tried."

"You just double the water to thin them out and add an extra egg and a dash of vanilla," Shannon instructed.

"Let's give it a try," Colleen said. "Where's the box of mix?"

"What box?"

"The box of mix, for the pancakes."

"You just mix up some 'gredients from the Hoosier cabinet," Kerry informed her.

"From scratch?" Colleen asked.

"Sure. That's how Dad always makes them," Shannon stated.

"But you have to start the bacon first," Kerry lectured, pulling her head out of the ice chest. "Dad always says to start the bacon before you make the mix."

And with that they began.

Brian woke from a few short hours of sleep, feeling more rested than he had in a long time. As was his custom since moving into this house, he rose and looked out the window, down the hill and over the marsh, then across the water, toward the little orange cottage that sat back from the shore at the far end of the lake. Squinting into the sun, he could see a fire ablaze in the fire pit, his father already busy picking up debris from last night's storm. As he peered out the window he could hear the voices in the kitchen, rising up the stairway. Three of them.

Brian made his way to the bathroom to grab a quick shower, and shave. Returning to his room, he heard the laughter escalating downstairs, and wondered what to wear. Brian Bailey never cared about what he wore. As long as it was loose fitting and comfortable, any plain-colored button-down cotton shirt with the sleeves rolled up was fine to go with his jeans and boots. He had an ample selection of shirts to choose from, white or blue, plus the fancy one with the thin gray stripes that Christine had bought him, just to muddle up his routine. Picking a shirt, Brian checked his hair in the mirror a second time before descending the stairs.

~

Making his way down the narrow back hall, Brian entered the kitchen, pausing in the doorway. The girls, wearing his old t-shirts for pajamas, were each perched atop a chair, Shannon busily flipping bacon on the stove, Kerry elbow-deep in flour at the chopping block. The smell of fresh coffee filled the room, carried toward him by the warming breeze that came in through the open window above the sink. She stood at the sink in his Packer sweats and white shirt, her back toward him, her long hair shining in the morning sun.

She turned to find him leaning in the doorway, staring at her. "Good morning," she greeted him.

"Morning," he nodded, returning her smile.

Hearing his voice the girls jumped off their chairs and ran to him. He scooped them up in his arms, planting kisses on their cheeks as they hugged him. Colleen leaned back against the sink and watched.

"Colleen's making Nueske bacon and Swedish pancakes, and we're helping," Kerry said proudly.

"Oh, is she now," he said, tousling Kerry's hair. Setting the girls back down on their chairs he made his way to the coffee, pouring himself a cup in the tall mug that was reserved for his regular use. "Coffee smells good," he said. "Sorry I slept in a bit."

"No problem," she answered. "As you can see, we've been making ourselves right at home." Colleen looked over the mess they had made of his tidy kitchen. "Your girls are charming," she said, "and helpful."

"So I see," he chuckled, used to having kitchen helpers.

"Looks like it will be a little while still before we pull everything together," she informed him as she added a dash of vanilla to the batter, "but we hope to have breakfast ready eventually."

"Great," he said, taking a sip of the thick coffee. "Good coffee, thanks. That'll get the old motor started. Speaking of which," he added, "is there time to check on your car before breakfast?"

"Oh sure," she replied. "The girls tell me the bacon has to be cooked slowly, until the grease starts to bubble."

"I think I'll run out to the shed, then, if there's time," he said, setting his mug on the cool Franklin. "I'll see if the car starts and grab your things, so you can change into your own clothes."

"That would be nice, thanks," she said as she looked over her outfit. "Just the one bag in the back seat."

"I'll have it right up," he called out as he headed down the hallway and out the back door.

He returned a few minutes later, her canvas duffel bag hanging from his shoulder. "Breakfast smells great," he said.

"You're just in time," she informed him. "Grab a chair." The girls noisily scurried into their chairs as Colleen set the food on the table, refilling the coffee cups before joining them.

Steam rose from the pancakes, disappearing overhead as two pairs of small hands descended on the plate of bacon, covering it from view. The pieces, once grabbed, were dunked into matching pools of sticky syrup.

"Girls," he reprimanded with a chuckle, "save some bacon for Colleen." He picked up the plate of Swedish pancakes. "So, who needs a panekoken?" he asked, placing a few of the thin pancakes on each girl's plate, then holding the platter out to Colleen.

Nodding in thanks, she placed a single pancake on her plate. "I hope they taste all right," she worried. "I've never made Swedish pancakes before, or any kind of pancakes from scratch, for that matter."

"They look great," he answered, directing her eyes toward the girls, who were busy gobbling down their syrup-drenched breakfasts.

"So, what are we going to do today, Dad?" Shannon asked.

"Yeah, you said we could have a special day today," Kerry added.

"And so we shall. What would the two of you like to do?"

"We could go to Cana Island, walk on the rocks, have a picnic lunch," Shannon suggested.

"And maybe stop at the ice cream store on the way home," Kerry hoped.

"Slow down," he laughed. "First we have to get Colleen's car running, then there'll be plenty of time left to spend a fun day together. A promise is a promise."

Colleen smiled to herself as she watched him exchange small talk with his girls – the light teasing, the hint of mischief in his manner, thrown right back at him. It was obvious the three of them were close, and enjoyed toying with each other. A napkin flew across the table, hitting him in the face. He returned the shot without missing a beat.

"Well, it looks like breakfast is over," he concluded. "Girls, clear your places and get dressed, then go outside and play for a bit while I do the dishes and talk with Colleen. Then we'll make a plan for the day." The girls dutifully obeyed, kissing him on the cheek before racing up the back stairs as he called out behind them, "And don't forget to brush your teeth!"

～

They sat quietly across the table from each other, comfortable in silence. After a time he rose, clearing her plate as he headed toward the sink.

"Let me help with the dishes," she offered. "After all, I made the mess."

"I think you had help," he laughed as he began to run the water. "Besides, you pulled cook and baby-sitting duty already this morning. Relax," he instructed. "I'll clean up while the girls use the bathroom, then you can shower and change."

Colleen settled into her chair, watching him as he put away the leftovers and set about washing and rinsing the dishes, neatly stacking them in the drying rack. After a few moments, he spoke.

"Your car didn't start," he said. "It must have been wetter than I thought. I'll pull the plugs while you're in the shower, to let them dry out, then we can drive you over to your brother's if you like," he offered. "I imagine he's probably expecting you by now."

Colleen sat, silently, and shook her head.

"You've come a long way," he said, recalling the Arizona license plates, "not to be expected."

She looked up at Brian. "He's not expecting me," she said softly. "Oh, he invited me often enough over the years, pleaded with me, really, to come visit him, spend some time here, though I never did. But no, he's not expecting me."

Brian noted the saddened expression on her face and remained quiet, allowing her to continue.

"My brother, Brenden," she said after a pause, "died last November."

"I'm sorry," he said as he turned and gripped the sink.

Death remained too close for Brian, consuming him still. He stood over the sink, water running, and stared out the window, down the hill, over the marsh, and across the lake. First his mother, then shortly after, his wife. Bang. Bang. Then thud, as his heart and soul and will fell away. If not for the girls, and his father, he doubted he'd have made it through a day, let alone the last few years. And now someone else sat before him, also deeply touched by death, though he couldn't imagine her loss without thinking of his own.

"He spent summers here," she continued, "for the past eleven years, working at some theater in the woods. He just loved it here, spent all his time away talking about coming back. In the spring he would get antsy to return, a bit like a caged animal waiting to be set free. But he waited, every year, for just the right time to come. 'You have to drive in for the first time each spring when the cherry trees are in full blossom,' he used to say."

Colleen shifted slightly in her seat. "After he died I was sure I'd finally come someday, though I didn't know when. First the funeral, then the holidays, and then it was winter up here. Then this past Friday I was sitting at work, staring out the window, and it hit me, and I knew it was time. I took some overdue vacation, packed a few things, and left that afternoon."

"You just left on Friday, and drove all the way, by yourself?"

"Yes. I thought about staying in Chicago last night and driving up this morning in the daylight, to take in the view. Brenden always said you should enter in style the first time each spring, to witness the beauty, and appreciate more fully why you came. But when I got to Chicago I got anxious and decided to drive straight through. I'd come so far already, and only had a little ways left to go, so I just decided to keep driving. Then I got lost in the storm, and my car died, and, well, here I am."

Brian dried his hands on the dishtowel, flinging it across his shoulder as he turned to face her. He stared at her for a moment and recalled lying in bed last night, thinking of Christine, and Colleen, until the two faces melted together in his mind.

"You could have drowned crossing that causeway last night," he snapped at her.

~

The rush of footsteps down the back stairs brought the girls, and the commotion, into the kitchen.

"She won't let me wear the pink headband."

"Well, it's mine, and she always stretches it out and it doesn't fit anymore."

"Why can't you just wear a clip?"

"*You* wear a clip, it's my headband."

"I'll cut off your hair, then you won't need either one!"

"Ladies, ladies," he interrupted as he crossed the room and put a hand on each of their shoulders. "It's early," he continued, "plenty of time for fighting later."

He led them across the room, taking a seat next to Colleen as he rested each girl against one leg and drew them in. "It'll probably be muggy today, after the storm moved through last night," he advised. "Why don't we pull your hair back in a braid to keep it off your neck. It might be cooler that way." Taking the brush from Kerry, he brushed out her long straight hair and began to braid it.

"I can give your hair a try if you like, Shannon," Colleen offered.

"Maybe I should wait for Dad," Shannon said. "He knows how to do it."

"Why don't you let Colleen give it a try?" Brian coaxed. "She has long hair. She must know how to braid."

"Well...," Shannon said, still uncertain about Colleen.

"Come on, let me give it a try," Colleen offered again. "If I do it wrong you can have your Dad redo it."

"I guess," Shannon agreed, "but don't pull it too tight."

Colleen expertly braided Shannon's hair, finishing well ahead of Brian and Kerry, to Shannon's delight. Completing the task, Brian gave each girl a light tap on the backside with the hairbrush before sending them off to play. "Don't get all dirty," he instructed, calling behind them as they rushed outside. "We'll be ready to go in an hour."

"They're a joy," Colleen observed after the girls had gone.

"Yes, they are," he agreed, "and a lot of work. But I'm thinking of keeping them."

Colleen chuckled as she rose, taking her coffee mug to the sink before grabbing her duffel bag. "I'll be ready to go in half an hour," she said as she headed down the hallway and up the back stairs.

Brian sat there, staring down the empty hallway.

Showered and changed, Colleen descended the back stairs, pausing at the bottom as she peered out the screen door. Brian and the girls stood across the barnyard, chatting as they leaned against the sides of a dilapidated old pick-up truck. Resting against the doorframe, she watched with envy as they laughed in unison. Knowing she'd had too few similar moments as a child, Colleen wondered if she would have enough as an adult. Pushing the screen door open, she stepped off the porch.

Brian turned at the thud of the screen door slamming shut. She crossed the barnyard toward him — wearing her cut-offs and sandals, and his white shirt — her long flowing hair bouncing across the tops of her shoulders with each step she took. He watched her, a mixture of his dreams and memories.

"All set," she announced to the group with a bright smile. Turning toward Brian, she added, "I hope you don't mind me wearing your shirt?"

"Not...at all," he stuttered slightly. "It looks good on you. Keep it."

"It just felt right," she offered.

"So, ladies," he said as he turned to address the girls. "Shall we take The Bucket? I feel like knocking around in her today."

"I get the window," Shannon yelled out quickly, reserving her spot.

Colleen surveyed 'The Bucket,' as he called it, and wondered about his preferred mode of transportation. Tailgate missing, fender rusted through, cracks spidering across the windshield. She doubted if the old pick-up could even roll down the driveway on its own, let alone make it up the steep hill on the road.

"Not much to look at, but it doesn't run that well either," he joked, sensing her appraisal. "Safe though, and the only way to fly down the back roads."

Noticing the placement of the two silhouettes inside the cab, he directed her toward the driver's side. "I'm afraid you'll have to slide across and sit in the middle," he said apologetically. "Shannon's kind of particular about her seating arrangement." Colleen climbed in ahead of him and slid across the seat, next to Kerry. Settling in behind the wheel, Brian pulled the choke, pumped the gas pedal, then turned the key a few times until the cold engine found the strength to turn over.

"Where to?" he asked. She gave him the address, he put The Bucket in gear, and the old truck limped down the driveway toward the road. Racing the engine a time or two, he pulled onto the empty road, not bothering to look for the passing cars that weren't there. The old pick-up sputtered up the steep hill leading away from the house, gaining speed slowly. They crested the hill at full speed, Colleen gasping as the road underneath momentarily left her view, replaced by the vast green waters they seemed about to plunge into. The Bay.

"Never get tired of the feeling you get going over that hill," Brian stated matter-of-factly, the road returning to view as they began their descent.

"It used to scare me," said Kerry, "when I was little."

Gliding down the hill, picking up speed as they rode over the bumps in the road that the worn shocks did nothing to hide, they shifted slightly in their seats. Colleen's leg brushed against Brian's, and rested there. "The Bucket must have had some suspension at one time," he commented, not moving his leg.

Gazing out the window as they ambled down the road, Colleen was struck by the plain beauty of the tiny country lane, lined with wildflowers on either side. No one detail of the scenery was by itself spectacular, just a series of simple environs that, when taken together, formed a patchwork of unified serenity. A corn field. A weathered barn. A stand of northern cedar. A rusted tractor. A solitary deer, grazing. A cherry orchard in full bloom. An overgrown baseball diamond. An abandoned wooden sailboat. Colleen was beginning to sense why Brenden had felt so at peace here, so at home, and why he had grown restless each spring, impatient to return.

Lost in the scenery, Colleen was unaware that they had slowed, and were now pulling up a short gravel drive. As they came to a stop the truck backfired, interrupting her solitude. She looked through the cracked windshield and stared at the dilapidated old shack before her, no bigger than a small shed. The grass grew tall around it, unkempt. A faded wooden bench lay overturned on the tiny front porch. A discarded rake leaned against the shaded window. A padlock hung from the latch above the door handle.

"Doesn't look like anyone's around," Brian said as he got out of the truck and held the door open for her.

"No," she answered, "Brenden lived here alone. Rented it from the farmer up the road. Paid a full year's rent in advance each year to assure it would stay his. Couldn't wait to get back to his 'castle,' as he used to call it." *Not much of a kingdom*, she thought to herself as she climbed out of the truck.

The girls ran off around the side of the shack to investigate an old swing that hung from the solitary oak in the side yard. "Would you like to go in by yourself?" he offered.

"No," she said quickly, grabbing his arm. "Come with me. It won't feel so empty if I'm not alone."

Colleen removed a single silver key from the front pocket of her cutoffs and handed it to Brian. He stepped onto the porch and unlocked the door, holding it open for her. She entered the darkness and paused, allowing her eyes to adjust. He stepped around her in search of a light switch. They both squinted at the sudden brightness of the lone bare bulb that hung directly above them.

The sparse shack was open, a single room, nothing but the four outside walls that surrounded them, and held the roof over their heads. To their right they found a small kitchenette, its tiny electric stove and half-fridge wedged on either side of a freestanding sink, which held no faucet. A single cupboard hung on the wall above the sink. Beyond, down the length of one wall, an old army cot sat, its neatly folded blanket and flat pillow resting on one end. On the back wall, set into the corner, an old overstuffed armchair provided the only seat, an end table and lamp set next to it. The remainder of space in the tiny shack was taken up by a grand piano, the dust-covered varnish aglow under the harsh light of the single bare bulb. Perched atop the piano, facing out into the room, to be seen from anywhere in the shack, sat a large color photo of Colleen.

Colleen retraced the arc of the room, taking in the scene. Brian stared at the photo on the piano. She looked younger, somewhat, but little different. Her hair was a bit shorter, but no less becoming, though he was glad she'd let it grow back.

Her picture smiled out at him, the smile the same as the one she now wore as she stood next to him.

"You OK?" he asked.

"Perfect," she answered as she crossed the small room and sat down on the old army cot.

He followed behind her, then hesitated, as if waiting for permission to sit. She looked up at him, smiled, and patted the space next to her, offering him a seat. They sat there a while, side by side in silence as Colleen pictured Brenden in his 'castle,' reading in the chair, cooking in the little kitchen, practicing at the piano. Brian noticed the tears welling up in her eyes and put an arm around her shoulder. She threw herself against his chest, clasping her arms tightly around him as she began to sob uncontrollably.

Colleen's crying subsided, giving way to sniffles alternating with gasps for breath. She raised her head from his chest and rubbed her eyes. He pushed back the few strands of wet hair that clung to her face, wiping her cheeks with the cuff of his sleeve.

"Feel better?" he asked.

"Yes. Thank you."

"Tell me about him."

Colleen scooted back on the cot and leaned against the wall. Catching her breath, she wiped her face once more, on the sleeve of his shirt that she wore.

"Brenden was my only brother, my only sibling, and in a way, my only true friend," she began. "We were each other's best friend's – had to be, I guess, for neither of us ever really had anyone else.

"My folks split up when we were young, probably about the age your girls are now. I was too young to understand what was happening at the time, but Brenden took me under his wing. He'd let me into his room late at night when I'd had a bad dream, give me his bed, then sit on the floor beside me, singing me to sleep. I used to find him there in the morning, lying on the floor, a pair of jeans tucked under his head for a pillow, a shirt drawn over him for a blanket.

"My father died a few years after he left us. My mother never really recovered, I don't think, from the break-up, or his death. I guess you could say she retreated within. She's in sort of a home now. Sometimes when I visit her she's quite sharp, but more often she just sits there and stares out the window.

"Anyway, when we were younger Brenden had to do many of the things my mother couldn't. I remember when he pulled the wagon, with me in it, down to the grocery store to buy cupcake mix when I had snack in Brownies. I remember how he took me to the library every week each summer. And I remember riding the bus downtown together to shop for ballet slippers when I took lessons at the Y."

Colleen rose from the cot and grabbed a box of Kleenex from the end table next to the chair. Brian stayed on the cot, remembering the special things his mother did for him, knowing Christine wouldn't be there to do them for the girls.

Colleen sank down in the over-stuffed chair and set the Kleenex on her lap, wiping her eyes once more before continuing. "When I was ten Brenden had saved up enough of his paper route money to buy us both a few piano lessons. I'll never forget how excited he was to start. That's how we learned to play," she said, nodding towards the piano, "on Brenden's extra paper-route money.

"As we grew older and Mom grew worse, Brenden and I grew closer. He was always there, watching over me, though never intrusive. Not that he was perfect, by any means. Oh, he had his share of human frailties, to be sure, most notably a temper that erupted without warning when he was tired. He made his share of mistakes along the way, but he was always there when I needed him.

"He stayed in town after he graduated, to see me through high school, I think. He worked at odd jobs, playing in clubs every night, practicing during the day. He somehow saved up enough money to help me through college, all the while still playing, still practicing. He just loved to play, anytime, anywhere, any kind of music.

"When I started college he began coming up here every summer. I guess he always thought I'd come with him, but by then I was too involved with my own life to come here and share his.

"Then, after I'd finished college, found a job, and settled comfortably into adulthood, he took his big chance and auditioned for the symphony. Self-taught, with no formal training, save for that one year of beginner's lessons paid for with his paper-route money. And he made it!

"I'll always remember the sheer joy on his face when he popped in at my office that day to tell me the news, and take me to lunch...."

The girls ran by the open window, startling Colleen as they shouted to each other, calling out who got the rope swing next. She turned toward the window, watching the girls until they faded from view, then returned her gaze to the piano, shifting herself in the old overstuffed chair before continuing.

"Joining the symphony gave him a measure of self-respect, I think. Oh, it's not that he lacked in that department to begin with, for he always had a quiet confidence in himself. But you could sense a subtle change had taken place within him, almost as if he felt the symphony was the reward for all his years of hard work, a validation that the sacrifices he had made, mostly for me, had been worth it.

"The other thing the symphony did was give him a steady income for the first time in his life. It wasn't like he made a ton of money, but what he made was regular, and when added to what he took in still playing the clubs on his off nights, for the first time in his life he had a little extra money that he could spend on himself, and not just on me.

"Oh, he didn't go crazy and spend it foolishly, but he had a lot of years of self-denial to make up for, and he was finally able to go out and buy himself some nice things back home. That's what makes the austerity of this place so shocking. He could have afforded something better for himself if he had wanted.

"But he kept coming back here each summer, to his 'castle,' to play folk songs in the woods or background music for some silly play, 'to recharge the soul,' he said. 'Come, Colleen,' he used to beg, 'come once and the place will never leave you.' But I never did come. And now I'm here, and he's gone." The tears began to well up in Colleen's eyes once more.

"You're here now," Brian offered after a while. "He knows it."

Colleen considered his words, then wiped her eyes one last time. "Well," she said, forcing a smile, "that was depressing."

"Feel better?" Brian asked.

"You know," she sniffled, "I actually do. I guess it's true that sometimes it's better to talk about things than to hold them inside. Thank you for listening."

"Thank you for telling me."

They sat there, worlds apart, lost in their separate memories of loss.

～

The clap of the front door startled them from their memories. Brian rose from the cot as the girls rushed inside.

"I have to go to the bathroom," Kerry announced.

"I could probably use a little freshening up myself," Colleen thought aloud. "I must look awful."

"I think you look pretty," Kerry said. Brian nodded. They all turned full circle, searching the shack.

"How bad do you have to go, Kerry?" Brian asked.

"Pretty bad."

"Outhouse bad?"

"Yuk! Not a pitter?" Kerry groaned.

"'Fraid so, my love. Take it or leave it. Want me to go with you?"

"Can Colleen take me? She has to freshen up."

Brian laughed to himself, wondering how much freshening up could take place in the old outhouse he'd noticed when they first arrived. He led his little entourage out the door and around the back of the shack, toward the outhouse that had sat dormant since last summer. The square hut, perched on a rise about fifty yards behind the shack, had somehow managed to survive the winter without falling over. Barely big enough for one, the door hanging at an angle from a single hinge, the frail privy was leaning slightly, and looked ready to collapse at any moment.

"I can take her if you'd prefer," Brian whispered to Colleen as they approached.

"We'll be fine," she assured him.

"You have to go in with her," he added. "She's afraid of falling in."

"So am I," Colleen confessed as she grabbed Kerry by the hand and opened the door.

Brian and Shannon made their way back down the small slope to Brenden's "castle," turning off the light and locking the door before going to sit on the back of The Bucket. Waiting for Colleen and Kerry to return from the outhouse, Brian picked up a long blade of grass and placed it between his teeth.

"Dad?"

"Yeah."

"Is something wrong?"

"What do you mean?"

"Was Colleen crying?"

"Yes. Yes she was."

"How come?"

"This was her brother's place."

"Was?"

"Was. He died last fall."

"And she misses him?"

"Yeah."

"Like you miss Mom."

"Yes. Kind of like how I miss Mom."

Brian ran the blade of grass through his teeth as he stared out over the back of the pick-up. Tossing the blade out, he bent down to pick up another.

"Dad?"

"Yeah."

"She reminds me a little of Mom."

"You too?"

Returning from the outhouse, Colleen and Kerry found Brian and Shannon sitting on the back of The Bucket, legs dangling over the edge where the tailgate was supposed to be, long blades of grass lazily stuck between their teeth. Kerry grabbed a blade of grass and hopped into the back of the pick-up. Colleen leaned up against the side of the truck.

"Everything come out all right?" he asked.

"No one fell in," she chuckled.

"What's next?"

"I don't know," Colleen contemplated. "I guess we can go. I'll come stay here for the week, but this has been enough for now. Nice, thanks, but enough. Besides," she added, "you promised the girls a day of fun. I'm sure they don't want to stay around here all day."

"All right, then," he said, hopping down from the truck. "Who's going to Wilson's with me for nachos and root beer?"

"Me! Me!" the girls shouted, dancing around in the back of The Bucket.

"Is Colleen coming?" Kerry asked.

"Come along?" he invited.

"Oh, I don't want to intrude," she said.

"Not at all," he replied. "Lunch is included in the guided tour."

"Please! Please!" the girls begged. "Come with us."

"That's two votes yes," he said. "What do you say? We'd love you to come."

"Well, all right then," she smiled up at the girls. "Let's go!"

The girls took their appointed seats in the cab, Colleen once again climbing in next to Brian. He backed out of the driveway, and they headed up the road together.

Chapter 3

~

*T*hey drove north, up the county lane that divided the peninsula in two. On their left, the tourist side; on their right, the quiet side. In a place that had more feet of shoreline than it did acres of dry land they could see no water, only smell it in the air. The warm sun beating down through the cracked windshield mixed with the damp breeze coming in through the open windows. They sat quietly, each lost in thought.

His wife. Her brother. Their mother. Him. Her.

Making a left onto a still smaller road marked by a wooden signpost, they curled their way through a working farm, white house on the right, red barn on the left. They wound around a crawling tractor that pulled an empty hay wagon, then headed up an incline to a stop sign perched at the crest of the hill. The deep green waters of The Bay glistened on the horizon. Below them sat Ephraim, its sailboats moored in the harbor, framed by the bluffs that encapsulated it.

Brian preferred to come into Ephraim from the back, to look down over the old town, blind to the rows of new shops that lined the main highway on both ends like a sprawling strip mall. The Door was about the serene beauty of itself, Brian felt, and not the diversions man had created. Coasting down the hill, he turned the truck off as they rolled into the parking lot in front of Wilson's.

The old soda fountain stood close to the road, facing out across the harbor. Early-season tourists leaned against the front porch rail, competing with the sun as their ice cream cones dripped onto the floorboards. A red-and-white-striped awning sloped down from the side of the building, covering a deck that had been added to accommodate summer visitors. The quaint setting drew Colleen in.

"Oh, can we eat on the deck?" she asked.

"Yeah, can we eat on the deck, Dad?" the girls chimed in.

Brian thought back to the countless stops at Wilson's over the years. "Your mother never liked to," he stated quietly.

"But she always did," Shannon reminded.

He nodded and jumped up the single step onto the deck, taking a seat in one of the painted metal chairs that circled the round tables. They ordered a large nachos supreme, extra napkins, and four tall root beers, plus an order of fries to go.

"Are the fries that good?" Colleen questioned.

"We feed them to the seagulls after we eat," Shannon informed her.

"Yeah, it's really fun," Kerry added. "You should try it."

"You get an order of fries just for the seagulls?"

"Kind of a ritual," responded Brian. "Been doing it for years. They're nice gulls here. The ones over in Fish Creek follow you around, begging, and the ones up at Gills Rock swarm in noisy circles like they're following a fishing boat, screeching for leavings. But the Ephraim gulls are a nice group, better mannered, if you will, so we feed them."

"What are we going to do after we eat?" Shannon asked.

"I don't know. What do the two of you want to do?"

"I think we should ask Colleen what she wants to do," Kerry said.

Touched by the child's thoughtfulness, Colleen looked from

one pair of expectant eyes to the next. "Don't change your plans on account of me," she said. "Didn't you have a fun day all planned out?"

"A day of fun, actually, but no real plan," he answered. "Just a day off together to do whatever. We're free and flexible. Anything else you wanted to do today?" he continued. "You know, about Brenden?"

Colleen fidgeted with her napkin, hesitant to take up more of their time. "But I don't want to ruin your day," she said.

"Nonsense. We've got no plans," he assured her, "other than just to hang out together."

"Well," she ventured, "I would kind of like to see where Brenden played during his summers."

"Of course. A theater in the woods, right? Not too many to choose from. Let's see. Birch Creek. Peninsula Players. American Folklore Theater."

"American Folklore Theater. AFT. That's the one."

"AFT? Really?" Brian said, surprised. "Why, we go there a few times every year."

"You know of them?"

"Know of them? I practically grew up with them. Used to be called Heritage Ensemble. Perform in the park across the harbor. Concerts, sing-a-longs, goofy original plays. Been going every year since – what, '71, '72? The girls love it. Why, we're practically there already, not five minutes from here. We can stop by after lunch, if you'd like," Brian offered. "I was going to drive through the park anyway."

"The play's in the park?" Shannon asked excitedly.

"With Mildred the Chicken?" asked Kerry.

"And Bob Bob Dirty Bob Bob?"

"The very same," Brian answered. "Would you like to go there this afternoon?"

"To see a play?"

"No, just to walk around and see the place."

"My brother used to play the piano there," Colleen explained to the girls. "I've never been there, and I'd kind of like to see what it looks like."

"But we've already been there a million times," Shannon said.

Colleen felt suddenly guilty for monopolizing more of the girls' day with what seemed to be a less-than-fun suggestion. "Hey, maybe you girls could go up on stage, if nobody's there," she offered. "Have you ever been up on the stage?"

"Neat," Kerry dreamed. "Can we go there, Dad?"

"Sure."

"Can we stop on the way," Shannon asked, "and climb the tower?"

"We'll see," he said, with some hesitation.

"What tower?" Colleen asked. The three of them turned their heads to look out across the harbor and up the bluff on the far side. She followed their gaze until she saw the tall, brown-logged fire tower poking its head through the tops of the trees, to look out over The Bay.

∼

Nachos finished, the bridges of their noses frozen by the frosty root beer, they waved for the waitress to bring them the check, and the order of fries to go. An old woman passed by their table as she was leaving, pausing to comment on how cute and well behaved the girls were.

"Such a nice family," she said, "and the girls just as pretty as their mother."

Colleen began to correct the woman. Brian raised his hand to halt her. He reached for his wallet, placed some money on the table, and pushed out his chair, walking off in silence as he stared across the harbor toward the tower.

Shannon watched her father cross the road. "Sometimes Dad likes to be alone," she said to Colleen as Kerry slid her pinky into the corner of her mouth.

Check paid, Colleen finished her root beer and tucked the fries under her arm. Taking each girl's hand firmly in her own, she led them across the road toward the water. Leaving the girls on the thick grass, Colleen continued on, toward the big white rocks that lined the shore, where he sat looking out across the harbor at the old fire tower.

"Anything I can do?" she offered.

"Other than not invoking old memories?" he stated dryly. Rising, he turned toward her and forced a smile. "Show time," he said. "Let's put on our game faces." With that he walked past her, calling out to his girls.

The girls stood a few yards away, waiting anxiously yet expectantly. Dad had his moments, they knew, but he could always pull himself together for them. "Ready. Set. Feed!" he shouted as they all stuffed their hands into the bag, grabbing a handful of fries. One at a time, in turn, they flung the fries into the air, pointing and laughing each time a patiently hovering gull lunged forward to grab one in midair. Colleen stayed back, watching the three of them as they enjoyed this ritual as if for the first time.

Kerry approached, offering the bag of fries to Colleen. "You gotta come try it," she ordered, "it's really fun." She grabbed Colleen by the hand and led her back to the others.

"Show Colleen your trick, Dad," Shannon begged, pulling at his shirt sleeve.

"Yeah, show Colleen your trick," Colleen egged him on.

"Dad puts a fry on his head and lets the gulls pick it off," Shannon explained.

"Except last time, when a gull tried to take some of my hair off along with the fry," he informed her. "Personally, I think that's why I'm thinning a bit on the top," he said, running his hand over his hair. "It's the gulls."

He perched a fry on top of his head, squinting his eyes in anticipation as the hovering gulls began to descend. "Ouch!" he cried out, feigning injury for the delight of his audience as a gull cleanly picked the fry from his head. He spun around, wounded, like a dying actor shot in an old western, milking the death scene for all he could. He dropped to the ground, the girls laughing as they piled on top of him and rolled in the grass.

The horseplay ended, the three of them lay on their backs in the deep green grass, gazing up at the light blue sky, its wisps of fluffy white clouds lazily rolling by.

"That one looks like an agillator," Kerry pointed out.

"Lie down and look at the clouds with us, Colleen," Shannon invited.

Colleen nestled into the grass between Shannon and Kerry. They lay side by side, the four of them, quietly watching the passing clouds, dreaming, remembering.

Lying there under the warm sun, the cool breeze that rose off the water gliding across her face, Colleen began to surrender to the long night before. She closed her eyes and began to doze off.

Drifting in and out, she could hear the muffled giggles, the suppressed laughter about to erupt. She opened her eyes to find the three of them standing at her feet, tumbling over with laughter as they covered her from head to toe with grass. She lunged out at them, startling the girls as she picked up some grass and chased them back toward The Bucket.

~

Brian started The Bucket and made a U-turn across the highway. They drove slowly, past the rows of condos and gift shops Colleen thought tarnished the beauty of the place. Up the hill and out of town, they entered the park, winding their way through the golf course, the harbor visible below, Wilson's staring back at them across the water as they approached the old fire tower.

"Can we stop, Dad, please?" Shannon asked hopefully.

"I suppose," he allowed, pulling into the small car park.

"I'm not going up," Kerry stated to no one in particular, determination in her voice as she scooted across the cab after Shannon and slammed the door shut.

"Who's coming?" Shannon invited as she took the first steps up the tower.

"Do you climb?" Brian asked as he looked up at the imposing tower.

Made of ancient round logs held together by metal cables, the old fire tower cradled a wooden staircase that zig-zagged its way up the middle, connecting the platforms that served as observation decks. Leaning against the lannon stone wall at its base, Colleen looked out over the expanse of The Bay, imagining the view from atop the tower.

"Sure," she replied. "Don't you?"

"I'm not real partial to heights," he answered. "Christine always went up with Shannon. I've only ever been to the top once in all the years I've been coming here. Kerry and I usually stay down below. When I was a kid my brother used to love to climb with my dad. My mom and I always stayed below. You can chart my childhood, and car styles over the years, by viewing the pictures my dad used to take from the top, looking down at my mom and me sitting on the open tailgate of the old family station wagon." He paused for a moment, then turned to Colleen. "Would you mind, terribly, going up with Shannon?" he asked as he looked worriedly up the stairs.

"Not at all," she answered. "I'd love to see the view."

Shannon was already on the first deck, peering out over the railing as she shouted down at them, asking who was coming.

"I'll be right there," Colleen called up to her. "Be careful. And don't lean over!" Turning back to Brian and Kerry, Colleen found both of them looking down at their feet, and the solid ground beneath. "Sure you won't give it a try?" she asked.

"No thanks," he begged off. "Too high if I fall."

"But not so high if you don't," she shouted over her

shoulder as she bounded up the stairs two at a time, trying to catch up to Shannon. Rising over the last step, Colleen paused. Fanning out before her lay the width of The Bay, its green waters dotted with still greener islands, and tiny white sailboats.

"Helloooooo," Shannon bellowed out as she leaned over the edge of the platform, waving. Colleen placed a hand on her shoulder as they both looked down at the two small figures below. Brian and Kerry sat on the back end of The Bucket, where the missing tailgate was supposed to be, their legs swinging back and forth. Colleen wondered what he might have looked like as a child, sitting on the tailgate of the old family station wagon with his mother.

～

Reunited on solid ground, the four of them got back in The Bucket, the seating arrangement now routine. Backing away from the tower, Shannon asked if they could sit in the back of the truck on the ride through the park. With ample words of caution Brian allowed them to move, winking at Colleen as he lectured the girls about safety. The window seat now empty, she remained in the middle of the cab.

He took Shore Road, which wound its way along The Bay, past the empty campsites, their fires smoldering, then turned up onto Skyline Road. A single doe, nibbling, paused to raise her head at the intruders, her fawn, in spotted spring coat, inching closer to the safety of its mother. Brian came to a stop by the side of the road, the girls crossing the bed of the pick-up for a closer view. They sat silently, watching the deer.

Looking across the cab, past Colleen and out the open window at the doe, protective of her fawn, Brian thought first of his own mother, and then of his girls, without theirs. His focus shifted back and forth as the doe's light brown coat melded with the soft shiny hair of the girl next to him, the fawn and her mother slowly moving out of the picture. He put the truck back in gear and lazily pulled away.

Taking a few more turns onto ever-smaller roads, they drove further into the middle of the park, stopping alongside a small, timeworn cemetery. Upright white headstones, faded by the years, stood in uneven rows before them, their engraved epitaphs barely legible.

"Christine used to love to come here on our bikes years ago, when we were first married," he offered quietly. "We would walk through here together, reading the old inscriptions. She always wanted to do a charcoal rubbing of a headstone to hang on a wall at home.

"Funny," he continued, "she so loved to stroll through old cemeteries, but I've never been back to her grave since the day we buried her. 'Forgotten lives, once we're gone,' she used to say."

"The memories aren't at the cemetery," Colleen ventured.

He pulled away silently, leaving the cemetery, and Christine, heading toward the amphitheater, and Brenden.

Curving his way through the tree-lined entrance, then down into the recessed bowl of the empty grass parking lot, Brian came to a stop. Turning to Colleen as the anxious girls leapt out of the back, he asked if she wanted to go in alone for a while first. "Thank you, no," she answered quickly. "Come with me, all of you."

Crossing the parking lot, climbing the timbered dirt stairs to the pine-needled trail, the girls began to run excitedly ahead as they reached the path to the amphitheater. "Girls," he called out, signaling for them to slow down. He dropped back a step as Colleen continued, passing the girls and going on alone.

The stately old pines that lined the way opened up before her, their tall trunks forming a perimeter around the open bowl of the amphitheater. Wooden benches filled the opening, sloping down the gradual incline, leading to a simple elevated wooden stage, a lone piano its only prop. Colleen leaned against the last bench, trying to envision Brenden playing on stage.

Brian approached and stood beside her. "I remember the early years," he began, "before the new stage, when the benches didn't have any backs on them. My folks used to bring us here when we were kids, smothered in bug spray. Folk concerts mostly back then, a different theme each year. Railroad songs, the history of logging in Wisconsin, tales of lonely sailors, that type of stuff. Always loved it here.

"You know," he realized, "I'll bet I saw him play at least a dozen times, since Christine and I started bringing the girls here."

"You saw him play?" Colleen said, turning suddenly in surprise.

"Was he a tall, lanky guy with a slight dimple in his chin?" Brian asked. "I remember he always wore a black beret, backwards, and dark sunglasses, even at the after-dark performances."

"That was Brenden," she nodded, a smile coming slowly across her face. They were both silent for a moment, he respecting her memory, she recalling the image she'd seen play so many times before. "He always played with those dark sunglasses," Colleen continued, her voice soft. "Sunday mornings at church alongside the bright stained-glass window, or late into the night in the back corner of some dimly lit, smoke-filled bar. He said that if you can feel the music you don't need to see the keys."

"I remember him softly playing background to an acoustic guitar ballad, or loudly banging out an upbeat show tune for some zany original play," Brian offered. "He would jump up and down on the stool and spin around, arms flailing dramatically, a huge smile on his face, as much a part of the play as the actors on stage. Sometimes I would find myself watching him, and not the play."

"That sounds just like him," she smiled as she tried to picture him here, where she'd never seen him play.

"He must have really loved it, to keep coming back each year."

"Oh, he did," she said. "Once I asked him if he thought he'd ever just move here, to stay, he loved it so much. But he said the leaving made the returning that much more special."

They stood there, she with a vision of Brenden on stage, he with the memories of coming here over the years – as a crew-cut kid with his parents and siblings, as a newlywed with Christine, as a father with his girls.

Shannon and Kerry climbed the steps onto the stage and huddled in the corner, whispering secretly to each other. "Ladies and gentleman," Shannon announced, "please take your seats as we present the famous and beautiful Bailey sisters!"

Brian took Colleen's arm, playing the role of an usher showing the lady to her seat. They strode down the main aisle to the front row, center stage. Brian released her arm, bowed, then kissed the hand she held out to him. She curtsied and took her seat as he sat down beside her. They laughed and clapped and whistled as the girls treated them to a variety show, complete with ballet dancing, Girl Scout camp songs, and mistold elephant jokes. The show – and numerous curtain calls – complete, the girls came down off the stage, sat on a bench, and announced it was time for the grown-ups to perform.

"Shall I sing?" Brian teased the girls, who groaned loudly.

"Dad *can't* sing," Shannon explained to Colleen. "Mom always said he likes Neil Young so much 'cause Neil can't sing either. It's the only music Dad can sing along with and not sound bad."

"They pester me when I sing along with one of Neil's

albums," Brian informed her, "but they know all the words, so I must be doing something right." Looking at the empty piano on stage, he turned to Colleen. "Do you still play?"

"A little, but I'm afraid not very well."

"Good," he replied. "You'll complement my singing perfectly. Shall we?" He led her on stage, where she took her seat in front of the piano, Brenden's piano. "You OK?" he asked.

"I think so," she replied as he made his way to the middle of the stage, taking his place in front of the imaginary microphone. "What key?" she asked.

"Off-key, if you please," he joked as he turned to face his audience. "Ladies and ladies, to end our show for today, I'd like to sing for you a little song my grandmother sang at bedtime to my mother, who in turn sang it to me, as I now sing it to you."

> *Over in Killarney*
> *many years ago,*
> *me mother sang a song to me*
> *in tones so sweet and low.*
>
> *Just a simple little ditty,*
> *in her good ould Irish way,*
> *And I'd give the world if she could sing*
> *that song to me this day.*
>
> *Too ra loo ra loo ral, too ra loo ra li,*
> *Too ra loo ra loo ral, hush, now don't you cry!*
>
> *Too ra loo ra loo ral, too ra loo ra li,*
> *Too ra loo ra loo ral, that's an Irish lullaby.*

As the song ended, the girls looked up at the two stoic figures on stage. Shannon bent down and picked up a discarded playbill from under the bench. Reading it, she looked back up at her father. He stared out over the top of her head, back into the pines that rimmed the amphitheater, back into time.

"Dad! They're doing a Clancy Brothers show this year. Tonight's opening night. Grandpa would love it."

"Oh shit, Grandpa!"

Chapter 4

≈

*S*ean Bailey rose early, put the coffee on, and sat in his chair, book in hand, looking out the bay window of his tiny cottage. Light morning waves rolled gently across Kangaroo Lake, lazily lapping against the shore, depositing their frothy white foam. The first rays of sunlight were just beginning to break through the trees, peering over the roof, casting their long fingers into the night. It was Sean's habit to greet each new day this way, for even four-plus years of retirement could not reset the internal clock that had been set during a lifetime of work.

It wasn't that he didn't sleep well. He did, which bothered him, for he thought maybe he should have suffered more sleepless nights since his wife had passed away. Maybe his son had enough sleepless nights for both of them.

As the coffee pot gave its final gurgle, Sean looked out over the lawn, surveying the damage from last night's storm. Brian was to stop in today to help hang a new ceiling fan, and Sean had a number of detailed preparations to make before Brian arrived, hell-bent on action and results. But first, it appeared, he would have to clean up the debris in the yard. He thought he'd best get an early start.

Pouring his coffee, heavy sugar, heavy cream, he laid his toast thick with peanut butter, creamy style. He sat at the table and ate quickly. Eating alone was bad enough – drawing the process out, worse still. Rising, he picked up the soap-filled scrub brush that lay across the back of the sink and wiped the dishes, setting them in the drying rack. Changing out of his pajamas, he put on his jeans, buttoned his plaid short-sleeved shirt over his white undershirt, and headed outside.

The damp ground squished slightly underfoot as Sean inspected the yard. Cottonwood branches lay strewn across his path, sticky to the touch as he placed them in the wheelbarrow and collected his tools from the shed. Pushing the wheelbarrow to the front yard, he lit a fire in the fire pit then began raking the debris into small piles, throwing them on the fire once gathered. The damp leaves temporarily smothered the flames, sending a thick line of sweet white smoke out over the lake, until the flames grew from beneath, regaining control.

Fire burning, Sean threw on the last of the green cedars, which crackled as their scent rose. Standing in front of the fire, hands folded atop the rake resting under his chin, he relaxed, having enjoyed this bit of early-morning activity. It struck him that the same activity would have felt like a chore only a few years earlier, a job to be fit into his hectic schedule back at the old house, a lifetime ago. Turning from the fire, he walked out onto the pier, glancing across the lake toward Brian's. He would be rising about now, Sean thought, or finally falling asleep.

After his mother passed away, Brian had taken it upon himself to play mother hen to his father, calling him daily to see how he was doing. He was the only child left in Wisconsin, and, as the oldest, felt a certain inherent duty that came with that position. Sean was initially appreciative of Brian's extra support and attention, and grew accustomed to it. He remained tolerant of it even after he himself had come to terms with his wife's passing. If the son needed to play mother hen, even if the father no longer required it, Sean could let it continue.

When Christine passed away a short time later, Brian intensified his paternal tendencies toward his father, as if holding more tightly to the shortening piece of rope on his life vest. The roles had since changed, subtly, without Brian's awareness, the son now requiring the extra support more than the father.

Though Sean had been bitterly stung by life's cruelties, his wife taken twenty years too soon at the age of sixty, they had had thirty-seven wonderful years together. Yet despite the fact that he missed her dearly, and was fearful of the lonely years ahead, Sean still had a feeling nearing completeness. He had loved, and been loved in return. His children were decent people, all of them, their mother so proud, and Sean was content to share in their futures, carrying his memories with him.

Brian, on the other hand, was more in need of receiving support than he was capable of giving it. Christine's death, so close after his own mother's, had devastated him so completely that he still had not yet begun to recover. They had been together for seventeen years, half their lives, but had lost the chance at the rest of their lives. Now, at thirty-six, Brian was far too young to live only off his memories, and not create new ones, though he still couldn't see that, holding on to Christine as he did. So now the father watched over the son once again.

Sean glanced across the lake toward Brian's one last time before leaving the pier and checking the fire. Satisfied, he loaded the tools in the wheelbarrow, set them by the shed, and went inside to read the ceiling-fan instructions. Calling Brian's and getting no answer, Sean grabbed a root beer and headed back out to the shed to collect the needed tools while he waited for Brian to arrive.

～

Hating the traffic and congestion of Fish Creek, Brian exited the park on the little-used road that ran along the back of the golf course, then cut across the peninsula, taking the shortest, fastest route to Grandpa's. It was nearly three o'clock, and he had promised Grandpa he'd stop by early to help install the new ceiling fan. Colleen's arrival, and the circumstances related to her brother, had caused him to forget all about the ceiling fan. If he didn't get there soon, Grandpa would probably try to install the damned thing himself.

Heading south out of Baileys Harbor, they rode through the old golf course Colleen had crossed the night before, past the plumbers with the huge black holding tank on the front lawn, then around the curve and past the sign for Kangaroo Lake. Colleen sat up straighter in the cab of the old pick-up, glancing at the surroundings.

"Been through here before?" Brian asked, sensing her awareness.

"I think I came through this way last night," she replied, taking a closer look at the vaguely familiar scenery, so peaceful in the light of day, so eerie in the midst of the storm the night before. A nicely tended wildflower garden sprang up on her right, followed by a closed music-box museum housed in an old barn. On her left three deer pranced along the line of cedars at the back of a cornfield. Continuing down the highway, they passed a mailbox, dotted with blue reflectors, then rounded a slight curve, a brown horse fence running alongside them. Brian slowed as they came to a homemade wooden signpost, carved in the shape of a kangaroo, 'The Dam Road' engraved in its pouch, then turned right onto a small gravel road.

He drove slowly down the shared road, dodging the numerous potholes, then turned onto a smaller drive carved out of the cedars, a strip of grass running down the middle between the gravel wheel beds. Brian pulled into the parking apron, stopping next to an old blue station wagon with wood-grain panels. The girls jumped out of the truck and ran off into the yard. Colleen slid across the empty seat and climbed out, stretching her legs as she surveyed the setting.

A small, quaint cottage sat proudly before her. A large screened-in porch sloped away from the simple square structure, a porch swing hanging from the rafters, facing out toward the lake. Through the porch screens she could see a deck off the front of the cottage, potted red geraniums lining its border. The cottage was set back on the lot, the long front lawn running away towards the lake. A number of boats, visible through the trees that hugged the shore, were moored alongside a pier. The smell of cedars filled her as she drew in a deep breath, taking in the scene.

A burst of noise grabbed her attention. She turned to see the girls running toward the shed in back, Brian's father poking his head out the open door. Stepping out of the shed, he knelt, opening his arms to receive the girls, and a kiss on each cheek. Sufficiently hugged, he retrieved a butterscotch candy for each girl from the pocket of his jeans then sent them off to play. Rising, he turned to face Brian and his guest.

"Hello," he approached, greeting them with a welcoming smile.

"Hey, Dad. Sorry we're late. Forgot all about the ceiling fan."

"No problem. All done, actually."

"Figured you might be."

"So, who's your friend?"

"Oh, sorry. Dad, this is Colleen. Colleen, my dad."

"Hi," she said, returning his smile. It was easy to see the resemblance, she thought, both in appearance and mannerisms. If she couldn't imagine what Brian might have looked like as a child, sitting on the tailgate with his mother, it didn't take much imagination to guess what he might look like in twenty-some years.

"Welcome," Sean replied, extending his hand. "Been a while since we've seen a smile as pretty as yours around here.

Come on in." He led the way across the lannon stone walk, holding the porch door open for Colleen. "Lemonade?"

Making her way through the porch, Colleen noticed the orderly nature of the contents, as well as the telltale signs that Brian and the girls spent a lot of time here. Four pairs of water shoes — two blue, two pink — were lined in a row along one wall, arranged by size. The garbage and recycle bins, sorted and marked, lined the adjacent wall. In the far corner, grill utensils and marshmallow roasting sticks hung from neatly arranged hooks on the back of the chimney, beneath a collection of driftwood. On the opposite wall, facing the lake, two tiny pink swimsuits hung in front of the screen, billowing lightly in the breeze.

Following Brian inside, the interior of the cottage opened up before her. The knotted pine walls led up to an A-framed ceiling of similar style, a lazily spinning ceiling fan hanging down between the rafters. The single room, partitioned into visible settings, was decorated in antiques, and invited warmth and comfort. A wooden butter churn, serving as an end table, sat next to a reading chair by the fireplace. An old wagon seat had been converted into a coffee table, a corner bookcase used to display a collection of flatirons. A wooden rocker faced out the bay window, overlooking the lake; an old school desk, with black metal legs, stood near the front door. It wasn't hard to see where Brian had acquired his tastes, Colleen thought.

He emerged from the tiny kitchen — compact for one, crowded for two — and handed her a glass of lemonade. Sipping the tart drink as the two men continued chatting in the kitchen, Colleen walked about the room, looking at the decorations. An assortment of old metal heat registers, painted black, hung on one wall. Opposite these, a collection of antique glassware and kitchen tins rested on the tiny shelves above the rafters. A hand-carved family crest hung above the mantel of the fireplace, next to a drawing of a thatched-roof Irish cottage. Small knickknacks sat on every available space around the room, along with various trinkets and craft-sale games. On the beam above her, a cloth goose curled its neck to peer down on the occupants below.

The far wall was framed by two doorways, hung with matching swinging doors, a small brown bag screwed onto the hinge of one. Climbing the wall between them, a built-in wooden ladder led to a loft above the bedrooms. Scattered across the wall, a collection of multiple-pose picture frames caught Colleen's attention.

Each frame appeared to hold a summer of memories, and chronicled a project a year as the cottage was slowly transformed. A shed one year, a pier the next, a deck, a paint job, new furniture, new carpeting, a boat, and so on, until the series ended with the cottage in its present form.

Colleen moved closer, studying the people and faces in the tiny pictures. Most showed laughter and fun, or relaxation and peace. Moving from frame to frame, she charted the growth of the girls, from pacifiers and diapers, through missing teeth, to long hair. Brian, younger and a bit thinner, sitting on the deck with his parents. His mother, playing cards in the loft with the girls, doing dishes in the kitchen with the grandmothers, lying in ready on the raft, squirt guns in hand.

Moving across the frames a second time, Colleen found herself focusing solely on the pictures of Christine. Brushing the girls' hair, playing Yahtzee at the kitchen table, reading a book on the couch, lounging on the pier. One picture in particular drew her in – Christine and the girls on the bridge of a ferry, laughing as they were sprayed by the mist of a passing wave. Staring at the picture, Colleen felt a melancholy sadness, at the thought of all that Christine had lost, and all that she herself was missing. Transfixed, she was startled when the front door burst open next to her.

"Grandpa, can we go tubing?"

～

"Sure," Grandpa answered after receiving a nod from Brian. "Grab your suits off the porch and get changed while I go ready the boat," he instructed. Turning to Colleen, he asked, "Boat ride?"

Colleen blinked, stepping back from the pictures. "I'm sorry?" she apologized.

"Care to go for a boat ride?" Grandpa repeated.

"Oh, yes," she replied. "Love to."

"Will you take us on topsy-turns, Dad?" Shannon asked.

"Not without your suits on," he chided as Shannon grabbed hers off the porch.

"Can Colleen go tubing with us?" Kerry asked.

"You'll have to ask her," Brian answered.

Kerry turned toward Colleen. "Would you go?" she pleaded. "It's really fun. You go really fast," she rambled on, "then Dad makes topsy-turns over the waves, and you go bouncing and flying in the air. Can you come, huh?"

"Sounds fun," Colleen said, smiling at the child's excitement. "I'd love to, but I'm afraid I don't have my suit."

"One of Aileen's old suits might fit you," Grandpa offered, referring to his youngest daughter. "She's a bit shorter than you, but just as thin. Worth a try, at least."

With that Brian disappeared into one of the bedrooms, Shannon and Kerry following close behind. The girls emerged quickly, prancing about the cottage in their little pink suits before slipping onto the porch to put on their water shoes, and grab their life jackets.

Brian reappeared soon after, jumping into the room with dramatic flare, striking a pose like an actor coming out of some changing tent on the beach in an old silent movie. His baggy, faded suit hung low on his hips. His legs and arms were beginning to tan, though his torso was whiter than the clouds. A small patch of dark hair lay on his chest, sprinkled with a few strands of gray. His stomach, a bit softer than in some of the pictures, hung slightly over the front of his suit. While not a threat to win the Mr. Universe contest, he didn't have to worry about the Ugliest Man competition either.

He held a small one-piece suit in his hand, which he offered to Colleen. "The best one I could find," he apologized. "You don't have to wear it, if it doesn't fit," he added, directing her toward the bathroom as Grandpa collected the girls and went to ready the boat.

Colleen entered the tiny bathroom and locked the door behind her. She turned toward the mirror and looked at the face that stared back at her. She studied her simple, plain features, so familiar to her, and wondered what she looked like to others. Undressing, she recalled the pictures of Christine, more full-bodied, with shapely curves that highlighted her profile. Standing there, Colleen wondered what Brian saw when he looked at his memories, and then at her.

She picked up the suit and tried it on. It was a bit small, hanging low in the front, pressing flat against her chest, though ample to cover her. She shook off the comparison with Christine, glad for the moment that she could take part in the fun. Picking her clothes up off the floor, she turned the knob and opened the door.

Brian sat in the rocking chair looking out the bay window, watching Grandpa and the girls ready the boat. Hearing the bathroom door open, he turned toward Colleen. She stood before him, a vision of everything he longed for, and all he had lost. He sat motionless for a moment, creating a memory, recalling another.

"Ready to go," she announced, holding her clothes out, asking, "where should I put these?"

"I'll take them," he answered, unblinking.

Taking her clothes, he slid into one of the bedrooms, closing the door behind him as he let out a deep breath. Drawing his breath back in, he could smell her scent as it rose off her clothes. He closed his eyes and leaned his head back against the door.

∾

They walked together across the front lawn, toward the pier. Standing alongside the boat, holding the rope as he watched them approach, Grandpa remembered a time, long ago, when the same type of peaceful smile had crossed his son's face.

Tossing the rope to Brian, Grandpa took Colleen's hand, helping her into the boat as the girls fastened their life jackets. Brian pushed the boat away from the pier, hopped in, and took the seat behind the wheel. Turning the engine over a time or two until it caught, he slowly pushed down on the throttle as they headed away from shore.

Coming to a stop in the middle of the lake, Grandpa threw the inner tube into the water, letting the towrope out behind the boat, making sure it didn't knot up. He helped the girls into the tube, positioning them in their usual spots, Kerry in the front, Shannon behind her. Grabbing the handles tightly, Shannon shouted out, "Let's move, people!"

Brian restarted the engine and pulled out slowly, tightening the slack. Rope taut, he floored the gas, the front end of the boat rising out of the water. The inner tube dipped down for a second or two as they started, then rose to sit atop the water, the girls screaming in delight. Gliding inside the wake, the tube followed behind the boat, mimicking its gradual turns, sending the girls back and forth, from the crest of the wave on one side then back across to the other.

Brian pulled back quickly on the throttle, the wake lapping up against the back of the boat, then turned the wheel sharply to the right as he pushed the throttle back down. A topsy-turn. Steering the boat back across the trailing wake, the slack rope tightened, pulling the tube into the crest of an oncoming wave, then up, into the air and over it, to skip in succession across the tops of the waves.

"Again!" shouted the girls, and so it went for the next few minutes.

Dripping on the seats as they climbed excitedly back into the boat, the girls shivered from the cold of the early season water. Brian wrapped their towels tightly around them and dried their faces as Grandpa pulled the tube in.

"How was it?" Brian asked.

"Great!" Shannon answered, "but we almost tipped over on that one turn."

"You should try it," Kerry added, turning to Colleen.

"I just might do that. It looked fun. How's the water?"

"FFFFrrrreeeezzzzing," they both shivered.

"Maybe another time," Colleen laughed.

"Lake tour? Shore cruise?" Grandpa asked as he stowed the towrope under the back seat.

"I get to drive," Shannon stated as she got behind the wheel.

"Slowly," Brian instructed her as Kerry lay down face-first on the floor between the front seats, her towel wrapped tightly around her, Brian spreading another one on top of her.

The full length of the lake lay before them as they headed north up the shore, past the place the family had rented when Brian was a child, toward the island at the far end. Quaint old cottages from another era dotted the water's edge, interspersed now and again with large new houses. Shannon hugged the shoreline for a while then took them out into the middle, around the shallow spot off the point, marked by the stone fireplace that stood sentry, looking out over its domain. They swung back toward shore, past more timeless cabins, and the boat launch, then headed off around the island.

Tucked behind the island, coming into view just above the water line, lay the causeway. A low road built up on piles of white stone, it cut the lake in two. On the far side, children fished among the lily pads, old bobbers and line hanging from the telephone wires above. Small lazy waves rolled away from the road, toward them, out across the lake. It was a setting so serene Colleen found it hard to imagine the fierceness of the storm the night before, the waves lunging across the road, pushing her car toward the edge.

"I have to go to the bathroom," Kerry announced from the front of the boat.

"Want to hop in?" Brian asked.

"Too cold," Kerry answered, shivering at the thought of jumping back into the icy water.

"Right. Home, James," he instructed Shannon, who grinned as she pushed the throttle down forcefully.

The sudden lurch of the boat caught Colleen by surprise, throwing her off balance. Straightening herself, she knelt on the seat, her head held up over the windshield. The sunlight reflecting off the lake highlighted the long shiny hair billowing out behind her as they skimmed across the sparkling water. Brian looked at her, Grandpa at him.

～

Returning to shore, Brian pulled into the lift and hopped out, grabbing the rope and securing the boat as they all got out. Walking across the front lawn toward the cottage, Grandpa invited, "Stay to supper? I've got chicken breasts thawing, enough for everyone."

Brian turned to Colleen, who nodded in approval. "Sure," he agreed, "start the grill. Old-fashioned?" he asked as he climbed the steps to the deck.

"What else?" Grandpa called back as he rounded the porch and went to grab the charcoal from the shed.

Brian found the chicken breasts thawing on the kitchen counter. Five of them. Grandpa had planned on their staying for dinner all along. Brian placed the chicken breasts in a bowl, covered them with teriyaki sauce, and began to mince a clove of fresh garlic. "Wild rice okay?" he asked over his shoulder.

"Great," Colleen answered, grabbing the borrowed white shirt from the bedroom, sliding comfortably into the already familiar garment. "Can I help?"

"Salad would be nice, if you don't mind."

"No problem," she replied, picking up the lettuce and washing it while Brian mixed the drinks.

"What's an old-fashioned?" she inquired.

"Brandy, sugar, bitters, sweet soda. Olive or cherry?"

"Olive sounds good," she answered.

"That's how my mom liked them," he said.

They stood there, side by side, chatting companionably. The grill ablaze, Grandpa sat on the edge of the deck, watching their backs through the bay window. Brian waved his arms with dramatic flare. Colleen tilted her head in laughter. Grandpa remembered, and wondered.

Brian stepped onto the deck, drinks in hand. Grandpa rose and set out two chairs, motioning Colleen to sit. Thanking him, she sat, stretching her legs out before her, leaning her head back against the chair as she closed her eyes to the sun that warmed her face, the unbuttoned white shirt falling away to her sides. Grandpa took the chair next to her, slowly drawing in the first sweet sip of the familiar drink. Brian descended the steps of the deck and headed across the lawn toward the pier, and his girls.

Sitting silently on the deck with Brian's father, Colleen listened to the quiet. The only sounds she could hear were the small waves rolling up against the side of the boat and the distant gurgle of water slipping over the tiny dam at the end of the lake. Opening her eyes, she looked out over the lawn, toward the pier. Three bodies lay belly-down, sideways across the pier, arms dangling down into the water, holding buckets to scoop up the minnows.

"Got one!" Kerry exclaimed excitedly.

"Special girls," Colleen offered.

"Special son, too," Grandpa stated.

Straightening in her chair, Colleen took a long sip of her drink and looked out over the peaceful setting. A fire pit sat on the front lawn, near the pier, closed off from the wind by a few sweet-smelling cedars. A lone sailboat, silhouetted by the late afternoon sun, drifted lazily across the waves in the distance. A tiny overgrown beach sat beside the water's edge in the far corner of the lot, near the cottage next door that seemed too close, as if encroaching on the solitude. "Neighbors nice?" Colleen inquired.

Following her gaze, Grandpa looked up at the cottage next door, then out toward the pier, at the three happy children playing in the water. "You could say," he answered. "Brian owns the place. Bought it, what, two and a half years ago now, shortly after my wife passed away, and just before Christine died. Don't think he's hardly been in it since," Grandpa informed her. "I live there in winter, when it's too cold to stay in this cottage."

"You live here all year?"

"Yep. Moved up here year-round after my Maggie died," Grandpa explained. "Didn't see much reason to stay back home with the memories, but without her."

"And Brian?"

"Tried to do the same, move away from the memories. But he hasn't been able to. Doesn't seem to know how to go on."

"He drifts off, I've noticed."

"We both had it all, for a time," Grandpa reflected. "Now we just have our memories, and each other." Grandpa took a sip of his drink before continuing. "I didn't have nearly as much time with my Maggie as I wanted, but what I had was good, and it will have to be enough for me. But Brian, his time with Christine was so much shorter, and he's still so lost."

"And the girls?"

"They're fine, doing as well as can be expected. He couldn't love them more. They keep him going, I think. But it's not the same. He's empty, hollow on the inside. Thick on the outside, but he's made of glass, brittle glass." Remembering the look on Brian's face as he watched Colleen in the boat, Grandpa straightened in his chair and turned to her. "Be careful," he counseled, "both for his sake, and yours."

Colleen raised her necklace to her chin as she looked out toward the pier.

~

The somber warning on the deck melted away in the frivolity of the meal. The tall, strong drinks, two each, helped set the light tone. Colleen listened to their playful banter, the good-natured ribbing and horseplay they exchanged between bites of tender juicy chicken. She imagined mealtimes had always been this way for him, and wished she had more happy family meals to recall from her own childhood, instead of the quiet suppers in front of the TV with Brenden.

Dinner finished, Brian rose and cleared the table. Kerry sat on Grandpa's lap, playing with his glasses, while Shannon stood behind Colleen, trying to braid her hair. "More milk, Grandpa?" Brian called out from the kitchen.

"More root beer," the girls chimed in unison.

"Tell Colleen the more root beer story, Dad," Kerry pleaded.

"Can I tell it?" Shannon asked as she began. "One time, on a really really hot day, Grandpa was cutting the grass while Grandma was making lunch. When Grandpa came in for lunch he was all hot and sweaty, and Grandma gave him a root beer. Grandpa was so thirsty he drank the whole bottle straight down in one sip, and when he finished he let out a huge burp, and Grandma said, 'Grandpa, what do you say?' and Grandpa said, 'More root beer!'" They all laughed at the cute little tale, Colleen for the first time, the rest for the hundredth.

"That reminds me," said Kerry, "about the show in the park."

"Oh, yeah," Shannon took over. "We went to the park today, you know, where they have the shows."

"Colleen's brother was the piano player at AFT," Brian explained to Grandpa.

"Anyway," Shannon continued, "we went there this afternoon, and I found a notice that said they're doing a Clancy Brothers show this year, and tonight's opening night, and do you want to go?"

"A Clancy Brothers show," Grandpa repeated. "Sounds fun. I'm game."

"Can we go, Dad, huh, can we?"

"Want to go?" Brian asked, turning to Colleen.

"I'd love to, if you don't mind me tagging along," she answered. "I did kind of want to see a show while I was here, and going alone doesn't sound like much fun."

"Great," said Grandpa, "what time's the show?"

"Seven-thirty," Shannon recalled.

"Just enough time to make it," Grandpa calculated, checking his watch, "if we leave now. Everyone in the station wagon!"

∽

Hurrying down the pine-needled path toward the amphitheater, they could hear the soft lilting of an Irish ballad rising to greet them. The show had just begun, the first song ending as they slid quietly onto a bench near the back. Four figures stood on stage in front of microphones, guitars over their shoulders, other instruments set behind them. To the side of the stage sat the unused piano, stool empty.

The concert proceeded briskly, a mix of rousing drinking tunes, songs about war and revolution and death, and ballads of love. The crowd sang along on many of the selections, Colleen surprised to find that the girls, so young, knew many of the words. She sat in the middle of the bench, Grandpa to one side of her, Kerry on his lap, Brian on her other side, Shannon on his lap. As the show came to a close, a chill ran through Colleen, as she listened to the deep, rich voices that rose on either side of her.

Oh, the summertime is coming
And the trees are sweetly blooming,
And the wild mountain thyme
Grows around the blooming heather
Will you go, lassie, go?

And we'll all go together
To pluck wild mountain thyme
All around the blooming heather
Will you go, lassie, go?

I will build my love a tower
Near yon' pure crystal fountain
And on it I will pile
All the flowers of the mountain
Will you go, lassie, go?

And we'll all go together
To pluck wild mountain thyme
All around the blooming heather
Will you go, lassie, go?

If my true love she were gone
I would surely find another
Where the wild mountain thyme
Grows around the blooming heather
Will you go, lassie, go?

And we'll all go together
To pluck wild mountain thyme
All around the blooming heather
Will you go, lassie, go?

Oh, the summertime is coming
And the trees are sweetly blooming,

And the wild mountain thyme
Grows around the blooming heather
Will you go, lassie, go?

And we'll all go together
To pluck wild mountain thyme
All around the blooming heather
Will you go, lassie, go?

~

They drove silently out of the park then across the dark interior of the peninsula, the two men sitting stoically in the front, alone with their memories. The girls, tired after a long day, rested their heads against Colleen's shoulders in the back.

Coming into Baileys Harbor, Grandpa slowed, turning his head toward the back seat, asking, "Ice cream?"

The girls quickly sat upright on either side of Colleen. Seeing the familiar sight of the Yum Yum Tree, they slipped on their shoes and readied to go. "Can we get some candy, too?" Kerry hoped.

Parking, they crossed the road to the ice cream store, the benches under the front windows lined with children licking at the cones that dripped down their arms. Grandpa opened the door, a cow bell rattling overhead as they passed under.

An old claw-foot bathtub, filled with salt-water taffy, sat across from a glass-topped counter, which offered homemade chocolate treats. The girls ran toward the opposite wall, and the buckets filled with candy, while Grandpa led the way past the jellybean display, to the ice cream counter in back. Their orders were taken by a tall college student with red hair shaved close to his head, paper hat resting on top at an angle.

Cones in one hand, candy bags in the other, the girls led Colleen back outside, to wait on a bench under the front window while Grandpa and Brian paid. Sitting on the bench between the girls, the three of them lazily licking their cones, Colleen thought back to the concert. "What was that last song they played tonight?" she asked. "I think your father was listening to it on the porch last night."

"It's called 'Will You Go, Lassie, Go?'" Shannon answered between licks. "Dad has a whole tape with only that song on it, both sides, and he listens to it over and over. They played it at my mom's funeral."

"And at Grandma's, too," Kerry added.

The cow bell on the screen door clanked behind them as Brian and Grandpa joined the group. "Nice night," Grandpa commented as he sat, licking his cone as he laid his wallet across his lap, organizing the wad of bills with his free hand.

"Be right back," Brian said as he opened the screen door and headed back into the store. He returned a few minutes later, a small white bag in hand, held out for everyone to see. "Booger Ball Bowling, anyone?" he asked, smiling mischievously.

"Yeah!" the girls shouted, jumping from their seats as Grandpa shook his head, groaning.

"What's Booger Ball Bowling?" Colleen inquired.

"It's a game Dad invented," Shannon told her.

"Yeah, it's really fun," Kerry added, "'cept Grandpa doesn't like it."

"You throw booger balls in the road and try to get the cars to run over them," Shannon explained.

"What's a booger ball?"

"Chocolate-covered malted milk balls," Brian answered.

"Really good, expensive, double-dipped chocolate-covered malted milk balls," Grandpa corrected.

"It's kind of tricky to get them to rest in the right spots, where the car tires go," Shannon continued. "You can roll one out almost all the way to the curb on the other side, and it'll roll all the way back to this curb. It's easier when it's really hot, 'cause the booger balls are slightly melted and they stay better on the road."

"You get two points for a boat trailer," Kerry stated.

"And two if your booger ball is sitting still when it gets run over," Shannon added. "Otherwise, it's just one point for a rolling booger ball and a regular car."

"How many points for a boat trailer running over a rolling booger ball?" Colleen inquired. They looked at her, puzzled, realizing they hadn't accounted for this scoring possibility.

"Let me have a few first," Grandpa said, reaching for the bag, "before you waste them all and mess up the road. I'm still not sure which is worse, the game or the name."

Grabbing a few booger balls, Grandpa walked off down the sidewalk, licking his cone, distancing himself from the activity, as if leaving the scene before a crime was committed. The girls quickly finished their cones, throwing their napkins in the garbage before holding their hands out to Brian.

"A few at a time," he instructed as the girls bent down at the curb to place their first shots. The road lay empty before them as they lightly rolled the first few booger balls onto the waiting lanes. Colleen leaned back against the bench and watched as Brian crouched down behind the girls. The first few shots rolled all the way across the road, pausing in front of Grandpa's station wagon for a moment before slowly creeping back toward them, coming to rest against the curb at their feet.

"Darn," Kerry said dejectedly.

"Softer," he instructed quietly.

Getting a feel for the playing field, the girls soon had both sides of the road dotted with sitting booger balls. They sat down on the sidewalk, feet sticking out over the curb, and waited.

"Southbounder," Shannon shouted.

Colleen followed the approaching car, which somehow managed to elude every single booger ball that lay in its path, save one, which it whisked with the side of its tire, knocking it into the other lane.

"Shoot," said Shannon. "Should we throw some more?"

"Patience," he counseled.

"Northbounder," Kerry exclaimed, rising to check the approaching vehicle. "With a boat!"

All three tensed in silent anticipation as the headlights approached, the booger balls waiting. The front tire of the car rolled squarely over a booger ball, flattening it against the pavement as the boat trailer squished another.

"A doubler!" Kerry shouted.

"With a trailer!" Shannon added as the three of them exchanged high fives.

Colleen watched them, wishing she'd had a father who took the extra time for the little things that matter to a child. Her father had always had big plans, and little time.

Brian held the bag out to her. "Try a shot?"

She rose from the bench and grabbed a few booger balls. Her first shot sailed clean across the road, coming to rest under Grandpa's station wagon. They all laughed, kidding her as they would each other. "Softer," he said, in the same instructing tone he had used with the girls. "Just lay it out there."

She rolled a second booger ball, which again headed for Grandpa's station wagon until it stopped, changed direction, and slowly crossed back over the center line, coming to rest in the tire track of the northbound lane nearest them. A car approached, its front wheel barely missing her waiting booger ball before the rear tire rolled squarely over it. They jumped in unison, Brian high-fiving Colleen as the girls hugged her legs.

Grandpa appeared from the darkness down the sidewalk in time to witness the celebration. "A new champion?" he asked as he side-stepped his way through the minefield of booger balls that littered the path to the station wagon. They drove noisily back to the cottage, the girls recounting the events of the night's bowling for Grandpa.

∼

They returned to Grandpa's cottage to find a pile of dirty dishes waiting for them in the sink. The light that escaped through the bay window revealed lawn chairs and towels on the deck, an uncovered boat by the pier.

"Looks like we left in a bit of a hurry," Brian stated. "I'll help you clean up, Dad."

Taking their cue, the girls climbed the wooden ladder to the loft, candy bags clenched between their teeth. Grandpa picked up the last of the dishes from the table as Brian ran the water in the sink.

"I'll help," Colleen offered, moving toward the kitchen.

"Guests don't do dishes," Grandpa informed her. "Sit. Relax."

Looking around the open cottage, Colleen was drawn again to the wall holding pictures of close-knit family fun over the years. Standing in front of the frames, she noticed a leather-bound writing book sitting on the old school desk by the front door, the words *Cottage Memories* stamped into the cover. She picked up the book and moved to the couch, snuggling into the corner by the lamp. She opened the book and read the handwritten inscription on the inside cover.

March 16
Dear Maggie,

I was so touched last fall by the tears that welled up in your eyes when Brian and Niall and I surprised you with a visit that first weekend you bought the cottage, the whole family together to share the special day. A real Norman Rockwell moment, Brian called it. I thought you might like a little writing book to keep at the cottage, to jot down all the happy memories that lie before us in the years to come. Happy Birthday.

Love,
Christine

Colleen fanned through the book, nearly filled, various styles of handwriting covering its pages. Wondering suddenly if she might be intruding on a piece of private family history, she closed the book. Grandpa noticed her uncertainty and tried to put her at ease. "It's okay," he said as he closed the blinds and headed toward the kitchen to help with the dishes, "you can read it." Colleen reset herself deep into the couch and reopened the book to the first page.

June 6

Thanks to Christine and Brian, and now baby Shannon, we can all jot down memories from our times at 'The Bailey's'. We're located at the far south end of Kangaroo Lake, about halfway between Jacksonport and Baileys Harbor. Jacksonport is much smaller, and its three main attractions are the Laundromat, Vi's grocery store, and St. Michael's Catholic Church. Baileys Harbor, on the other hand, is a "full-service" town with a wonderful old hardware store, a movie theater, a bank, library, filling station, and barber shop, the Harbor Market, St. Mary's of the Lake, and many restaurants and gift shops.

I'm going to backtrack so that we have a history of our times at the lake. They've been fun times for the whole family, and we hope — and know that we will — have many more fun times to come. Starting with this weekend, three — no, four — generations have shared in this enjoyment. This was Shannon's — in all her newborn beauty — first trip to the cottage. She seems to be surviving it just fine, on this her "first-month" birthday.

We feel bad that the two great-grandpas, Charles and Ray, never had the opportunity to join us here — but then again, because of their love for us and for Door County, we know they're here with us each time any of us is here. We hope that our children, and grandchildren, and great-grandchildren have many fun times at this cottage, and are left with many wonderful memories.

Family — and friends — feel free to share your memories and fun times with us in this book. And remember to thank the Lord for providing us with this beautiful place — this piece of heaven on earth called Door County.

Maggie

Colleen settled more deeply into the couch, covering her legs with the handmade Afghan that hung over the back as she flipped through the book, stopping here and there to read. The treasured memories of others flooded out at her, of happy times spent together, of projects worked on, of peaceful moments spent in the quiet setting. She read on, learning the personalities of the various writers as they described quiet weeklong vacations alone, or short busy weekends, the whole family crowded happily together in the tiny cottage. Surely no family could be so close, she thought, to a place, or each other. Closing the book, she thought of her own crumbling family, wishing there were more happy memories to recall.

"Gotta close up the boat," she heard him say, "then we'll go get your car."

Colleen looked up to find Brian standing before her. "I'm fine," she assured him, reopening the book as the two men headed out the front door into the darkness. She read on, with more interest in the various members of the family than she'd ever had for the characters of her romance novels. After a while she came again to a particular passage, in Grandpa's handwriting, one she had seen before but not read, as if unconsciously avoiding it.

...and then, at 10:35, the worst thing that ever happened to me happened, and it happened to the best thing that ever happened to me. Mary Margaret Corchran Bailey, R.N., Ph.D., Maggie, my wife, my friend, my love, the mother of those great kids and proud grandma of Shannon and Kerry, and little Bailey, left this world. God be with her!

Colleen leaned her head against the back of the couch and closed her eyes, thinking of Maggie, and Brenden, and Christine. She thought too of Grandpa, and herself, and Brian, each having to go on in life without their special friend. A chill ran through her and she felt suddenly sad, very sad. And tired, very tired.

Boat closed up, towels hung on the line, lawn chairs put away, father and son walked through the porch and entered the cottage. Grandpa paused, a finger held to his lips as he turned toward Brian. They both stood in the doorway a moment, looking across the room. She lay on the couch, head resting on the cushion, the Afghan drawn over her outstretched legs, the cottage book clutched tightly to her chest.

Brian crossed the room to the wooden ladder that led to the loft, calling up softly, "Girls?" Getting no answer, he climbed up the first few steps, opened the swinging doors, and peered in. Closing the doors, he turned to Grandpa. "Asleep," he said.

"Stay the night?"

"Looks that way. Thanks."

Locking the doors and turning off the lights, they crossed the darkened room in silence, heading toward the twin sets of doors on the far wall.

"Good night, Dad."

"'Night, son."

Opening the bedroom doors, they entered their separate rooms, alone.

Chapter 5

~

Colleen lay on the couch, drifting between sleep and consciousness. The smell of strong coffee filled the room as the low whisper of voices rose over the crackle of a small fire. Lying still, she concentrated on the voices coming from the kitchen, interrupted now and again by the tumble of peanuts being poured from a jar.

"Pretty girl." It was Grandpa.

"Nice girl." Brian.

"Pretty nice then. Or nice and pretty."

"And hurting. Her brother passed away recently. She came up here from Arizona to see where he spent his summers."

Silence.

After a time, Grandpa spoke again. "You're still young, Brian."

"We've had this discussion, Dad."

"It's life, son. You've got to go forward, move on."

"And you?"

"We're not talking about me. But if we were, I'd tell you that, though I didn't have enough time with your mother, what I had will be enough to last me the rest of the way. But you ... you're still young ...." Grandpa paused. "Your mom would want you to be happy again," he added.

"And Christine?"

"Her too, I think. They're watching, you know."

"You think so?"

"I know so."

Another pause.

"It doesn't diminish what you once had," Grandpa offered eventually, "to love again."

"I just don't think I could," Brian replied slowly. "Not like before."

Silence.

Colleen lay still, pretending to be asleep. She was embarrassed, not because she had heard the conversation, but because of the stirrings she had allowed herself to feel over the past day. He was still hurting so from the loss of his wife that he couldn't bring himself to look past her memory. It was quite probable that he hadn't been looking at her when he drifted off at times, but through her, back to Christine.

The creak of the loft doors overhead provided Colleen the opportunity to stir. Kerry climbed down the ladder, then up into her father's arms, yawning. "I have to go to the bathroom," she said loudly.

"Shh," he scolded her lightly, pointing toward Colleen.

"It's all right," Colleen said, rubbing her eyes as if just waking up.

Kerry headed off to the bathroom as Grandpa poured himself another cup of coffee. Brian sat in the rocker, staring across at Colleen as he rocked back and forth. Sitting up, she rolled her head, working the kinks out of her neck, her long golden brown hair tumbling across her shoulders. She stood, the Afghan dropping to the floor, exposing her long tan legs. Placing her hands on her hips, she arched her back, Brian's white cotton shirt pulling tightly across her chest. She took a step toward the bay window and looked out at the morning.

Gray clouds rolled swiftly overhead. Brisk waves lunged across the lake, beating against the side of the ski boat. A yellow paddleboat, tilted on its side, leaned against an old cedar. The jon boat, overturned, lay in its stationary berth, the raft bobbing in rhythm with the waves beyond.

"Coffee?" Grandpa called out from the kitchen.

"Thanks," she said as he brought her a steaming cup. She turned again to look out at the foreboding weather. "Gray day," she said, taking a sip from the warm mug she cupped between her hands.

"Too early to tell yet," Grandpa replied. "Never know what the weather's going to be like till noon. Some days break with full sun and glassy water, then turn to rain by afternoon as the clouds roll over the lake. Other days start out like today, gray, then the clouds part and open to the sun."

"Of course, some days are just gray altogether," Brian stated flatly as he stared out the bay window.

The loft doors creaked open again. Brian rose to greet Shannon, who was climbing down the ladder just as Kerry came out of the bathroom. He wrapped an arm around each girl, pulling them close to him.

"So," Shannon asked sleepily, "what's for breakfast?"

"How about I treat at the Sandpiper?" Grandpa offered.

"How about we take Colleen back to her car," Brian suggested, "and get her on her way."

Brian and the girls crowded into the bathroom to wash up while Grandpa went into the bedroom to change. Colleen stood alone in the empty room, setting it to memory. She folded the Afghan across the back of the couch and picked up the cottage book, placing it on the old school desk that stood under the wall of pictures. Scanning the pictures one last time, she realized she was focusing only on the photographs of Maggie and Christine. There had been two women in Brian's life, both now gone. She doubted there was room for a third.

"Freshen up?" she heard him ask as he emerged from the bathroom, offering her a towel and washcloth. "I don't recall seeing a shower over at Brenden's."

"I'm sure I must need one," she answered, suddenly self-conscious about her appearance.

"You look fine," he assured her.

"I've slept in this shirt the last two nights."

"You wear it well," he said, thinking it looked right.

Collecting the items he held out to her, Colleen entered the bathroom, locking the door behind her. The cool water of the shower, smelling sweetly of minerals, did little to relieve the warmth that rose from her chest. On the shelf she found a nearly empty bottle of strawberry-scented shampoo, evidence that the girls showered here frequently. Washing her hair, she stepped from the shower and quickly dried off.

Dressed, she searched the wicker cabinet for a hairbrush. Finding none, she turned and looked at herself in the mirror. She had always been comfortable with her appearance, though never vain about it. She was aware of her simple good looks, though she did not flaunt them, preferring instead to present herself plainly, without make-up or jewelry, and be taken at face value. Standing there, she wished she had her cosmetic case. Flipping her hair out from under the collar of Brian's white shirt, she collected up her things and exited the bathroom, hair tangled and wet, unbrushed.

Brian watched her emerge, unruffled by her unfinished appearance. Christine had always spent more time preparing herself than Brian had thought necessary, though in truth he knew it had not been too long. Yet all the time she spent could never have changed the way she looked in his eyes. To him Christine had always looked beautiful, whether dressed for a fancy party, hair curled, or cleaning the oven, greasy hair dangling in her face. To him Christine always looked as she had the first day he met her. It was the picture he carried in his mind, and the only one he ever saw when he looked at her.

But Christine had never seen herself through his eyes. Unaware that her preparations did little to alter his vision, she had always taken the extra time to try to look nice, for him. He'd appreciated the sentiment, though he wished she had understood it was unnecessary.

"Just about ready to go," Colleen said as she slipped into her sandals. "I'll brush my hair out on the way." Brian stared at her and realized the comparison he was making.

"When are we leaving?" Kerry wondered as she climbed down from the loft.

"Would you like to stay a while longer?" Brian asked.

"Can we?" Shannon replied as she peered out the open loft doors.

"Yeah, we're making a house of cards in the loft," Kerry added proudly. "It's gonna be *so* cool."

"A house of cards," Brian repeated, turning toward Grandpa. "Would you mind watching them for a few hours?" he asked.

"As always," Grandpa replied, as if it were a frequent request.

"Thanks," Brian said, explaining, "I think it might be easier to get Colleen's car going without a couple of helpers."

"You're leaving?" Kerry pouted, looking up at Colleen.

"Time to move on," Colleen answered. "Don't want to overstay my welcome."

"Will we see you again?" Kerry asked, her fingers automatically rising to her mouth as she began to chew on the tips of her worn nails.

"I hope so," Colleen said, suppressing the hand that wanted to reach for her necklace.

"Me too," said Kerry as she gave Colleen a hug good-bye.

"Nice to have met you," Grandpa offered, resting a hand on Colleen's shoulder. "Hope to see you again."

Brian called up the loft to Shannon, who had been watching from above. "Aren't you going to say good-bye to Colleen?" he asked.

"Good-bye," Shannon said, staring down at Colleen for a moment before closing the swinging doors behind her.

~

They climbed into The Bucket and headed out the gravel drive, the cab of the truck feeling overly wide as they sat by the doors on either side. Picking up speed as they left the shared road and turned onto the highway, the damp morning air rushed in through the open windows. Colleen began to brush her hair, the scent of strawberry shampoo filling the cab.

They drove off in silence, through the old golf course, over the causeway, then past the marsh and up the hill to Brian's. Stopping by the side door, they exchanged keys. She entered the house to get her bag; he headed across the barnyard to the shed and her car.

Moving through the empty house, collecting her things, Colleen took one last look around the kitchen, remembering her uncertainty that first night, and the fun-filled breakfast the next morning. In the few short hours she'd spent in the room she had grown to feel comfortable here. And now she was leaving.

She walked down the narrow hallway, lined with coats and boots, then pushed her way through the screen door onto the porch. Her car sat idling gently, Brian leaning back against the driver's door. She came down the steps and walked toward him.

"I've had a really nice time," she said.

"Me too," he replied. "I guess this is good-bye, then."

"Or so long," she restated. "Listen, I want to thank you for everything," she continued. "I don't know what I'd have done if I hadn't found you that night."

"Found someone else, I suppose."

"It wouldn't have been the same," she said thoughtfully. They stood there a moment, looking at each other.

He moved toward her and took her bag, placing it in the back seat, holding the door open for her as she got in, watching her curl her long tan legs under the steering wheel. Closing the door behind her, he rested his hands on the frame of the open window.

"When are you heading back home?" he asked.

"Friday."

"What are your plans until then?"

"I don't know," she shrugged. "Clean out Brenden's place, pack up his things, visit a few places he always talked about. No firm plans, really. Just be where he was. I kind of just drove up here on a whim," she explained, looking up at Brian. "Not really sure why I'm here."

"Do any of us, really, know why we're here?"

"We find out."

"Do we?"

"In time."

Brian stepped back from the car, stuffing his hands in the pockets of his jeans as he looked down at Colleen. She smiled up at him as she shifted the car into gear and slowly drove down the gravel drive, waving her hand out the window.

Brian stood in the barnyard watching Colleen's car as she made her way down the driveway and out onto the road, disappearing over the top of the hill. He thought for a moment about what she'd said, then turned to face the old homestead, house on his right, barn to his left. Between them, set back behind the corncrib, stood the shed, where her car had sat. For how long? Thirty-six hours? Not even. Less than a day and a half. Was it possible the place could look so different in such a short time?

The morning clouds began to roll away. Standing there, squinting in the bright Tuesday sun, he tried to form an image of her in his mind. He thought of the first time he'd seen her, dripping wet, her hair matted flat against her face. He thought of her sitting on the deck, chatting with Grandpa. He thought of her sleeping on the couch, the cottage book tucked under her arm. And he thought of her with his girls, making breakfast that first morning, climbing the tower the next day, Booger Ball Bowling that night. Was it only just Sunday they had met, or was his vision more timeless?

~

Colleen turned her car into the short drive and pulled up to the dilapidated little shack, Brenden's "castle." Turning off the engine, she sat behind the wheel and looked out at the meager setting. What was it, she wondered, that drew Brenden back here each year, to live the summer alone in the dim austerity of this place, no running water, outhouse out back? And why, she wondered, was she here now?

Grabbing her bag from the back seat, she climbed the single step to the porch, unlocked the door, and entered. The sunlight that came in the open doorway highlighted the dust that lay thick atop the contents inside. She thought maybe she should clean up a bit, then pack some of Brenden's things. Raising the shade on the single window that broke up the walls, she looked over the sparse contents of the small shack. There was little to clean, less to pack. The old armchair would not fit in her small car, nor would the beat-up army cot. The few dishes in the tiny cabinet could likely use washing, or simply be thrown out. The piano and two cardboard boxes that held Brenden's things were the only items worth attending to, the only belongings that needed to be kept.

She slumped down into the overstuffed chair, a feeling of loss overtaking her. She had come here to see the place Brenden so loved, and to take back tangible reminders of him. But there seemed to be few. The memories of Brenden in life, not the items left behind after his death, were all she would have to take with her.

Yet, as she sat there, she felt as if something was missing, felt as if she wanted, needed, more. There must be more than just this little shack, she thought, that drew Brenden back here every summer.

Sitting in his chair, Colleen thought of Brenden, of the stories he had told of The Door, of the places he had been, of the people he had met. She stared out the open doorway, thinking the key to Brenden's love of this place must lie somewhere out there. Tomorrow, she resolved, she would drive The Door.

~

Brian left the barnyard, climbed the steps onto the porch, and went inside. The kitchen seemed strangely different somehow, he thought – large, cavernous, and empty. He remembered the breakfast scene the morning before, the room abuzz with laughter, the girls perched atop their chairs, Colleen turning to greet him, flour on her nose. He smiled at the thought of the kitchen come to life again, then felt suddenly ashamed by the feeling. He must tell her, he thought, though he was sure she already knew.

Crossing the kitchen, Brian pushed through one of the swinging doors, into the hallway that ran alongside the front steps. Ducking his head, he settled into the tiny alcove under the stairs, turning on the light above the darkened computer. Taped to the monitor hung a small note.

Brian,
Thank you for the kindness you showed me over the past few days. I shall cherish the memory of the time I spent with you and the girls, and Grandpa.
Colleen

Brian removed the note from the monitor and sat in front of the keyboard, letting out a long breath before he began to type.

June 17
My Dear Christine,

Sometimes I can see your face so clearly it feels as though I could reach out and touch you, while other times I feel as though I'm losing the memory of you, confusing the faces before me with the vision in my mind. Sometimes I feel you with me, other times I feel you slipping away. Sometimes I feel nothing at all, other times old feelings I haven't felt since you left.

Do you remember that day we first met, in the bookstore, and how I later told you I knew right then we'd be together always? I've had that same feeling again, and it scares me to death. Don't leave me, Honey, and don't let me forget you.

My Love Always,
Brian

Brian saved the letter on the computer, filing it away with the rest. He turned off the monitor, tucking the note from Colleen in the bottom drawer of the desk, next to the letters Christine had written him when they first started dating.

～

Grandpa and the girls sat at the kitchen table, unwinding with a game of Yahtzee after their busy day.

"So," Grandpa said as he passed the dice cup to Shannon and marked his score sheet, "Colleen seems nice."

"Yeah," Kerry answered, "and pretty, too."

"Do you think so?" Grandpa asked.

"Well," Kerry joked, "she certainly isn't ugly."

"Full House!" Shannon exclaimed as she removed the cup from atop the dice.

"I never get those," Kerry grumbled as she picked up the cup for her turn.

"I always have trouble with four-of-a-kind," Grandpa assured her.

"Can I have a root beer?" Shannon asked.

"Boy, Colleen really liked the 'more-root-beer' story," Kerry commented.

"I think she enjoyed the whole day," Grandpa considered.

Kerry sat at the end of the table, the dice cup sitting idle in her hand. "Do you think my dad likes her?" she asked Grandpa after a long pause.

"What do you mean, 'likes her'?" Shannon responded briskly.

"What do you mean 'what do I mean'?"

"I mean, do you mean he 'likes' her, or he 'Likes her, Likes her'?"

"I don't know," Kerry replied. "I just mean that Dad seemed different yesterday."

"Well," Shannon retorted, "Mom always said Dad was different."

"You know what I mean," Kerry continued. "Did you see the way he looked at her? It reminded me of how he used to look at Mom."

"Dad would never do that to Mom!" Shannon shouted as she slammed her root-beer bottle down on the table.

Grandpa sat quietly during the exchange, allowing it to take place. After a time he leaned forward, arms resting on the table as he spoke. "You know, girls," he said reflectively, "things get pretty lonely around here sometimes since your grandma's been gone."

∽

Brian arrived at the cottage to find Grandpa and the girls sitting quietly around the table in their swimsuits, heads lowered, the empty dice cup between them. "Did someone die?" he asked as he entered the room.

"Colleen get off OK?" Grandpa inquired.

"Fine. Car started right up," he replied. "She had a lot to do. Left right away. Gone."

"You look like you've seen a ghost," Grandpa observed.

"Maybe I have," Brian uttered, taking the empty chair and peering at the score sheets.

"Stay to dinner?"

"No, thanks. Got stuff to do at home," he lied, thinking he'd rather be alone. "You guys have a nice day?"

"We went to Cave Point," Shannon told him, "and walked along the rocks."

"And Grandpa slipped in up to his knee, and got his pants all wet," Kerry added, laughing.

The girls scooted up to the loft to change. Brian rose from his chair. Grandpa loaded the dice into the leather cup, laid the pencils in the box on top of the score pads, and placed both in a plastic bag, knotting the twister tightly as he watched his son walk toward the bay window.

"Thanks for taking the girls today," Brian said as he stared out across the lake.

"No problem," Grandpa replied. "Let me know if you need more time alone."

The girls descended the ladder from the loft, dropping their candy bags down ahead of them. They hugged Grandpa good-bye, hung their suits on the porch, and headed out to the truck. Brian turned from the window, looking like the little boy Sean used to hold on his lap.

"Christine would want you to be happy," Grandpa offered after the girls had gone. Brian took a long look back at his father, then walked out the door without responding.

Arguing as they waited in the cab of the old pick-up, the

girls quieted when Brian got in. They had learned from experience that it was better not to annoy him when he was in one of his moods. As they drove silently home they knew there would be no horseplay tonight, no wrestling matches on the floor, no frolicking in bed as he read them a story. He was brooding, and they sensed it was best to leave him alone, to drift off to that place he often went, without them.

~

Colleen woke as the first rays of morning sun slipped in through the open window. She felt surprisingly refreshed for having spent the night on the old army cot, though she thought her relaxed state had more to do with the length of her sleep than the comfort the meager bed offered.

Crossing the room, she peered out the window. A farmer's field grew behind the shack, the tall spring hay billowing lightly in the gentle morning breeze. In the corner of the field a stand of cedars framed the scene on two sides. She breathed deeply, catching the fresh scent of the cedars wafting toward her over the top of the hay, and pictured Brenden doing the same as he rose each morning.

The peaceful setting was shattered as her gaze traveled up the gentle slope, coming to rest on the old outhouse. She shuddered at the thought. Turning from the window, she faced the empty kitchen, which offered no running water for coffee, nor food for breakfast, and recalled the fun-filled morning at Brian's two days before. Having resolved last night that she would drive The Door today, to see the place that was so dear to Brenden, she decided it was best to get an early start. Closing the window, she summoned the courage to make her way up the slope.

Returning from the outhouse, Colleen stopped at the pump on the far side of the shack and quickly washed her face in the icy water. Back inside, she changed her clothes, laying Brian's white cotton shirt over the back of the overstuffed old arm-chair. She put on a pair of University of Arizona gym shorts and an Arizona State t-shirt, then pulled a Grand Canyon sweatshirt over her head. Grabbing the Door County map Brian had given her, she turned out the light and was off.

She drove west down the little lane toward Juddville, not really a town, then north up the highway into Fish Creek. Rounding a curve as she descended the bluff that rose beside her, she came to rest at a stop sign at the bottom of the hill. A series of white shops, connected by woodchip walkways, sat to her left. The harbor, dotted with large sailboats, lay a few blocks ahead. Turning right, she parked across the street from the old general store. Relaxing behind the wheel, she watched the tiny tourist town spring to life for a while before getting out of her car and going inside.

Coffee and muffin in hand, she got back in the car and continued on her way. The road was lined with tightly packed tourist shops calling visitors inside, offering little chance of escape. As she drove past the clutter, the sign marking the entrance to the park beckoned her. She turned off the highway and drove along the shore road, the waves rolling gently along with her, serenity returning, growing stronger as she drove farther into the park. Slowing as she passed the old fire tower, she thought of him sitting at its base, on the back of the pick-up with Kerry, on the back of a station wagon with his mother.

She wound her way through the golf course and out of the park, then down the hill into Ephraim, past more tourist shops, and Wilson's, then up out of town. A quaint mini-golf that time had forgotten passed by on her right, an out-of-place modern one on her left. She climbed her way up another hill, then descended through the traffic down into Sister Bay, past the restaurant with the goats on the grass roof, then up again, out of town, back into open country.

The peaceful surroundings returned, the once cozy towns – now overcrowded with tourists – behind her. Farm fields and cherry orchards passed by, the air once again fresh, and still. Cresting the rise that led down into Ellison Bay, a view of the water briefly greeted her, then disappeared quickly as the road cut inland toward Gills Rock, each town becoming smaller the farther north she drove. The road led on, to end in Northport, just a restaurant set down to occupy the tourists as they waited to board the ferry that crossed over to Washington Island.

Colleen parked her car and watched the old ferry take leave of its cargo, only to fill up once more and head off again, passing its returning mate as it headed out across the cold, deep water. Families waited, anticipation on the faces of the children, who, once onboard, hurriedly ran up the metal steps to the upper deck, where they could look out over the water toward the island, or pose to have their pictures taken near the railing.

Sleek modern cars crowded the lower deck of the ferry, bright nylon jackets filling the frames of the color photos being taken. Sipping her coffee, Colleen wondered how many times the old ferries had witnessed the scene. She imagined an old black-and-white photo of a crew-cut Brian, standing in a light cotton jacket alongside a dark square station wagon with his mother. She wondered how many similar photos lay in a box in some attic, forgotten.

Alongside the railing of the upper deck, a mother posed with her two little girls, who looked up at her as she drew them close to her. Colleen wished such a photo existed from her own strange childhood, and longed for one to be taken, her in the middle. She wondered how the children on deck felt as they looked up at their mother, how the mother felt as she held her girls tight. She thought of her own mother, and of Shannon and Kerry. And she thought of Christine, erased from the picture.

Colleen took the back roads home to Brenden's, avoiding the highway as best she could, winding her way down the quiet side of the peninsula, along the desolate, serene curves of

County Q as it swung out, away from the commotion, back in time. She stopped at Cana Island, hopping across the rocks that rose just above the water, walking around the small island, its lighthouse now automated, living quarters empty.

She drove south into Baileys Harbor, past a restaurant lighting the fire for its nightly fish boil, then over the flattened booger balls that freckled the road in front of the ice cream store. A neglected grocery store sat dormant on her left, the width of the harbor opening behind it. A proud, stately church was built up on a hill to her right, its doors left wide open, to let God enjoy the view. She continued through town, past the old filling station with the blue tarp tied over its forgotten electric sign, and the quaint little park where families used to picnic before there was drive-through. Rounding the curve by the tiny fifties-style motel, she followed the highway up out of town then headed down the quiet lane and over the causeway that crossed the calm waters of Kangaroo Lake. Turning, she slowly climbed the hill as she passed Brian's — his old pick-up standing alone in the barnyard at the top of the tree-lined drive — then sped down the hill toward Brenden's.

~

Eyes ablaze, hair sticking out in all directions, Brian stood in the bathroom doorway, yelling at the girls about some harmless hairbrush left out of place. He had been a real bear all day, sulking moodily by himself, snapping at the slightest provocation. The girls stood silent, frozen and stung by his latest tirade. Outburst finished, shoulders slumped, he took the girls tightly in his arms, shaking as he held them close to him. They were glad the long painful day was finally drawing to a close.

~

Grandpa sat in the rocker and gazed out the bay window as the last of the sun's rays glistened across the glassy water. The clouds on the horizon cast a pink hue above the far shore as daylight slipped below the trees, engulfed by night. Across his lap sat an old shoebox, its tattered cover tied up with string.

Since his Maggie had passed away it had become his habit to read through her old love letters during those times when he missed her most. Tonight, he needed her.

He had been troubled all day, wondering what to make of the events of the past few. Rocking in his chair, he thought of Brian, of the lost look on his face when he came to pick up the girls. He thought of the girls, of the conversation during the dice game. He thought of Colleen, and Christine.

And he thought of Maggie, and his need for her guidance. Slipping the string from the box, he opened it, randomly pulling out a letter.

Dear Sean,

Do you remember how we both felt that night we met at the frat party? I remember the instant attraction, and the butterflies in my stomach, and the sleepless first night, wondering if you'd call.

Yet I also remember that feeling we later talked about, that comfortable fit when you just know something is right, and was meant to be. We both recognized that feeling from the start, and it hasn't betrayed us over the years.

I had that same feeling last night, when Brian introduced us to Christine. She just seems so right for him, that perfect match that was meant to be, and I can't help but wonder if we may have just met our future daughter-in-law.

I'm happy for him, that he may have found that special

someone. Some people never do find that perfect fit, like we did, or don't recognize it when it's right in front of them. I'm so glad we did, and so pleased that Brian may experience the joy that we have known.

My Love,
Maggie

Grandpa gazed out the window once more. The moon had risen through the clouds, casting shadows across the lake, silhouetting the cedars that guarded the pier. He folded the letter, missing Maggie even more than before.

~

Brian spent the morning trying to make up for his behavior the day before. He made the girls a special breakfast, then treated them to a short shopping spree for new summer clothes, and ice cream. Now he was taking them down the path that led away from the house, toward the trail they so enjoyed walking together.

He had put the trail in last summer, shortly after they had moved in, hacking and cutting away at the trees and brush, working off his anger as part of the grieving process. Forming a circle around the perimeter of the large homestead, the path lead away from the barnyard then down the hill toward the marsh, winding its way through the trees and along the little stream before it climbed back up to the front of the house.

They walked together, between the shed and the corncrib, through the field that led to the head of the trail. Spring came late to The Door. The thick grass, which by fall would stand taller than Kerry, its brown shoots waving in the breeze, now barely rose to her knees. Reaching the base of the hill, and the wall of cedars that stood before them, they slid through the tiny opening that marked the secret entrance to their private path, curling around the remnants of the rusted barbed-wire fence that had long ago framed the old cow pasture.

The trail made its way through the sweet-smelling cedars, the intermittent shafts of sunlight providing brief respites from the mosquitoes, allowing a moment's pause, to scratch. The firm footing of the old pasture slowly changed as they walked on, the decaying moss-covered underbrush spread thinly atop the bedrock that had held ancient glaciers at bay, and gave the peninsula its form. They walked single file, Shannon, head down in determination, setting the pace, Kerry falling behind as she stopped to inspect each new site.

Ageless limestone pushed up through the carpet beneath, reaching out to trip them as they passed over. Gnarled bare branches were strewn about the forest floor, fingers of the hands that waved as they walked by. Rotting logs lay crumbling beside them, the once proud remains of lives gone by, white mushrooms clumped at the ends, the headstones of nature's graveyard.

The three silhouettes moved on, marching in formation, through the eerie darkness of the cedars and occasional white birch, over the low sand dune with the crawling scrub brush that bit at their ankles, then down into the marsh and the warm light of the sun. Cattails stuck their heads up through the tall grass, red-winged blackbirds perched atop, lightly bending the shafts to one side. The trail, now covered with wood chips, sponged beneath their feet. A lone duck swooshed up out of the stream beside them, rising over the trees beyond. The path wound its way alongside the lazy little stream then curled out to a point, where a solitary dormant goose egg, undiscovered by a raccoon, sat atop a tuft of grass, the gray and yellow feathers of its departed mother and siblings stuck to its side.

They paused for a moment to look at the egg, the forgotten life left behind, and recalled the walks they had taken earlier in the spring, when the nest was full of life. The mother goose, who had protectively warmed her clutch, then nurtured her playful brood until she set them free, had herself now departed, leaving the empty nest behind. Brian thought of his mother, and of himself and his siblings, left behind without her. And he thought of Christine, and his girls, too young to be left behind without her.

"Do you think we'll see Colleen again?" Kerry asked thoughtfully.

Brian crouched down and picked a dandelion, blowing its white seeds out over the creek, where they were carried away by the wind.

"I have no idea," he answered reflectively, "no idea."

The scene too close to home, he led them away from the nest, taking their hands in his as they made their way down the remainder of the solitary path. Reaching the end of the trail, they slipped back through the tiny opening and out onto the front lawn, climbing the hill up toward the house.

Colleen turned off the little country lane and drove up the tree-lined gravel drive, toward the now familiar old farmhouse that stood waiting for her atop the hill. The Bucket sat alone in the deserted barnyard, sheets billowing in the breeze on the clothesline beyond. She was pleased by the signs that they might be home, and that she would see him again.

Parking her car next to the old pick-up, she waited for someone to come out and see who the visitor might be, then smile when they saw it was her. When no one appeared she got out of her car, reached into the back for the bag of groceries she had bought, and headed towards the porch.

"Hello," she called out as she peered in through the screen door. "Anybody home? Shannon? Kerry? Brian?" Receiving no answer, she opened the door and went inside, making her way down the narrow hallway into the kitchen. "Hello?" she called out again, her voice echoing through the empty room as she set the bag of groceries on the chopping block. Retracing her steps, she stood at the foot of the curving back stairs, grabbing the railing as she leaned up. "Hello? Anybody up there?" No answer. Returning to the kitchen, she began to unpack the groceries.

Job complete, she went to check the rest of the house, pushing her way through one of the swinging doors at the far end of the room. The tiny alcove that hid itself under the stairs sat darkened, the computer turned off. She made her way down the hall to the front of the house and peered into the living room. The sofa bed lay open, waiting for the sheets that hung on the line. "Hello," she called up the front steps, no longer expecting an answer. Reentering the kitchen, she stood before the other swinging door that formed the corner of the room. The dining room, she reasoned, the door opening off the kitchen as it did, making it easy to serve for parties. The door was probably little used these days, she thought. She pushed it open slightly, to confirm her appraisal.

A walnut roll-top desk sat beneath a window against the far wall, flanked by an oak file cabinet and a pine bookshelf. The desktop was neatly organized – computer in the middle, papers and magazines piled to one side, computer printouts on the other. The chair, turned away from the desk, faced the opposite wall, every inch of which was covered with a collection of photographs held in handmade wooden frames. The shrine.

Colleen let the door swing back and forth behind her as she was drawn toward the wall. The pictures, tightly packed, spanned a wide course of time. Christine, in a white dress drawn down over her tan shoulders, a red rose in her hand, Brian beside her, looking out of character in a blue sport coat, his long hair resting on his shoulders. A youthful Maggie, long black hair and cat glasses, posed next to a buzz-cut Brian, backpack in hand. Brian, wearing purple sunglasses and a red beard, on the deck of a cruise ship, a bandanna pulled back over his head, snow-capped mountains in the background, Christine by his side. Maggie, in a man's trench coat and hat, eyes crossed, tongue sticking out. Christine, in a hospital bed, beaming, newborn Kerry in her arms, a curious Shannon beside her. An older Maggie, playing cards in the loft with the girls, the only grandchildren who would ever remember her. Christine, perched atop a sign in front of the Medical College. Maggie, in cap and gown, proudly displaying her doctorate diploma. Christine, in front of the Christmas tree, the colorful lights reflecting off her long shiny hair. Maggie, in an old black-and-white photo, asleep on the couch in her visiting nurse's uniform. Christine, long hair corn-rolled, lying on the beach in some tropical setting. Maggie, in her wedding dress, the girl Grandpa had married. Christine, posing with the girls, on the deck of the ferry.

Colleen moved across the wall, arms held tightly around herself as she gazed at the memorial to the two women in his life. A certain warmth, then sadness, came over her as the pictures began to blur.

Touched by the display, she felt suddenly intrusive, more so than that first night, when she'd peered at the computer in the alcove under the stairs. She knew him now, as she had not then. She backed away from the pictures and left the room, slowly closing the swinging door behind her.

Stepping out onto the front porch, Colleen noticed the little tape player sitting on the top step, where she had first seen him. She hit the play button, the soft lilting of the now familiar Irish folk song surrounding her as she leaned back against the post that supported the metal porch roof. Tilting her head slightly, she gazed out over the front yard, down the hill, and across the marsh. In the distance Kangaroo Lake glistened in the golden light of early evening.

≈

Leaving the trail behind, Brian and the girls climbed the hill in the front yard that led back up to the house. Reaching the summit, the house coming into view as they crested the slope, they saw her. She stood on the front porch, leaning against a post, looking out past them.

"Colleen! Colleen!" Kerry shouted. "Dad, Dad, it's Colleen!" she yelled behind as she raced ahead to greet her. Shannon stayed back, with Brian.

He paused, mesmerized. She wore a cotton sundress the color of fall corn, the thin straps running over the soft curves of her shoulders, the low neckline revealing the gold cross that lay flat against her bronze chest. Her long, tanned legs reached down to the thin leather sandals he had already grown accustomed to. Her shiny brown hair, pulled back at the nape of her neck, was streaked with a few strands of summer sun.

"Wow!" said Shannon. "I didn't think we'd see her again."

"Me either," Brian mumbled, recalling a different sundress.

Colleen descended the steps to meet Kerry, who flew into her arms. Brian and Shannon followed behind, arriving amidst shouts from Kerry.

"Dad, Dad, Colleen's back!"

"So I see," he laughed, patting the child on the head as he turned toward Colleen.

"Hello," she offered tentatively.

"Hello," he smiled back. "And to what do we owe the pleasure?"

"I've come to ask a favor," she said, "and to thank you, again, for your kindness. I've brought dinner."

"Dad, Dad, is Colleen really gonna stay for dinner?" Kerry asked excitedly.

"Well, we can't have her cook and then just leave, now can we?" he teased. "Who will do the dishes?"

"Yeah! Yeah!" Kerry shouted as she took Colleen by the hand and led her into the house.

~

Entering the kitchen, they found the groceries she had brought, neatly stacked on the chopping block. Brian led the girls to the sink to wash up. "So," he called back over his shoulder, "what's for dinner?"

"Stir-fry okay?" she wondered, unsure of the meal she had chosen.

"Great."

"Can we help cut stuff up?" Kerry asked, pulling a chair up to the chopping block.

Colleen looked to Brian for guidance. Nodding, he turned to Shannon. "Wanna help?" he urged.

"I suppose," Shannon replied unenthusiastically as Brian took a seat at the table.

"I hope you don't mind that I just dropped in," Colleen ventured. "I wanted to do something nice for all of you, to repay you for taking me in. And to ask you a favor. And...." She paused, fondling her necklace.

"And?"

"And to see you all once more before I leave."

"You're leaving?" Kerry pouted.

"Tomorrow morning," Colleen nodded. "I have to drive back home," she explained, "get back in time for work Monday."

"And the favor?" Brian asked.

"The piano," she replied. "The old farmer Brenden rented the shack from said I could leave behind anything I wanted — dishes, cot, chair — but I'd like to try to save Brenden's piano, if I can. I was hoping maybe you could pick it up and store it in the barn for a while, until I can make arrangements to have it sent down. The shack is rented through the summer, so there's no hurry. The farmer said no one but Brenden would want to live there anyway, so he wasn't too worried about when the piano gets moved. I thought, with The Bucket and all, maybe you could pick it up for me. I could leave you the key."

"Sure, no problem," Brian said. "Grandpa and I can grab it sometime. He loves my projects."

"Thanks. I hoped you wouldn't mind. Oh, one more favor to ask, if I may," she continued. "I forgot to pick up a bottle of wine for dinner. Could you make a couple of those drinks you made at Grandpa's? Old-fashioneds, wasn't it?"

"Coming right up," he said, rising from his chair. "Olive, wasn't it?" he remembered, then, "Kiddie cocktails?" to the girls.

"A party!" Kerry yelled out, jumping up and down on her chair.

He mixed the drinks at the dry sink, listening quietly as Colleen chatted with the girls, holding Kerry back, drawing Shannon out. Drinks made, he handed Colleen's to her, an olive perched atop the floating ice cubes, then made a big production of presenting the girls their kiddie cocktails, acting the gay waiter bringing champagne to the little queens as they all laughed loudly.

"Do you have a wok?" she asked.

"Walk this way," he said effeminately, hands on hips, elbows jutting out sideways as he strutted across the kitchen, wiggling his fanny.

They enjoyed a fun-filled dinner, with much laughing and good-natured kidding. Shannon softened after a while, and joined in the fun. They sat together after the meal, chatting for a long time, enjoying each other's company, no one eager to leave the table. It was the way Brian remembered family meals when he was a child, the way Colleen had hoped they had been.

Darkness crept in through the window, supplanting the light. Brian pushed back his chair and rose, clearing the dishes, stacking them high in the sink. He wiped the table with a wet cloth, lifting Colleen's drink to wipe under it, the lone olive barely afloat in the bottom of the glass.

"Bedtime, ladies," he informed the girls.

"Can I have your olive?" Kerry asked, her hand already fishing in the bottom of Colleen's glass.

"Can we do a fashion show for Colleen," Shannon begged, protesting the call to bedtime, "of the clothes we bought today?"

"Yeah, can we, Dad?" Kerry joined in.

"Yeah, can we, Dad?" Colleen laughed.

"All right," he conceded, knowing he'd already lost the battle. "But be quick about it. It's getting late, and Colleen's got to leave early tomorrow morning." The girls darted out of the room and up the back steps. Brian smiled to himself as he sat back down to wait for the show to begin.

"Nice dinner," he complimented her. "Thanks."

"My pleasure. It was fun." She paused, taking the pendant of her necklace between her fingers and running it across the chain. "And nice," she ventured, "to see you again."

"Yes," he replied, looking across at her. "It was nice to see you again, too."

The stampede down the back steps announced that the fashion show was about to begin. The open floor of the large old kitchen provided a runway for the models to strut their stuff, which the girls did, dramatically playing their parts amidst suppressed giggles. They modeled light cool sundresses and bib overalls, matching shorts and tops, and new sandals, the style of Colleen's. Brian whistled as they applauded the dames, Colleen observing, in her best upper-crust voice, "Oh, it's simply daaarling, isn't it, my deeaaar. I reaaally must have it, you know."

The fashion show complete, the last of the bows and curtseys over, Brian guided the girls across the room toward the back hallway. "Nice job, ladies," he said, kissing each on the forehead. "Now say good night to Colleen, then run along and get ready for bed. I'll be up to tuck you in as soon as I've finished the dishes."

"Could Colleen tuck us in?" Kerry asked.

He turned to her. A gentle smile came slowly across her

face. "I'd love to," she said, touched that Kerry had asked. Colleen rose, gathering the girls in as she marched them down the narrow hall and up the back stairs. Pausing after a few steps, she leaned her head back into the hallway and winked at Brian. He stood there after she'd gone, leaning against the doorframe, staring down the empty hallway.

∾

Brian stood at the sink, lazily washing the dishes as he listened to the laughter floating down the back stairs. How long had it been, he wondered, since he'd heard the sound of three female voices float softly by. Was it only yesterday morning, or longer ago than that, before the mourning.

Wiping the last dish dry, setting it back in the pie safe, he realized the laughter upstairs had long since died down. A bedtime story, he thought to himself as he went to the back stairs, or maybe a good book. "Girls?" he called up the steps as he climbed them, two at a time. Coming down the hall to their room, he quietly pushed the door open and peered in.

A tiny nightlight on the far side of the bed gave the room the soft glow of twilight. He found them asleep, all three, their heads resting lightly on the pillows that lay across the bed, Colleen in the middle, a book across her chest. Three ducks in a row, he thought, the same picture he held in his mind, the middle face slightly different.

"Colleen," he said softly, nudging her shoulder.

She woke and looked up at him, then rolled on her side, a smile crossing her face as she closed her eyes.

"Colleen," he said again. "Wake up."

"Be right down," she yawned, rubbing her eyes as she inched her way between the girls, toward the end of the bed. As he left the room she could see, from behind, that he was wiping his eyes.

∾

She found him, as she had that first night, sitting on the front porch, listening to his tape. She sat down in silence and leaned back against a post.

"Your girls are sweet," she said after a long while, merely stating a fact, not expecting a reply.

"They get that softness from their mother," he said quietly, the words trailing away.

"You miss her so, still, don't you?"

"Daily."

"Care to talk about it?" she offered. "I found out the other day, thanks to you, that it actually helps. Better than keeping everything bottled up inside."

"No," he responded after some thought. Then, after another long pause, "Thanks, but she's my memory."

They sat quietly together for a time, looking up at the stars. At length he came around, and they chatted companionably for an hour or so — about the girls, about Brenden, about The Door — never reaching for conversation, comfortable together during the peaceful lulls that cropped up, no need to fill the void. Eventually she rose, readying to go.

"I've got an early start tomorrow," she said. "Long drive ahead of me, work Monday."

"I'll miss you," he said, then, catching his admission, "we'll miss you."

"It's been a nice few days, hasn't it?" she reflected.

"Yes," he agreed, "it has been nice."

He rose and stood before her, heart racing. Leaning closer, he opened his mouth, as if to speak, or.... She closed her eyes, moving toward him, then stopped as he began to back away.

"Well," she suggested, catching her breath, "I suppose I best be going."

"I suppose it's best," he said.

They walked side by side across the barnyard, under the glow of the light that hung from the silo, each wondering what came next, she afraid to ask, he afraid to think about it.

Reaching her car he gave her a brief hug good-bye, which lasted longer than he intended, and felt better than either of them could have imagined.

"Drive safe," he instructed as she climbed in and started the car. He closed the door behind her, his hands resting on the open window as he looked down at her one last time. "And let us know you made it home okay."

"Oh, you'll hear from me again," she said as she put the car in gear and slowly headed down the gravel drive.

Brian stood in the empty barnyard and watched her drive away for a second time, following her taillights until they disappeared over the top of the hill.

Part II

~

Chapter 6

～

June 22
Dear Shannon and Kerry,

Hello from Arizona! I hope all is well with the two of you back in beautiful Door County.

I wanted to let you know that I got home safely, and send you some gifts I picked up on my way back. Not much, I'm afraid, but I felt like getting a little something to say thanks for all the fun times I had with the two of you on my trip. I hope you like them!

Say hi to Grandpa for me.

Love,
Colleen

～

June 22
Dear Brian,

I arrived home late this afternoon, exhausted from the long drive back, looking forward to climbing into my own bed after sleeping on Brenden's cot, but find that I can't seem to unwind.

The memories of my trip to Door County keep running through my mind. I'm so glad I finally made the journey to visit Brenden's "castle." Now I have a picture I can recall when I think of him and all the summers he spent in Wisconsin. I think I'll pull out my journal and tell him about my trip.

Enclosed is a little thank-you for the kindness you showed me during my stay, and for helping me find what is special in the place that was so dear to Brenden. I shall remember warmly my week with all of you in The Door.

Love,
Colleen

∼

June 22
Dear Brenden,

Well, I finally made it to your beloved Door County!

I'm so glad I made the trip to see your "castle," and to visit some of the places you used to talk about all winter. Now I know what you were always waiting to go back to. I'm sad, as well, though, that I never went when you wanted me to come, never spent time there with you.

I'm sitting here, sweating in the dry heat of home, recalling the cool damp of The Door, and the feeling I had when I passed the sign that said "Leaving Door County, Please Come Again." I wonder how you could ever leave, and know now why you couldn't wait to return.

While my memories will never be the same as yours, I too, like you, found something special in The Door. I shall recall warmly a big old farmhouse perched atop a hill, and a cozy little cottage set back from a lake. And I'll never forget the faces of two little girls, or the one I'll probably never see again.

I wonder, can you see Door County from where you are?

Leeny

∼

June 25
Colleen,

Thank you so much for the thoughtful gifts you sent. The girls love their Arizona t-shirts, and I'll save a special spot on the tree for the ornament from Phoenix.

We all so enjoyed the few days we spent with you, a bit like a little vacation for us too. Please feel free to stop by again should you ever find reason to come back to The Door.

I came across this book in a little gift shop the day after you left, and thought of you. I hope it brings fond memories of your time here with us, and of Brenden. Enjoy!

Brian

∼

June 30
Dear Brenden,

I received a book in the mail today, titled Door County Collage —
A Pictorial Remembrance of the Way It Was. *It is filled with
glossy color photos of harbors, sailboats and sunsets, and soft
black-and-white pictures of old weathered barns, dry-docked
wooden fishing boats, and dormant cherry orchards.*

*Paging through the book, I nearly came to tears when I found a
picture of your "castle," framed against an angry sky, dark clouds
rolling overhead, the old outhouse visible in the background.*

*Do you remember when we were both little, and I was scared of
thunderstorms, and you loved them? I recall one dark stormy
night when you took me outside and we sat on the back stoop,
under the eaves, and you tried to show me the beauty, and allay
my fears.*

I now have a book of The Door, though not all the pictures are in it.

Leeny

~

June 30
Dear Brian,

*Thank you so much for the thoughtful picture book you sent. It
sits proudly atop my coffee table, and I flip through it often,
fondly recalling my time in The Door.*

*Would you believe I actually found a shot of Brenden's little shack
in the book, his "castle" as he used to call it. What a wonderful
reminder of something I will never forget.*

Other memories of my trip, however, are already beginning to fade. I wish I had taken some pictures of my own when I was in The Door — of the stage in the park, or the old fire tower, of Grandpa's little cottage, or of you and the girls. Sometimes I can barely remember your faces, the whole trip seeming somewhat like a dream.

Love,
Colleen

∾

July 5
Colleen,

Well, the holiday's finally behind us. If I eat another bratwurst before Christmas it will be too soon! The Fourth parade in Baileys Harbor was a smash — as usual — then we went over to Grandpa's and shot fireworks off the pier at night, out over the lake.

The girls say hello and send last year's Christmas picture along. Now, instead of not being able to remember us clearly, you'll probably get sick of looking at us!

Well, that's about all the news from here. I guess we can stop sending thank-you-for-the-thank-you letters now. It was nice having met you. Take care.

Brian

∾

July 8
Dear Brenden,

I miss you tonight.

Why are good-byes so hard? Why do memories stay with us, and leave us wanting more? Why can't we just be happy with what we've had, and move forward? Why can't we go backwards sometimes?

Why do I have to say good-bye? Why can't you be here tonight, helping me say good-bye? Why did I have to say good-bye, to you?

Leeny

∽

July 14
Dear Brian,

Your last letter said we could stop sending thank-you-for-the-thank-you letters, so I won't thank you for the Christmas picture you sent, even though it was much appreciated.

I've been thinking about Brenden the last few days, and about good-byes, which your last letter seemed to be saying. Both of these thoughts brought me back to The Door, and left me wanting more. I'm not ready to say good-bye yet, to Brenden, or The Door.

I wonder what it looks like in the middle of the tourist season. Are the blossoms all gone from the cherry trees? Has the water warmed up in the lake? Do the booger balls stick to the pavement any better?

Will you send me news of The Door? Will you send me more memories to hold on to? Will you send me another letter?

Love,
Colleen

~

July 18
My Dear Christine,

I know I can't hide myself from you as you look down on me, watching over me as you do, knowing all that happens to me, all that goes on inside me. You are with me still, a part of me that I keep and carry with me, always. You run through me, filling my heart with your love.

And what if a tiny corner of my heart is beginning to twinge with a feeling only you have given me? Is it right to let that feeling rest there beside you? Or will it push you aside, and take your place?

I'm so scared of losing you, Honey. It's been so long now, I can barely remember your voice.

My Love Always,
Brian

~

July 18
Colleen,

The Door looks pretty much the same in summer as it does in spring. Yes, the white blossoms have fallen off the cherry trees, replaced by the red of the ripening cherries. The water in the lake is a little warmer, warm enough that even Grandpa went tubing the other day. And the booger balls do hold a bit better to the pavement these days, though still not as well as in the heat and humidity of late August. Other than that, if you can overlook the condos and gift shops that seem to reproduce quicker than rabbits, things are pretty much the same here — except for the tourists and Illinois license plates. The Door never really changes that much, which is nice.

The girls are doing fine, tan as they get every summer, their swimsuits the only clothing they seem to wear, except for the t-shirts you sent. Send them a letter sometime — they'd be thrilled to hear from you again. They mention you often, Kerry especially, and how nice it was to have you here.

The house seemed so different when you were here, so full of life, like when Christine would cut fresh wildflowers and place them all around. The house feels a bit empty now, like a Sunday night. Christine used to hate Sunday nights, when the weekend of family fun was coming to an end, and all there was to look forward to was the long week ahead, all of us separated by work and school. Why is it that we don't get to spend more of our time with the ones we love?

As to whether I'll send you another letter, I guess I just have. As to whether I'll send another after this, I don't know.

Though the thought of hearing from you from time to time sounds nice, it might feel strangely disrespectful to Christine if we became regular pen pals. That said, letters are still nice. They allow for a more leisurely pace of exchange, providing time to think about what one might want to say, or hear. Anyway, I once knew two people who wrote long-distance letters, and it all went pretty well for them.

Brian

≈

July 23
My Dear Christine,

Happy Anniversary, Honey! It's fifteen years today that we've been married, or would have been. I guess we are still, in my heart.

I wonder, what would we have done today, if only we could have celebrated together? Would we have gotten a sitter and gone out alone, just the two of us, for a romantic candlelit dinner at some fancy restaurant? Or would we have spent the day together, the four of us, as we used to do? I remember my favorite anniversary, the year the girls decorated the boat for us — floating candles, old-fashioneds, and an Irish tape — the Moonlight Café they called it. Do you remember lying there together, naked, the moonbeams glistening toward us across the water?

Oh, how I wish that hadn't been our last anniversary together.

I dug out our wedding album today. Do you recall how hot it was, taking pictures in the park as we drank warm champagne from paper cups? All the hopes and dreams and fears we shared as we began our life together. I remember looking at you that day, on the wooden footbridge that crossed the little stream under the willow tree, thinking how beautiful you'd look in fifty years, bouncing one of our grandchildren on your knee.

Oh, Honey, I miss you so.

My Love Always,
Brian

July 28
Dear Shannon and Kerry,

It was 111 degrees at my house today. I was so hot I thought I'd like nothing better than to put an ice cube down my shirt, or jump into Kangaroo Lake off Grandpa's pier. I imagine the two of you now, playing by the pier all day, the water much warmer than that day you went tubing when I was there.

Are you starting to get ready for school yet, or is it still too early to think about the summer ending? I remember when I was a kid I used to hate when the freedom of summer came to an end, but also love the promise the start of a new school year held.

I was over at a friend's house the other day and the whole front of her fridge was covered with pictures her kids made in school. When I got home I noticed that the only thing on my fridge was a magnet from the Chinese restaurant where I order take-out. I wonder, do the two of you like making art projects? I'd love some pictures to cover my blank fridge door.

Take care of your dad, and say hi to Grandpa for me.

Love,
Colleen

∾

August 2
Colleen,

Enclosed are some pictures the girls drew for you. Kerry said no one should have to suffer from Fridge-Door-Disease. I'll bet you didn't even know your fridge suffered from a named malady!

Grandpa and I picked up Brenden's piano today and returned the key to the old farmer. I was going to store the piano in the shed, covered with plastic to protect it from the pigeons, but Grandpa worried about the moisture and wood rot, so I decided to keep it in the living room until you can make arrangements to have it sent down. With a slight bit of furniture rearranging it fits real nice, almost as if the spot had been meant for it.

Funny, Christine always wanted a piano, but I always balked at the idea. Now I've got one, but not her. Anyway, Shannon thinks she may want to take piano lessons at school, so we might actually get some use out of it. I hope you don't mind.

Back here the only big news is that football season has finally started! First pre-season game's in a week! Can life get any better than that?

The girls and I took Grandpa down to Green Bay yesterday to watch the Packers practice. It was kind of neat. In this day and age of spoiled, high-priced athletes and pushy, obnoxious owners — who treat the game as if it were actually just a business, and not a religion — two thousand people showed up to stand behind a wire fence and watch practice. The best part is the kids, clad in their favorite players' jerseys, toy helmets on their heads. They lend their bikes to the players after practice, to ride back across the parking lot from the practice field, back to the hallowed ground of the frozen tundra that is Lambeau Field. Nowhere else in sports will you find such a love affair with a team as you do here, a team so closely tied to the community that owns it, a team so rich in history and tradition, a team that's won more championships than any other team in the history of the NFL, the only team to win three consecutive championships, an unmatched feat they've accomplished twice.

It's nice we finally won another Super Bowl, so people can live again in the present and not just off the memories of days gone by.

Take care,
Brian

~

August 7
Dear Brenden,

Ironic, isn't it, how irony is such a funny thing.

Funny, isn't it, how some people don't hear what they're saying, while others don't know what they see.

I see someone who loves football, and history, and tradition. I see someone who's deeply attached to his family, though missing part of it. I see someone who has suffered a loss, and is having trouble moving on.

I know some of the major facts, yet few of the minor details. I know I want to know more, yet I don't know if I'll be allowed to find out. I know where I want to go, yet I don't know how to get there.

Leeny

Chapter 7

≈

August 8
Dear Shannon and Kerry,

Thank you so much for the wonderful drawings you sent. I've taped them up all over my refrigerator, so it no longer suffers from Fridge-Door-Disease. You are both such wonderful artists.

It's amazing how a few pictures can add so much life and color to a room, and brighten my outlook. Thanks again.

Love,
Colleen

P.S. — I was sorting through some of Brenden's things the other day and came across a couple of his old piano lesson books from when we were kids. Since your dad tells me the piano is now in your living room, I thought you might like to use the books. Enjoy!

≈

August 9
Dear Brian,

Thank you for moving Brenden's piano for me. I hope that it wasn't too much trouble. I was happy to hear that you're keeping it in the house, and that the girls may get some use out of it. I hope it brings them as much joy as it brought Brenden. I look forward to hearing them play the next time I find myself in The Door.

It struck me when I read your last letter, describing your love of the Packers, how little we actually know about each other. In a way I might already know more than I could ever learn from a brief biographical sketch, the days we spent together in The Door revealing so much about what's important to you — your girls, Grandpa, a slower paced lifestyle. Yet other things I don't know, simple little things, like what your middle name is, how old you are, where you grew up, when your birthday is, and so on. I thought to myself, here I am writing a few letters to someone I spent a couple of really nice days with, and I don't actually know all that much about him.

My name is Mary Colleen O'Connell. I'm twenty-nine years old, single, and live alone in Phoenix. I work for a large accounting firm doing estate planning for clients — trusts, wills, that kind of stuff. My hobbies include bike riding and swimming, I like to read romance novels, and my favorite movies are Sleepless in Seattle, The Sound of Music, *and anything with Cary Grant in it.*

Sounds kind of goofy now that I've written it, as if next I'm supposed to say, "And my dream, if elected Miss America, is to work for world peace and feed all the starving children in Africa." At this point the announcer says, "And next, in the formal evening gown portion of the competition, Mr. Wisconsin." Your turn.

Love,
Colleen

～

August 14
Colleen,

My name is Michael Brian Bailey, and I am the son of Mary Margaret Bailey (nee Corchran), aged 60 years, born to eternal life this day (three years ago), loving wife of Sean, devoted daughter of Agnes (Ray), caring mother of Brian (Christine), Niall (Claudia), Ciaran (Patrick) O'Flannery, & Aileen (Ryan) O'Rourke, and proud grandmother of Shannon and Kerry Bailey and Bailey O'Flannery. Further survived by other relatives and many friends, who shall also one day pass on, until there will come a time when there will be no one left on this god-damned earth who remembers her life, and she will be left a forgotten headstone in an overgrown cemetery, where some young, love-struck couple will do a charcoal rubbing of her engraving, without realizing how much she meant to those she loved, and who loved her.

It's funny what you remember about a person, and what you don't. When I think about my mom I picture her now only as Grandma to my girls, and can hardly remember anymore, try as I might, the younger, thinner, cute little mother who watched over her house full of children. It's not that I've forgotten the memories. They're still there, just slightly hidden from view.

Her bringing a TV tray into the den when I lay sick on the couch. Setting the timer for one of her fifteen-minute catnaps in the living room. Being dipped and kissed by my dad in front of the kitchen sink. Holding chili a half-hour longer as she peered out the window watching Niall and me play football into the darkness on a Sunday afternoon in the fall. Shuffling her feet across the carpet on her way to the bathroom, her long flannel nightgown nearly tripping her as she checked up on me when I came home in the middle of the night from some high school party, drunk. Making her famous turkey stuffing at Thanksgiving, allowing us to snitch our favorite items from the bowl. Waiting for us to come home from grade school at lunchtime, places set and waiting for us. Driving me to high school in the winter, just because I hated to take the bus, her coat pulled tightly over her flannel nightgown, the heater in the old green station wagon never kicking in until she pulled back into the driveway. Sitting at the kitchen table as we talked on after family meals, slicing the leftover piece of chicken in half as she ate it, then in half again, then again, until the whole thing was gone. Her proud face beaming each Easter morning, sure that she'd gotten Dad the biggest chocolate egg ever made, until she opened the one he'd bought her, always slightly larger.

On and on the memories can be brought back, if I try real hard. Yet, when I hear her name, or think casually of her as I still do so many times each day, the image that always comes to mind is the last time I saw her before she went in the hospital, the proud grandma playing on the floor with my girls, her smiling face bright with delight as she stuck out her goofy elbow, laughing as she slid the newfound lump from side to side, grossing out my girls.

I am who I am because of her. I quit work to stay home with the girls because of the example she'd set, to provide a happy, stable home life for her children, putting herself and her career goals second for the benefit of others. And I try, as best I can, to create for my girls the same feeling of warmth that comes over me when I think back on my own childhood, hoping I can do half as well as she did to let my girls know they are special, and loved.

I don't really get mad that she's gone, like I do about Christine, or wonder why she had to leave us so soon. She hasn't, I know. Instead, I get sad, not from the memories of times gone by, but for the memories that never will be. The four-generation picture that was to come next, her seated in the rocking chair, holding her great-grandchild. The peaceful, quiet retirement the folks had dreamed of at the cottage, sitting together by the fire, reading, so comfortable with each other they need not talk, but only glance up occasionally from their books, and smile. Long walks around the lake with Grandpa, looking at the color of the fall leaves. Holding hands in the car, still, after all these years, as they came to my house to eat my Thanksgiving stuffing. And the long-awaited trip to Ireland that Grandpa will take, without her.

I wanted to care for her as she grew gracefully older, to return to her the maternal love she gave to me. I had long ago decided she would never be put in a nursing home after my father one day passed on, but would move in with me, to drive me crazy as she aged, just as I must have driven her crazy when I was young. Now I'll never get the chance.

I wanted to write something about her after she died, something Grandpa could have to hold on to, something to say what she meant to me, something to tell my brother and sisters what I saw during those horrible days in the hospital and after. I was going to write a poem called "The Twelve Days of August," but like so many other good intentions it lives only in my head, unwritten. It does no good to recount those terrible days in detail, some memories best forgotten, the roller coaster too scary even to think about riding again. Yet some impressions of that time seem as real today as they did surreal then.

Arriving at the hospital the morning after her surgery to find my father standing over her, sobbing uncontrollably as she lay motionless, her head wrapped tightly in a bandage, once white, now soaked through with her own red dye, Dad holding a blood-filled pouch that lay across her chest, a piece of tape with the word "brain" attached to it. Aileen, in the hospital cafeteria, unable to eat, an untouched plate of fries before her. Niall, not taking our advice to wait, but rushing back home to be by her side, back here with all of us. He was back, my brother, and I felt whole again, as I always do when he returns, only to realize that he was alone, Claudia stuck in California. Niall made us all feel together, even though a part of him was missing, and another was leaving. Ciaran and Patrick, cut off from the family during the long lonely nights of worry, staying with Grandma Corchran so she wouldn't have to be alone. Frail Grandma Corchran, life slowly leaving her as she watched her daughter die, unable to lift her own hand and separate it from the lifeless one she held. Christine, shaking uncontrollably in bed one night, so hollow she couldn't feel the touch that wanted to comfort her. The girls, so young, confused by the whole affair, knowing only that Grandma was very sick, and that Dad wasn't coming home at night, but sleeping at Grandpa's. The blueprints I drew up in my mind while sitting in the hospital with Mom, telling her I would add a wheelchair ramp to the cottage, and teach Dad how to cook. A midnight chat with Grandpa on one of the first nights, when we still had hope, him unable to imagine his life without Mom, refusing even to think that she wouldn't get better and be back with us, the same as always. And the note, copied from Mom's medical chart, written on the inside cover of the book Dad was reading, first so he could remember the words exactly, then to let us read the words he could not speak. The note that told us Mom was getting worse, not better. The note we made him throw away.

The next day, as the surgeon told us that Mom wasn't going to make it, the birthday balloon I had bought for Aileen slowly deflated, the air that had given it life seeping from it, from all of us. We went down to the hospital chapel, what was left of the family, Dad and the four lives he and Mom had created, a circle, now broken. I slumped in a chair and took in the scene, part of it, yet detached from it, as if looking down from above. Ciaran keening, Aileen staring, Niall pacing. Dad succumbing, dying inside, his forehead resting against the wall in the corner of the room. I recall burying my head in his chest, holding him tight, so as never to lose him. It reminded me of the feeling of comfort I felt as a child, when he'd pull me close against his white t-shirt as he cut my hair on the step stool in the laundry room of the basement.

And then, when I finally let go, I had to drive over to Grandma Corchran's and tell her that by the same time tomorrow, her daughter would be dead.

That night I sat frantically looking through stacks of photos for pictures of Mom, unable to see her clearly through the tears, fearing I'd forget her face. I didn't come across one good shot of her from the hundreds of pictures I searched through, finding only pictures of her on the periphery of the scene, just at the edge of the photo, always waiting on others, never the center of attention. How was it possible that I never found a way to get her in the center of a picture, this woman who was so central in my life? I panicked as never before, mind racing, heart pounding, breath waning. I went outside for some air and stood in the driveway for a long time, hugging the basketball pole for support as I cried uncontrollably, knowing I'd never take her picture again. I slumped to the ground, curling up in a fetal ball on the cold pavement, until I fell asleep.

The next day, as we prepared to leave for the hospital — to turn off the machines and let her slip away — I was struck by the absurdity of worrying about my clothes, which I never do, wanting to look nice for Mom. What does one wear to a death? *I thought as the girls got dressed and I explained to them about Grandma.*

In a way, the end was as beautiful as it was sad. We were all together with her, the family, crowded around her bed, all those who loved Mom, and whose lives had been filled with the love she gave. Her mother. Her brother. Her children. Her grandchildren. Each of us there with the special person in our lives to support us. Except for the man who stood in the corner of the room — the man whose life had been so complete, filled as it was by the love of the only woman he had ever loved — the man who now stood alone.

As they turned off the machines that had kept her alive long enough for us to say good-bye, she slipped from our lives, but not our hearts, her eyes opening for a moment, as if to look up at us all one last time, then slowly closed shut, to open no more. We all walked silently from the room, leaving Dad alone with Mom for a moment. I paused in the doorway as he softly kissed her forehead one last time. "I will definitely see you again, Honey," he said to her as he left the room, closing the door behind him.

We all gathered back at the house that evening, needing to be together in our loneliness. Dad was sitting at the computer, looking past a game of solitaire that stared back at him as the phone rang. Some telemarketer on the other end of the line introduced himself, asking, "How are you doing this evening, sir?" "My wife just died today, how are you?" Dad answered as he hung up the phone. I crossed the room behind him, putting my arms around his shoulders, and lightly kissed the top of his head. "Oh, Grandpa," was all I could say as we cried together.

I got real drunk after that, not to avoid feeling the pain, but to try to feel nothing at all. As Christine drove us home, a Neil Young song I wasn't familiar with came on the radio. I haven't heard the song much since, and don't know what the whole thing means, but four lines from the song hit so close to home that night that the rest of the words couldn't matter. Those four lines still pop into my head now and then, when I think about Grandpa.

> *I'm singing for the stringman*
> *who lately lost his wife,*
> *there is no dearer friend of mine*
> *that I know in this life.*

Mom had written a poem at the cottage the previous fall, the last one she would witness among us, one of those eerie signs we try to make sense of after the death of a loved one. It seems strangely foretelling, and you almost have to wonder if she knew her time was drawing near.

Morning Solitude

From my window I see the quiet business of fall:

A single seagull, its white, windswept wings silhouetted
Against the vibrant colors of the changing foliage,

Skimming the jewel-blue water, barely touching it before
Rising again, to be carried away by wings and wind.

A single leaf, disturbed, then detached by the breeze,
Colorful in its last moments of life,

Struggling to remain a part of this scene, turning and twisting
With the current, yet falling faster to its end.

The business of fall: so quiet and serene after
The joyful noise of summer.

Mary Margaret Bailey
October 4

I used to so love autumn. Now the gently falling leaves simply remind me of the cold harsh winter that lies ahead.

I see her still, not a vision or a ghost, but real, with us, in the places she's supposed to be, but never will. In Ireland, with Grandpa. At the girls' graduations, or weddings. At my old house, washing the holiday dishes with Christine. At the cottage, playing cards with Grandma Corchran.

But mostly I see her with Grandpa, holding hands twenty years from now, two gray-haired old people shuffling out to the end of the pier to view the sunset, together.

Brian

∽

August 15
Colleen,

I'm sorry for the long letter I dumped on you yesterday. I was in a bit of a mood, in case you couldn't tell. I've never fully expressed my thoughts and feelings about my mother's death to anyone before. Since Christine's been gone I sometimes feel like I have no one left to talk to. I know I should have been talking about things with Grandpa instead of writing to you, but it's often easier to bare your soul to someone who isn't there.

Thanks for being there.

Brian

∽

August 19
Dear Brenden,

I'm sitting here on the couch with an old-fashioned and a letter, getting to know someone.

I don't know how old he is, though I know he's aged considerably in recent years. I don't know what he does for a living, though I know the pain he lives with. I don't know his tastes in music, or literature, or movies, though I know there's a writer within him. I don't know if he'll ever write to me from the heart again, though I know I wish he would.

I know a lot more about him than I did — yet...I wonder.

I wonder how much more I would have learned from a brief biographical sketch, and how much less important it could possibly be. I wonder how hard it must be to move on after the loss of a spouse, knowing how much I miss you. I wonder how well you can really get to know someone through long-distance letters, when a smile speaks a thousand words?

And I wonder, how was it that you led me across a storm-battered causeway and dropped me on a particular front porch, when there were countless other front porches I could have walked up to.

Leeny

~

August 24
Dear Brian,

I'm sorry it's taken me a while to respond to your last letter(s). I'd like to say that I've been busy at work and simply didn't have the time to write, but that would be a lie. Quite honestly, I was deeply touched by your letter about your mother and didn't quite know how to respond. Your letter was so sad, yet so beautiful in so many ways. I'm glad you were finally able to put into words your thoughts and feelings about her, and I'm grateful that you chose to send them to me.

When Brenden was killed in a car accident last fall I experienced the full gamut of emotions you are all too familiar with. And though his loss was bad enough, what was worse still was that I had no one to share my grief with, no one to console me when I needed support. Like you after Christine passed away, I felt I had no one left to talk to.

My father left us when I was young, and my mother, unable to cope with his rejection, became a shadow of her former self, living somewhere between her memories and her dreams. Brenden filled the void, and provided my childhood memories.

When I look back on my childhood, I realize that all the happy memories include Brenden. He stands out like a glossy color photo stuck in the middle of the otherwise drab mural of my youth.

I recall him coming to the pretend tea parties I'd host under the basement stairs when I was very young, always staying for a second cup, asking for sugar. I recall the smell of glue as I'd lie on the floor of his bedroom, watching him build his model airplanes. I recall the feel of his sweater on my cheek as I rode on the back of his bike, holding on tightly as he took me to some new playground I'd never been to. I recall him sitting with me by my bedroom window on rainy weekend days, watching the droplets run down the glass. I recall how he always put butter on top of scrambled eggs, and could never find two socks that matched. I recall how messy his closet was, how neat his desk. And I recall how he took me to my first dance, corsage and all, when no one else had asked.

I suppose I'm guilty of idealizing my memories of him, and suppressing his faults, which he was not without. But he is the memory I carry with me from my childhood. Without the idealization, I'm left only with the reality – my parents fighting all the time, Dad storming off, Mom retreating within.

Brenden was the one who wiped away all the loneliness and filled the emptiness with happy memories. When he died I learned firsthand the difference between simply being alone, and being lonely.

I guess that's what brought me to The Door, that feeling of utter loneliness. I wanted to be near him again, to find a way to fill the void with new memories. I believe I did.

Love,
Colleen

~

August 28
My Dear Christine,

Whatever happened to that little boy that I used to be?

I have memories of my childhood I saw from the perspective of a little boy. I never saw those memories from my parents' point of view. Now I have their perspective, and can't see new memories through the eyes of the girls.

Whatever happened to that little boy that I used to be?

I can warmly remember lying on the floor under the Christmas tree and looking up through the branches at the rainbow of lights, though now I look down at the tree from above, and miss all the ornaments on the bottom. I can fondly recall raking the fallen apples from under the old metal swing set of my youth, though I can't begin to imagine how the girls will look back on gathering chestnuts beside their fancy wood play set.

Whatever happened to that little boy that I used to be?

Can I ever look back at the small boy I was, and see who my

parents saw? Can I ever truly know what memories the girls will hold dear, not seeing events through their eyes? Can I ever go back and see life again, through the eyes of the child I once was?

Whatever happened to that little boy that I used to be?

I've lost that little boy somewhere along the way, and I don't know how to find him.

My Love Always,
Brian

∽

August 29
Colleen,

Sometimes I get too caught up in my own grief over my mother and Christine to realize that others have suffered similar losses. I know I do that with my dad, too hurt by my mother's passing to offer any real comfort to the man who lost his wife. Your loss of Brenden is so much more recent that I should have been listening instead of talking. Bad habit of mine. Please accept my apology.

People die every day — maybe not the people who are dear to me, but people who are nonetheless dear to someone. If you look around, everyone has a personal tragedy to deal with. Mine is unique only to me.

I found the letter I wrote you about my mother to be a great release for me. It seems that writing it all down provided an outlet for my feelings, a way of thinking it all through, a form of closure, if you will. I hope that your letter about Brenden provided some of the same for you.

Yet I must admit that alongside the warmth I could feel in your letter when you spoke of Brenden, I also felt a certain melancholy sadness from the description of your childhood memories, or lack thereof. I'm sorry you didn't have the happy childhood I was fortunate enough to experience. If you'll allow me, I'd like to tell you about my own childhood, not to contrast it with yours, but to highlight how wonderful the memories can be. For, while you have childhood memories of your own to recall, you will also one day create them for others, and should know how special they can be.

I grew up shortly after the Camelot the history books tell us were the Kennedy years, in the Camelot of my wonder years. No real tragedies or worries, no major fears. Just a sense of comfort, of belonging, and of feeling loved.

I grew up in a big old house, the place I always think of when I hear the word home. *It was filled with laughter, and love, and just enough tears. We had great family parties with my grandparents and cousins, and quiet family times together, just the six of us. I proposed to Christine in that house, hoping that together we could recreate for our own children the happy childhood my parents had given me there. The house was, I know, simply four walls and a roof – a place that others had lived in before us, and others would after. But the life that was lived within stays with us long after we've left those four walls.*

There was a vent pipe that ran from the first floor powder room up to the attic, and my brother and I used to sneak up the curved stairs, past the push-button light switch, and holler down the tube to my dad in the morning as he crouched down in front of the angled mirror to shave.

A church pew rested in the front hall, beyond the leaded glass door we used to slowly swing shut, trying not to ring the wrought iron bells that hung on top. We would stand on the church pew to look up onto the shelves in the closet, to choose a game from the pile that sat stacked next to the phone books. Mom would stuff the round Hoover vac between the garment bags that hung in the closet and set up a folding chair to reach the game, which she'd play with us on the floor, losing each time.

Running up the side of the stairs, behind the radiator, was the railing where Dad hung his tie each night when he came home from work. We would sit on the steps and peer through the rungs of the railing, to watch company pass under the wrought iron bells as they came, or went. Up the stairs, on the landing at the end of the railing, a stained glass window looked down at us, its permanent hole a waiting receptacle for gum wrappers as we passed by.

At the top of the stairs, past the attic door, were my sisters' rooms, which I didn't spend enough time in. My room, which I shared with my brother, was down the hall, between the triangular closet and the bathroom. Red carpet, black-and-white checked curtains, and a football clock, which hung between the windows that looked down over the backyard. Two antique school desks gave us each our own space, mine in the corner next to the other window that looked out over the driveway, where I used to stare out and cry as I tried to do the math homework I didn't understand. And the bunk beds, where my mother would kneel with my brother and me as we said our good-night prayers.

My parents' room, always neat and tidy, held the big bed we all climbed into on Sunday mornings when I was little, to read the paper. Sometimes we'd set up a TV table and bring breakfast in bed to my folks, black coffee and black toast. Next to the bed was the upstairs phone, where I spent hours talking to my girlfriend in grade school. The folding card table, where the Christmas and birthday presents got wrapped, sat opposite the bed, near the dresser, where my sisters played with Mom's jewelry in front of *the mirror. The closet held Dad's ties, and the fairy-tale story-books of his youth, which he read to us on special nights.*

The first floor held an expansive living room, leaded-glass French doors at the far end, in the corner where the Christmas tree always stood, looking comfortingly the same every year, surrounded by packages we opened in turn, prolonging the excitement of the moment. The slide shows we all loved took place there as well, old Grandpa Bailey asleep in his chair, old-fashioned in hand, Grandpa Corchran in the opposite chair, Mom and the grandmas lined up on the couch, my brother and sisters and I strewn across the floor. It was the party room, where countless birthdays were celebrated, extra chairs pulled in to hold the extended family that would gather.

The den, in contrast, was the immediate family's room, where we sat at night watching the news and Carson, Dad and Niall with their bowls of ice cream, Mom and I with our bowls of cereal. Mom always sat in the wooden rocker, never back deep in the chair, but always on the edge, ready to get up and grab whatever someone needed. Dad would sit across from her in the opposite corner, near the panel of light switches whose order I could never remember, Niall on the floor beside him, rubbing his feet.

Next to the den was the dining room, the table covered with stacks of books and papers and mail most of the time, except when dutifully cleared before parties, when we all gathered and ate. Mom would fill the buffet table that we lined up behind to pray, then run back and forth to the kitchen all meal long, refilling the dishes to be passed for the second helping. She would usually first sit down about the time the rest of us finished our meals, and we would stay and talk as she ate. After the meal was complete and the conversation died down, the kids would clear the table, then drift off as the grandpas retired back to the living room for a nap, Mom and the grandmas chatting at the table, Dad rinsing the dishes.

Beyond the dining room sat the kitchen, inconvenient and out of date when I was young, modern and efficient and foreign to me when I grew older and it was remodeled. The old kitchen was my childhood. The pencil marks on the door frame that charted my growth, the tall cabinet that held the clothes-pinned red napkins, the table we all sat around each night, telling the others about our day, each member of the family as interested to hear of the other's day as they were to tell about their own. That table was what family meant to me when I was young, the place where we carved pumpkins and colored Easter eggs, made Christmas cookies and Thanksgiving stuffing, the place we excused ourselves from to go spit our peas out in the powder room toilet, or pretend to wash our hands. That table was the place we all gathered each night to be together, my family. No one ever seemed to rush away from that table; we all lingered after meals, enjoying being together. I still have that old table, in my basement here at this house, unable to let go of it even now, as if the memories might leave with it.

Off the corner of the kitchen, the back stairs led down to the basement. A dark cubbyhole sat on the landing, filled with footballs and basketballs, frisbees and baseball gloves, unhung hooded sweatshirts stuffed in the corner. The damp 'green room' at the bottom of the stairs — filled with antique flat irons, ski boots, golf clubs, and old glassware — was no less eerie when I grew older than it was when I was young.

Dad's workshop was straight ahead, behind the folding gate that kept small fingers out of harm's way. Just beyond the gate sat the incinerator, where Niall and I learned to light matches. Keys that had long since lost their locks hung from the cabinet doors that closed off the dormant coal chute. Baby food jars filled with nails and screws and nuts and bolts, all neatly sorted, hung on a peg board on the opposite wall, above the cigar boxes that held the prizes from long-ago rummage sales. Dad's workbench, tools hung in order on the wall behind it, chaos on top of it, sat against the far wall, next to a smaller workbench, where two small boys learned to pound nails.

Mom's laundry room was around the corner, next to the unfinished bathroom my sisters never liked to use. A wash basket sat on the floor under the clothes chute, waiting to catch the clothes and shouts we sent down from the second floor. Clean shirts hung on hangers from the exposed pipes that crossed the ceiling, folded laundry sat on the little table next to the dryer. A broken clock hung on one wall; on the opposite wall, above the washtubs, two windows allowed Mom to look up into the backyard and watch us play as she worked.

The playroom, never finished, never needed to be. The alphabet zoo picture on the wall, the homemade knock-hockey board and beanbag target, the folding ping-pong table, the hanging shelves. The blackboard, where we played school, and which later announced the birth of my two girls. On the far end of the room, under the window where the leaves would collect in the fall, a homemade wooden bench covered the radiator. I used to lie across the top of the bench on stormy winter nights and feel the heat rise through the round holes. The playroom.

The side porch, where my sister once ate a stick of butter left by the milkman, ran alongside the driveway. Our cat, Fig, used to wait patiently on the porch for my dad to leave for work, proudly presenting him with a dead bird each morning, the extra brown paper lunch bag Dad carried ready to whisk the thoughtful present into the garbage.

Outside, in the backyard, the swing set stood under an apple tree, which held our tree fort, built of wood and love, where we'd have secret meetings, or throw apples down at my sisters and their friends as they played on the swings. The basketball court, hoop secured above the garage doors, got little rest when I was young, lighted at night, shoveled in winter.

The garage, offset from the house, its doors barely wide enough for the cars to fit in, seemed cavernous and unending when we'd have to empty and clean it each spring, and fall. Alongside the garage was the garden, its raspberry bushes and pole beans needing constant picking. Around back wound the dark scary path that led to the upper backyard, once made into a golf course with holes in the lawn, most times a football field that seemed so large when I was young, playing ball with Niall after Packer games in the cool fall air, Mom watching out the kitchen window as she stirred the chili.

The front porch held numerous lemonade sales, and twice donned a pink towel to signal the arrival of my sisters, inviting the ladies of the block to ascend the steps with their casseroles, which were never as good as Mom's. Next to the porch, the tall prickly bushes that scratched us as we raked leaves stood under the front windows of the living room, where Dad used to tuck his shirt into his underwear for all the world to see. A canopy of elm trees hung over the street, a dome to play football under in the rain.

Across the street was an alley, where kick-the-can was the game of choice. Down the block, the scary overgrown property we never once set foot on, certain the grumpy old man would snatch us from our parents if he caught us retrieving lost balls. The duplex we ripped the vines from one misguided day, the motorcycle I tipped over, poking a hole in the oil pan. The nice old people near the far end of the block, who always had a piece of hard candy for us when they let us help pick grapes from their vines. The refrigerator-box wedding chapel where I was first married, at the age of seven. The names of some of my playmates back then escape me now, though it matters only that they were the friends of my youth.

A few blocks east, Lake Michigan, where we'd ride our bikes and climb the cliffs, sliding down the wet clay into the frigid water. A few blocks in the other direction, between the churches of other faiths, my school, and the playground where we spent summers playing strike-out. Beyond that, the park — kickball in the summer, ice-skating in the winter.

The house, the yard, the neighborhood. The scenes of the Norman Rockwell painting that was my youth.

Yet while that big old house was the setting of my childhood, it's not the scene, but the people in it, who make the picture what it is, and create the memories we cherish.

I owe those memories to my parents, to the life they created for me. I hope that my girls will one day look back on their own youth with the same warm feeling I have for mine, and that you may some day have the chance to create special childhood memories for children of your own.

Brian

Chapter 8

∼

September 2
Dear Brenden,

I've been thinking about memories, about the ones we cherish, and the ones we create. I've been thinking about perspective, about the one we bring to life, and the one we take away. I've been thinking about special people, about the ones we hold on to, and the ones that slip away.

I'm packing tonight, getting ready to go away for our annual Labor Day camping trip!

A couple of friends from work invited me to their cabin near Flagstaff, knowing, I think, that I always spent the weekend with you. Nice of them to ask, but at the time I was still half-thinking about flying up to Wisconsin and going to The Door. In the end I chose the certainty of tradition over the insecurity of doubt.

I'm not sure where I'll camp. Should I go up to the mountains, or out to the desert? Either way, I'd like to find a spot we once stayed at together, so I can camp with you one last time.

Leeny

∼

September 6
Dear Brian,

I hope you and the girls and Grandpa had a nice holiday weekend.

I maintained tradition and went camping. Brenden used to come back from The Door on Labor Day weekend, and we always went camping together, just the two of us. I thought it might be good for me to go with him again, one last time.

I decided against going north to the mountains, and instead went south into the desert. While I prefer the companionship of the trees, Brenden loved the barren emptiness of the open expanse, and I thought he'd have chosen the contrast of the desert if he were here, having just returned from The Door.

I left Phoenix late Saturday morning, leisurely winding my way farther away from civilization on the tiny two-lane highways Brenden loved. I found an abandoned old campsite at the end of a dirt road and had the place to myself all weekend. I suppose I was probably on someone's private grazing lands, but nobody came and kicked me off, so I guess it really didn't matter.

I was feeling a little down when I arrived, having driven through the lonely desert, missing Brenden, and The Door he would have just left.

I arrived at my destination in the glow of the early evening twilight, the setting sun highlighting the colors of the butte that formed the backdrop of the campsite, adding more shades of brown and orange and red than seemed possible to the already abundant spectrum. The parade of colors transfixed me, giving me pause to see anew the beauty that exists in the midst of this barren landscape. Turning my back on the empty desert, I studied the butte, the layers of color, the strata of life gone by over time, each built upon the layer before.

I think in that moment I finally came to terms with Brenden's death, and put it behind me.

His life is wasted only if I allow the butte to weather and crumble, to be overcome by the grief of the desert. He is not a thing of the past, but a building block to the future, a foundation that will support me as I go forward. I know now that I'll make it, that I can move past my sorrow and pain over Brenden, and look forward again.

Though I'm not sure where life will lead me, I have an idea of where I want it to go.

I guess I did get one last camping trip with Brenden!

Love,
Colleen

～

September 9
My Dear Christine,

Do you remember walking in the woods, together?

I took a walk on the trails tonight, alone.

Night walks are rare, reserved for reflective nights when the moon is full, their infrequency the source of their uniqueness. The moon rose high over the cedars, casting eerie shadows through the slits in the corncrib. Shafts of darkness fell on the tall marsh grasses, which gently swayed in the cool breeze as the clouds parted, opening new views.

Do you remember how we both felt the one time we broke up?

How long did that break-up last? Twenty-four hours? Thirty-six? That feeling of emptiness, that hollow pit in the stomach we both said we never wanted to experience again, ever. That same feeling I have tonight.

We can't run back into each other's arms this time, as much as I wish that we could. That feeling is with me again, but I have no one to run back to.

I took a walk on the trails tonight, alone.

My Love Always,
Brian

∽

September 10
Colleen,

I hate Labor Day weekend. I re-bury my mom every Labor Day weekend, when we take the boat out of the water. It was her boat, in a way — she wanted it, Grandpa didn't. The year they bought it we put it in the water with such fanfare on Memorial Day, and by the time we took it out of the water on Labor Day, she was gone. I wonder how Grandpa feels about the boat, if it brings back happy memories of her, or if it's a painful reminder that she's not with him anymore. He said one time that we should name it 'Maggie's Revenge.'

I'm happy for you that you had the experience you did over Labor Day weekend, that you seem to have made the adjustment to the loss of Brenden, and are now able to look forward. I went through a similar experience when I wrote you the letter about my mother. I wonder if someday I may get over the loss of Christine, and be able to move past her.

Brian

∽

September 14
Dear Brenden,

Where does Mom go when she stares out the window? I think I'm starting to go there.

I stopped by to see her on my way home from work today. She was sitting in that over-sized yellow rocker you moved from the house, looking small and frail and old as she sat gazing out the window, the same blank stare on her face as the one she wore when she'd sit at the kitchen table years ago, a long, bending ash hanging unnoticed from the end of her cigarette.

I recalled all the times as a child when I'd ask her a question and she wouldn't hear me, even though I was standing right in front of her.

I wanted her to hear me today, and I wanted to hear her. I wanted to understand her better, question her less. I wanted to try to see her from a new perspective — not just through the eyes of a child who didn't understand, but through the eyes of a woman who's lost a love, or never found one.

But today she would not let me look inside her window. Maybe Sunday will be a better day.

Leeny

~

September 16
Dear Brian,

How about that Packer game today! Wow!

I stopped by my mother's after church this morning for my regular weekly visit. We got to talking about Brenden and The Door, and she told me about a Packer bar on the edge of town where they carry the game on TV each week. Evidently she used to go there once in a while with Brenden, who had grown to follow the Packers during his summers in Wisconsin. I guess maybe it tied him back to The Door during football season, over the months he was away.

We decided to go to the bar (her first outing in nearly a year) and had a really nice time together. She was in good spirits today, the best I've seen her in a long time. It almost felt like when I was young, before my dad left.

Anyway, we strolled around the bar and she told me about all the old pictures and memorabilia on the wall, about Lambeau and Lombardi, about Titletown and the Glory Years, and about the history of the team, owned and loved by the people, America's Team before there was such a thing. Funny, I never knew my mother was so knowledgeable about football.

We watched the whole game together, drinking beer and eating brats while she tried to explain the game to me. I'll admit that I don't know much about football, but it was great fun. Maybe I'll go back again.

A certain parallel came to mind as she tried to explain the strategy of the game to me. "Don't go for it all in one big shot," she said. "Take what you can, what they'll give you, a little at a time, and eventually you'll reach the end zone."

I've been thinking about that advice as I sit here tonight, and I think maybe there's a lesson about life in that game plan. We both pushed so hard in our earlier letters, my needing to get past Brenden's death, you seeming to come to terms with your mother's passing. We each needed that at the time, I think, and I'm glad we were there for each other. But that was a lot of long bombs in a row, and I'm wondering about the short pass.

I think back fondly on the time we spent together in The Door, and I've come to value our friendship over the course of our letters. The need for our friendship may have passed, but the desire is still there.

I know you're still hurting over the loss of Christine, and that you still love her deeply. I won't ask about her, nor do I expect you to tell me about her. I'm not looking to take her place, not that I could. Nothing like what you had with her could ever grow out of a few letters separated by a few thousand miles.

I'd simply like to stay friends with someone I've grown fond of. Can we try the short pass?

Love,
Colleen

~

September 20
My Dear Christine,

I sat on the front porch tonight, reading a letter from a friend.

The dew began collecting on the lawn in the cool, damp air, the night mist settling over the marsh below. Fall is coming swiftly to The Door, the leaves on the trees fast coming into color, a few already beginning to fall to the ground.

Two leaves floated down toward me, landing at my feet. One leaf was mostly red, the tips of its ends still holding to the green of summer. The other was mostly green, with only a hint of color beginning to come over it before it fell to the ground prematurely.

I sat on the front porch tonight, thinking about the short pass.

My Love Always,
Brian

∼

September 20
Colleen,

The brief biographical sketch you requested on Mr. Wisconsin was regretfully never completed. I hope this one has been submitted on time.

I forget which part of the Miss America pageant was next, swimsuit or evening gown. You've already seen me in a swimsuit (you'll recover in time), and I already know what I look like in a formal evening gown (it isn't a picture you want to remember). I'm thinking maybe I might be best suited for the covered-from-head-to-toe-in-a-burlap-sack competition!

I'm thirty-six years old and have two wonderful daughters, who some days make me feel like I'm sixty-three! I like spicy food, strong coffee, and kids. I'm either retired or un-employed (vacation requests are easier to fill that way), enjoy reading the occasional romance novel (a bad habit Christine got me hooked on a number of years ago), and love watching old movies (if the lead actors are still alive, the movie is probably too recent for me). My favorite hobby is staying home with my girls. If elected Miss America I would use my crown to work tirelessly to restore nickel movie nights and rid the world of mission statements.

Seriously, your last letter hit a number of nails right on the head, maybe too many for my own comfort. But I too have grown fond of our correspondence and friendship and don't want to see it end either, as long as you understand the extra baggage I carry with me. I could never let go of Christine, but I sure could use a friend now and then.

You said once that we already know so much about each other, but also very little, and I agree. I'll try to fill in a few of the empty spaces on the biography you requested. To summarize beforehand, I like that warm safe feeling one gets when snuggled under a blanket, the covers pulled up tight under the chin, the world blocked out. It would be nice if someone else was there beside me to share that feeling, but sometimes just holding yourself tightly is good enough.

My musical tastes are varied and open, with a few exceptions. First, I have no use for country music, although I must admit I do enjoy southern rock. Second, I don't like anything that requires you to dance, unless it's at a wedding, after a couple dozen drinks. Finally, I'm having a little trouble listening to the stuff the girls are starting to play in the car. (And I wondered why my parents never liked the music I played for them when I was a teenager! I must be getting old.)

Exceptions aside, I'm open to just about anything else, though I do have a particular affinity for Irish music, and also enjoy old show tunes, folk songs, and Christmas music. The true test of one's musical tastes, however, is the car radio, and mine has only two of the five buttons pre-set, one to National Public Radio, the other to classic rock from the '60s & '70s.

Great songs take you away, to a place inside you that other art forms don't reach. Sometimes it's the music, unleashing primordial dances deep within your soul. Other times it's the words, stirring unconscious thoughts deep within your being. Sometimes the two meet, and your mind races faster than your feet.

Mostly I love great lyrics, words that cause you to pause for a moment, and think. I guess if I had it to do all over again I'd come back as a singer/songwriter. Oh, to be the poet of a generation, and touch so many lives. Then again, I suppose life isn't about how many lives you touch, but how you touch the ones you do.

Yet when all is said and done, I'm a Neil Young fanatic to the core. I just hit a certain zone when I play his albums, and feel comfortable inside. I think I like Neil because it was the music I grew up with. I like the feeling I get when I listen to him, a feeling that takes me back to a simpler time, when life wasn't so complicated. It's funny when you stop to think about it, though. He's had a long career, and his music has grown, yet I'm still stuck in the past, listening to his old stuff. Maybe there's a lesson somewhere in there for me.

I love old movies, my favorite cable channels being the ones that carry the classics, and carry you back to a simpler time. Old black and whites from the '40s and '50s, the great actors and actresses of Hollywood's Golden Age, or future stars appearing in their first minor roles. No graphic sex or blatant violence. Give me the old movies that left as much to the imagination as was shown. That's the drawback of the new movies, trying to show you everything in the story.

Art — meaning movies and music and literature, not just painting — is as much about what you perceive in your own mind as it is about what the artist gives to you. Once you take imagination out of the equation, and rob the audience of their own creative process, the work dies. That's why movies are never as good as books. As much as I love the old movies, movies in general take away from the viewer the chance to create the work in his or her own mind, like you can do with a song or a good book.

The only new movies I really like are romantic comedies, which give some of the feel of the old movies. You know the part in The Sound of Music *when Maria and the Captain are dancing on the patio, the moonlight shining off her face and hair as they struggle to catch their breath. Or the scene in* It's a Wonderful Life *where Jimmy Stewart and Donna Reed are close together, sharing the same phone just before they kiss for the first time. The best movies are the ones where the only kiss is the freeze-frame at the end of the movie, when you know a lifetime of happiness will follow.*

I guess I'm just an old romantic at heart, wishing for love and happiness. Take the romance novels Christine got me hooked on. I don't like the rough ones, with a lot of graphic sex, or when one character starts out treating the other badly, only to fall in love in the end. Give me the classic formula: boy meets girl, they fall in love, tragedy separates them until they come back together in the end, and you know they will live happily ever after. It's funny, though, how all the romance novels depict only the coming together of first love, when the greater gift is not in finding each other, but in staying together throughout a lifetime, that newfound love changing, being tested, growing. Then again, why is it that we get to experience the wonder of first love only once? Ah, but that's another letter.

I like the past better than the future. I like antiques for the simpler times they convey. Old methods, old techniques, old tools – the solidness of a well-built wooden hutch, an old farmhouse, a sturdy barn, a slanting shed. Would that we could all go back to those simpler times that never existed when they took place, but are created only afterwards, in our memories.

I used to be a jock in high school, playing all sports all year long.

Now I've grown old and fat and lazy. Beer will do that to you, I guess. For exercise now, in addition to searching for the remote, I enjoy an occasional round of golf with Grandpa. But mostly I like walking, with the girls, or by myself. There's a peacefulness you get when you walk in the woods, or along an empty shoreline, not unlike the feel of three o'clock in the morning, when the rest of the world has gone to bed, and it's just you, alone with yourself.

I guess that should fill in my biographical sketch for a while. I've covered music and movies, reading and recreation. Religion and politics we can save for another letter. That way we can look forward with anticipation to our first fight!

About the only other thing I can add that would help to describe me is the love I have for my girls, which I trust was evident when you were here. My folks used to say "wait until you have kids of your own," and I never quite knew what they meant, until my girls were born. It's a feeling one just can't describe, the moment you hold that tiny new life in your hands for the first time, then watch your child grow. I'm sure I won't be able to let go when they're fully grown and ready to leave home.

You really should get married some day, Colleen, and have kids of your own.

Brian

Chapter 9

~

September 23
Dear Brian,

I am pleased to inform you that the wonderful biographical sketch you submitted was received in time. However, while your thoughtful discussion of the covered topics was appreciated, the judges have informed me that before we may proceed with the talent portion of the competition you must answer the remaining questions about politics and religion.

I'm not sure I ever gave either much thought. I've always just been what I've been, without really thinking too much about it. Being from Arizona, I'm a Republican. Being Irish, I'm Catholic.

Are we about to have our first fight?

Love,
Colleen

~

September 27
Colleen,

It is not my wish to file an incomplete application and annoy the judges, for I am so looking forward to the talent portion of the competition. I've been practicing a little baton-twirling number while I sing "God Bless America," and am certain it is pretty good, if only I could find the right tutu.

Neither is it my wish to engage in our first fight, even if politics and religion seem the most likely subjects to differ on.

Politically I am neither a Republican nor a Democrat, but an American, which means I am a card-carrying member of the group that chooses not to get involved in the entire process, but reserves the right to bitch about the whole mess. Truth be told, they say all politics is local, and I live in a dictatorship. It's really not all that bad, though, because I'm the dictator, though I imagine the peasants may try to mount a revolt about the time they hit their teenage years!

I loved early American history when I was in grade school — the pilgrims, the Declaration of Independence, the Continental Congress and all that. I think one of my favorite family vacations when I was young was when we went to Washington, D.C. and Williamsburg during the summer of the bicentennial.

When I was in high school I got all charged up about politics, a '60s wanna-be, a post-Watergate idealist. I thought, like everyone at that age — all full of piss and vinegar — that I was going to change the world. As I got older I found out it was enough of a chore just to keep one's own little piece of the world afloat, and that making a difference didn't involve doing grand deeds that got your name in the history books.

I'm comfortable living in anonymity, not mentioned in the history books used in schools, my place to be found in the history book of a family tree. Bringing my girls up to be solid people who know right from wrong will affect a lot more lives than any legislation passed in Washington. Trickle down morality, if you will, which brings us to religion.

My religious convictions make me a member of the Confucians, which is to say, I'm confused. I was raised Catholic, attending a Catholic grade school and high school, being brought up in the culture at home, though my parents were neither fanatic zealots nor Sunday-only Christians. Religion to me means the moral grounding I received at home, the lessons my parents taught me — the difference between right and wrong, the compassion one should feel for others, the respect one should have for life, and the hope that something more lies beyond this life.

To me, the difference between Catholic and Protestant, Hindu and Buddhist, is all just smoke and mirrors, making little real difference in the end. I'm a Catholic because my parents were Catholic. Had I been born in India, I'd be a Hindu; in Saudi Arabia, a Muslim; in Tibet, Buddhist. The particular differences among the various religions matter little. What unifies them all, and makes them one and the same, is the common thread of a belief that there is something more to life beyond life itself, be it a Supreme Being, a natural order, or a continuing spiral of life.

While I'm not real regular about going to church, I practice my religion almost daily, on the nights when I stay up late and review all the chances I missed that day to act upon my faith.

Religion is about what is inside you, not whether you are inside a church. Prayer is expressed internally, in the desire to be a better person. Communion is about giving to others, not receiving for the self. Confession is made to yourself, in admitting your faults and shortcomings.

Religion is not about how often you go to church, but about how you act outside of church. Religion is about always changing the toilet paper roll. Religion is about letting the other car go first at the stop sign. Religion is about taking the time to play with your child, when they want to play. Religion is about your need to know when someone else is in need.

I've always had an interest in the theory of evolution, in particular that point in time when we one day changed from being apes to being humans. I think the watershed event must have been when Lucy, or one of her friends, first thought that there might be something more out there beyond this life. What a day that must have been, when the last ape first pondered what life was really all about, and became the world's first human, and invented the world's first religion.

Would you believe a priest once told me I think too much to have faith? Think about the implications of that statement the next time you ponder the concept of God. Then think about the fact that Christine's faith brought her an inner peace, which I will never have.

We all need something to believe in, and we believe in what was taught to us when we were too young to think for ourselves. Religion is not something you decide upon. You don't go to the mall when you reach the age of majority and pick out a religion from the faith store. If you did, I might choose some type of Native American belief system, so complete they are in their simplicity, so unified in their belief that the Creator exists in all things.

I guess in the end I'm a Godian, believing in some form of an undefined Supreme Being, for my conscience leads me through life, and my heart wants to believe that there is something more out there awaiting us after death.

Yet I don't suppose we ever really learn what life is all about, until after we are dead.

Enough of a sermon for today. Take care.

Brian

∾

September 30
Dear Brian,

The weather has finally started to cool a bit here in Arizona, though not enough; the stifling heat of summer now merely oppressive.

It may sound funny to you, but the climate here robs us of the seasonal stereotypes that live in our American psyche. The reality of the seasons is wherever you live, but the ideal that exists in our minds belongs to those of you in the North. Think of Christmas songs. "I'm dreaming of a white Christmas." "Chestnuts roasting on an open fire, Jack Frost nipping at your nose." "Sleigh bells ring, are you listening, in the lane, snow is glistening." How many Christmas songs do you know that talk about palm trees swaying in the winter heat? Christmas cards show a family dragging a freshly cut tree through the snow, or skating on a frozen pond, or snowflakes clinging to a window.

And it's not just winter that belongs to you, but all the seasons. Kids swimming in a cool pond in the summer, a rope swing hanging from an old oak tree on the shore. A haystack in the fall, pumpkins placed around it, a pile of smoldering leaves in the background. The April showers that bring May flowers, the corn knee-high by the Fourth of July, the newborn calf nibbling at the budding green grass. These are the images that come to mind when one thinks about the changing seasons.

It's not that there aren't changes that take place here, or elsewhere, throughout the year. The changes are different, depending upon where you live, and each setting has its own unique seasons that are dear to those who experience them. But you live in the Grandma Moses paintings of the seasons, in the place we all wish we lived in our childhood.

I've been trying to picture The Door, what it might look like in the fall, the leaves all changing colors. I was only there less than a week and know little of the changes that occur, of what it might look like now. The book you sent me has a number of pictures of the fall colors, but it doesn't capture the feel of the season. I wish I could come back for a weekend and see your fall. Please describe it for me.

I do so miss The Door.

Love,
Colleen

~

October 2
Dear Brenden,

Did I tell you I took Mom to the Packer bar a few weeks ago? We had a really nice time together, talking about football, and you. I think the two of us being together in a place with memories of you was good for both of us.

She talked a lot about you that afternoon, and I was surprised to hear all the detailed memories she recalled from our childhood, memories I thought she'd been unaware of. She asked a lot of questions about you as well, and about my trip to The Door. I got the feeling she was trying to picture you there. I try to picture myself there, too.

In the meantime I wait for news of The Door, and find myself flipping through the mail each day, searching for the postmark.

I do so miss The Door

Leeny

~

October 4
Colleen,

Autumn is not a single season. It is three distinct periods that share only a common name. You cannot visit Wisconsin, spending a weekend driving through the colors, and think you've seen fall. Rather, you have to live here across all three months, and then you can experience autumn.

September is the bridge between summer and fall. The heat and humidity of August slowly begin to melt away as the kids adjust to going back to school, and footballs replace baseball mitts in the parks. Cooler air descends from the north, letting the leaves know their transformation is to begin. The sumac is often the first to change, its small leaves a brilliant red, covering the sides of the highway, a carpet laid out down the sides of the path. The deep greens of summer begin to lighten, yellowing the birch and ash leaves. Pockets of orange and red and brown begin to appear on the maples and oaks, dotting the hillside with small bursts of color. The squirrels sense the change, scurrying about to gather their winter fare of acorns, hickory nuts, and horse chestnuts. Jackets come out of the closet for the first time in months, and the air conditioner is finally turned off in favor of the cool breeze that blows in the bedroom window, billowing the curtains like the sail on a boat. And if the football gods are pleased with what they see, with a little luck the Packers are 4-0 at the end of the month.

October, I think, is my favorite month of the year. The transformation that began in September is now in full swing, the air growing crisp as the full parade of colors fills the trees. You could never imagine all the shades one color can have. Are there nine shades of red, or ninety? Oranges and yellows and browns mix with the reds, stubborn greens the exception, hanging on to a memory. The geese of spring hope return, now the geese of fall remembrance, their formation heading in the opposite direction. Indian Summer brings a few last days of warm sun on your face, giving you a chance to look back over the bright summer before you turn to face the dark winter that lies ahead. Christine and I used to take the girls for an all-day ride in the country on the Sunday of Indian Summer, going in no particular direction, a lonely country lane the busiest road we would travel as we marveled at the colors, stopping to let the girls play at some ancient park that was new to them, in some forgotten little town that was mostly now a memory.

October is the giant leaf pile I would gather for the girls, to throw them into, or bury them under. When the horseplay was over we'd burn the mound, the sweet smell of the pungent smoke lazily drifting across the yard. October is the cornstalks and hay bales we'd set up against the split-rail fence, and the ghosts we'd hang from the trees. October is the trip to the apple orchard and pumpkin farm, the fresh honey we'd eat every day, the squash and the gourds and the Indian corn. October is the Sunday vat of chili that simmered all day, warming the house with its aroma. The end of October brings the end of daylight savings time, and the beginning of darkness.

November dawns gray, the cloud-filled sky hanging low above. November is unique for its barren stillness, for the quiet it brings. The leaves have mostly fallen, the branches bare. I love to walk in the woods in November, such a contrast to the budding hope of spring, the lush green canopy of summer, the bright pallet of early fall colors. When you walk in the woods in November you can see through the trees, back into the darkness of remembrance. I like to sit on a bed of damp leaves, my back against the trunk of an old oak, and look up through the empty branches, watching the gray clouds race swiftly across the sky, pushed by the cold winds that signal the final change of autumn.

The smell of the turkey that fills the house brings an end to fall. The cars that pass by on the road show the change, one weekend carrying deer on their roofs, the next weekend Christmas trees. As November comes to a close so too does autumn, and we all shut our doors and retreat within. The wonder that is Christmas lies ahead, followed by the long winter months of introspection. Spring is the hope that leads us through winter, autumn the memory that sustains us.

Autumn. Three months, three seasons. Autumn. An experience, not an event.

Brian

∽

October 8
Dear Brian,

Is it possible to have a mid-life crisis at 29? I'm really getting down on my job, starting to hate the day-to-day drudgery of the rat race. All the sexy glory I once dreamt of is beginning to fade away. I read a quote the other day that said something to the effect that no one ever dies wishing they'd spent more time at the office, and it hit a bit too close to home for me.

I rise before the sun and am off to work by seven, to meetings and power lunches and more meetings. Then I lug a briefcase full of papers home to fill the empty evening hours, dragging it back to work the next morning to do it all again. Ah, the circle of life!

It all seemed so grand when I started. The book lay open before me. I was going to make my mark on the world. Now the world has made its mark on me. A robot, a number, a body that fills a chair at a desk, a chair where someone sat before me, and where someone will sit after me.

Isn't there supposed to be something more to life? What do you do for a living?

Love,
Colleen

∼

October 13
Colleen,

What I do for a living is live.

I remember when I was a junior in high school, in the locker room at halftime of a football game. We were losing, getting killed actually, as we usually did. The coach was disgusted beyond words, and opened the floor for discussion. The senior captain of the team gave a rousing speech, a real Knute Rockne job, about goals and effort and commitment. I don't know to this day if it came from his heart or if he was just saying what he thought the coach wanted to hear, but he had fire in his eyes and he was pacing, ranting and raving at us, talking about how the second half would define the rest of our lives. It was just a damned high school football game, like hundreds of others played that night, like thousands of others played before it, and countless others that would come after it. It was not the defining moment in his life, or any of our lives, though he didn't know it at the time. I smiled to myself at the absurdity of it all. The smile inside must have escaped, for when I looked up he was standing before me, arm cocked, ready to punch me out for my cavalier attitude. I laughed in his face and he came after me, the coach separating us, me lying prostrate on the floor beneath the guy, him ready to teach me a lesson about life. As we walked back out on the field for the second half the coach pulled me aside and said something to the effect that most people don't have the ability to take a step back and view things from afar, with a larger perspective on themselves, and their lives.

I think, in retrospect, that for me that was one of those few defining moments we go through in our lives, for I knew right then that there is more to life than the events of a lifetime. The bubble burst that day, the dreams of glory vanished, and I began to question the purpose of our short time here on earth. From that day forward I never wanted to be anything, I just wanted to be.

Why is it that we should have to spend ten of our sixteen waking hours each day, five of seven days a week, fifty of fifty-two weeks a year, away from those we love, doing what we'd rather not be doing? I think the hunter-gatherer societies of old were probably much smarter than we pastoralists give them credit for. They lived for hundreds of centuries spending most of their day surrounded by the people they loved. We, in a few short decades, have created a life for ourselves that separates us from the special people in our lives most of the time. And they were primitive?

Since that day in the locker room I've never really had any career ambitions, no dreams of glory, no desire to leave my mark on the world, or let those who come after me know I was here. I've just wanted to be. Be a good person, be happy, be with the ones I love – and be able to look back on my life, before I die, and say with satisfaction that I did it right.

To be truthful, I suppose everyone, including myself, longs for their fifteen minutes in the sun. I had five minutes saved for Shannon and five minutes saved for Kerry, to walk them down the aisle between Christine and me, or to hold their children, my grandchildren, for the first time. I'd saved the other five minutes for Christine, to thank her, in the twilight of our years, as we looked back over our long lives together. If I had an extra five minutes I might have wished to write a book, something that would give the reader pause to think about the nature and purpose of their existence, make them appreciate the gift that is life, and motivate them to use it properly.

As you may have guessed, I've had considerable occasion over the past few years to ponder life's imponderables. I've had deep thoughts – about the existence of God, the purpose of life, the unknowns of death. And I've had small insights – about caring for others, about seeking peace, about accepting being loved. But I still haven't found the meaning of life.

Yet I find that my search often takes me back to that long-ago day in the locker room, and the question of perspective – of how we view ourselves and our lives, and how that view is created.

Much of our perspective comes from within, from that person we are inside us, though I think a greater portion comes from outside us, from the special people we let into our lives, for they help create what is inside us.

Of course, our perspective changes when those special people are no longer here. My mother and Christine look different to me now than they once did. Life looks different to me now than it once did.

Grandpa tells a riddle he heard after my mom died that asks if you know how to make God laugh. The answer: tell him your plans.

You only get one chance, Colleen, and life's too short to worry about the details if you miss the big picture. A job is a job. There are plenty of them out there. Don't define your life by what you do, but by who you are.

Find out what's dear to your heart, the people you love, and spend your time with them. The present is all we have, and it affects both the memories we recall — and the new ones we create.

In closing, I'll suggest a little game I play from time to time. When I start to slip, when I begin to forget who I am, or why I'm here, it always helps me focus, and regain perspective.

A hundred years from now, when no one who knew you in this life is still alive, someone will come across your headstone and pause, to read the summary of your existence. What words do you want carved in your little piece of granite?

Brian

～

October 19
Dear Brian,

Thank you for your last letter. I was feeling a bit low, as you noticed, and needed a shot in the arm. Your letter hit the spot, and provided the perspective I needed.

"Find out what's dear to your heart," you wrote, "the people you love, and spend your time with them."

There are two people I've loved in my life. The first was Brenden, and though he's now gone, his love is a happy memory. The other is my mother, Brigid, whom I never quite understood, or fully appreciated, until now.

I know I've told you a little about her, how she retreated to a world within after my father left us. She's getting older now, noticeably weakening physically, and I sense that the sand is slipping through her hourglass.

Yet something's changed in her of late, or maybe in me. I'd always seen her through the eyes of a child, and only saw someone I thought was unable to give. I'd never seen her through the eyes of one who'd suffered a loss, and had given more than she could bear. I'd never understood her before, because I never shared her perspective on the loss of a loved one, until Brenden died.

Now that I can better appreciate living with loss, I'm developing a new appreciation of my mother. I'm beginning to understand that, while she may not have been able to do the things I wanted her to do, she did the things she could do.

No, she may not have been able to be the Girl Scout mom, or the volleyball coach, or the head of the PTA dance committee. And when I got older she may not have been able to take me out shopping when I was down, and needed a new pair of shoes. She was not a public person.

Yet I'm slowly coming to realize all the little things she did do, and find meaning in them.

My school lunch was packed every morning, a brown paper bag religiously waiting for me on the corner of the counter, the napkin neatly folded on top, a little note tucked inside the waxed paper wrapping that held the sandwich with the crusts dutifully cut off. I was always the first girl in my troop to have my scout patches sewn on my sash, my volleyball uniform was always washed in time for my next game, and my permission slips were always completed the day I brought them home. And I remember that whenever I woke in the middle of the night when I was young I would usually find her watching some old black & white movie on TV as she ironed my dad's white shirt for work, or my dress for school. Oreo's never tasted so good as on those nights.

Seeing her now, from a new perspective, I see that these are the special memories of her that I will carry with me.

Having found my mother, I can better appreciate how difficult it must have been for you to lose yours, and the girls theirs.

Love,
Colleen

~

October 25
My Dear Christine,

Happy Birthday, Honey. No cake, or candles; no presents, or balloons. Just me, alone, with my thoughts of you.

The girls did well on your birthday this year, not like the first one we spent without you, the three of us stumbling aimlessly around the house all day, crying. It's sad to say, but remembering your birthday without you here with us is becoming more routine each year. I thought the memories would never leave me, but they're starting to fade.

I kept the girls out of school today, as I do each year on your birthday. We went driving around The Door, stopping at spots we rarely frequent anymore, places we used to go when the four of us vacationed here. Though it's sometimes painful, I like to go to the spots that bring back happy memories of the times we spent together.

Do you remember the first year we spent your birthday together, when I hitchhiked back from college and surprised you? I'll never forget the look on your face when you saw I'd come back. I knew right then that you'd be my best friend, my soul mate for life. I mistakenly thought it would be for the rest of my life, not just the rest of your short life.

I think I'm fast acquiring a new friend. It feels nice, because I've been without one since you left. But I'm guarded. A friend I can surely use. Anything more scares me. Be happy for me that I've finally got someone to talk to, but please don't worry that I'll ever leave you. There could never be another to take your place in my heart. I love you so, still, and miss you terribly. Happy Birthday.

My Love Always,
Brian

Chapter 10

~

October 26
Colleen,

Yesterday was Christine's birthday. I'm afraid I'm not in the right frame of mind to write a letter to another woman.

The girls put together this little package for you and asked me to send it. It was a big secret. I'm not sure what lies within, or ahead.

Brian

~

Colleen

Kerry thought you might like to try some of our pumpkin seeds. Dad makes the best ones in the world, from Grandma's recipe. We only have about two zillion of them, so if you like them we can send you more. Dad loves to carve about a hundred pumpkins and put them all on the porch roof with a candle inside. He says it's to decorate the house for Halloween, but I think he does it just for the seeds.

We put up the Halloween decorations the other day, taping witches and jack-o-lanterns on all the windows and hanging ghosts from the trees. I'm going to be a witch for trick-or-treat and Kerry's going to be a kitty. Dad helped us make our costumes. Not as good as when Mom used to make them, but OK.

Dad's starting to get ready for the holiday season. Next it will be pork sausage stuffing for the turkey, then it's Christmas cookie time! We make about 15 batches of cookies every year, sugar cookie cut-outs and spritzes and gingersnaps and pecan fingers and you name it, we make it. The only kind we don't make anymore are those peanut butter cookies with the chocolate kisses in the middle. Those were my mom's favorite, and Dad doesn't like making them anymore.

Anyway, Christmas is really fun around here. We decorate two trees and make cut-out snowflakes for all the windows and put about a million Santas from Dad's collection all over the house. Dad says a person should always have happy childhood memories of Christmas to carry through the years. He even keeps an ornament hanging around the house all year long, just to remind us of the spirit of Christmas. What do you do for Christmas in Arizona without any snow? It must not really seem like Christmas without snow.

My hand is getting tired from all this writing. I think this is the longest letter I ever wrote in my whole life. Hope you like the pumpkin seeds.

Love,
Shannon

∾

Dear Colleen

It was my idea to send you the pumpkin seeds. I'm going to be a kitty for Halloween.

When are you going to come back and visit us? My Dad seemed happier when you were here.

Shannon says I have to finish my letter now. Can you come back and visit us again sometime?

Love,
Kerry

∽

October 28
Dear Brenden,

I sit here tonight in his white shirt, an old-fashioned in my hand, a bag of pumpkin seeds on my lap, and I wonder.

I wonder — what is to become of me when Mom slips away, you already gone?

I wonder where the future will lead me. I wonder if his future lies in the past. I wonder what he sees when he looks at his memories, and then at me.

I wonder about the long flowing letters he writes, and why he sends them to me. I wonder if he'll send any more of his lyrical epistles. I wonder about the short note, just received.

Leeny

∽

October 29
Colleen,

What is life all about? I've spent mine trying to answer that one question, and gotten nothing but more questions as the answer.

What happens to us when we die? Why have we lived? What is the purpose of our time here on earth? Is there really a God? Are we nothing but water and chemicals? Do we simply return to the earth, ashes to ashes, dust to dust? Where does our conscience come from? Where does it go when we die? Is there life after death? Do the deceased now watch down over us? Are we reunited with the ones we love after we die? Can any of these questions be answered?

I have an old photograph of my house, from around the turn of the century, past occupants posed in the front yard under a stand of old oaks, now gone. The stout matriarch, in her apron, stands next to her aging husband, seated, white neck beard sticking out proudly below his chin. At their feet sits the family dog, who once roamed the fields my cat now patrols. A few middle-aged adults stand behind them — a son, or daughter, with spouse, children at their side. An odd gentleman, by himself, leans up against a tree — a cousin maybe, or an unmarried son, or a hired hand.

Who are these people who once lived in my house? Or am I now living in theirs? Does one of the youngsters in the photo, now quite old, drive by occasionally and fondly recall the childhood spent here? Who were these people in my picture? Does anyone remember them?

My Grandmother Bailey is in a nursing home, her mind slipped back to infancy. She doesn't recognize my dad when he visits, doesn't remember her husband, who's been dead ten years, or know that my mother has passed away, or Christine. Has she slipped into the old photo of my house, her life a forgotten memory, the people she knew now just nameless faces in a discarded photograph, the same fate awaiting the picture I will take tomorrow?

I acquired an old briefcase a few years back, filled with turn-of-the-century newspapers, kept by a great-grandfather I never met. A few of the newspapers chronicled world events, items important at the time, none now in the history books. A few more mentioned significant moments in the lives of family members — a grammar school graduation, an engagement, a relative from Ireland come to visit. Most, though, were papers that held death notices of various family members.

When I was young we had a large extended family of relatives who got together at various gatherings once or twice a year — Mom and Dad's cousins, my grandparents' siblings, assorted relations I didn't know I had. I remember being amazed as a child that the old people there could recall every name, every relation, and where people fit on the family tree. It all seemed so overwhelming and confusing to me at the time. Then, when I got older, my girls got confused over the names and places of their distant relatives, though I couldn't understand why, for they were the people who were dear to me in my youth.

I see these people infrequently now, sometimes at a wedding, more often at a funeral, and we don't much know what to say to each other anymore, except to explain the relation one has to another, as if setting the places at the table makes everyone accounted for, the family tree complete. Yet with each successive funeral one more leaf has fallen from the tree. I've always wanted to chronicle my family history, but never have. By the next family funeral I still won't have started, and one more branch of the tree will be lost.

Most of the newspapers in my briefcase chronicle a life gone by, mentioning dates and places and relations — quantitative data, not qualitative information. We learn nothing about the essence of the people who are no more — no description of their life, of the things they held dear, of what they feared, of how they felt, of whom they loved. We know about them, but we don't know them.

One death notice was for my great-grandfather's dad, my great-great-grandfather, who came from the old sod to the new world in 1854. I know he came from Ireland, though I know not from what part, from what county. A mere five generations back and I don't even know what type of life my forefathers lived in the old country. I don't know if they were fishermen living by the sea, or farmers living up in the hills. Five generations! I have pieces of furniture that are older than that. My house is nearly that old as well, five sets of lives having passed briefly through the front door, from nowhere to somewhere. Who now recalls the people from five generations ago? And what of us, five generations from now?

In a time before headstones and death notices, the old cultures of most societies had a storyteller who could trace history back orally, not five generations, but five hundred years, and bring the faces of ancestors to the minds of their listeners, as if they'd seen them only yesterday. "She was a jolly, gregarious woman who loved her husband dearly, but she liked to play tricks on him." "He was not a talkative man, his face set in stone as it was, but when he did speak, softly, the people of the village all listened." "What a fiery young lad that one was, the wild red hair matching the fire that burned deep within his eyes, and he knew early on that his life was to be a short one, and that he must act fast."

Why does this happen no more? What has happened to the storytellers of old? Who shall ever recall, for those who come after, those who have gone before? Who shall say "Maggie was a soft, giving woman who met a nice man, and they loved each other in return, having four children anyone would be proud to call their own, so right was the love they gave them, but she died too early for them all and left her nice man heartbroken and alone"? Who will recount that "Christine was soft on the outside, though tough on the inside, and gave of herself to others, but in the end time was not her friend, and she left this world far too soon for everyone in it, most of all for her two darling angels, who lost the mother they barely remember"? And will anyone tell of "the father and son who were left with only a memory to love, along with each other"?

How many leaves have fallen from all of the trees over the course of time, and been carried away by the wind?

Brian

~

November 3
Dear Brian,

You lament photos fading. I grieve over pictures never taken. In a way, it's the same.

I have no photos to fade, as you worry yours will, now that no more can be taken. I have a brand new camera, but an empty photo album.

I have no snapshot of the happy family sitting together on Santa's lap, or the four of us wearing mouse ears at Disney World; no beloved kitchen table stored away in the basement, no Sunday walks in the park after church. Yet I long to take pictures — of a spaghetti-faced toddler, of a first day at school, of a grandchild on my knee, of the deck of a ferry.

I've never known the special love one can only receive from a child, or share with a spouse, though I'm finally beginning to understand the love of a mother who gave me my own special childhood memories. I feel so fortunate about my newfound relationship with my mother, so sad that you can't have more time with your mother, or Christine. You will never forget them, just as I now will always remember my mother.

Love,
Colleen

~

November 8
Colleen,

After my mom died, my dad started reading a lot of those books one tends to read after the death of a loved one, books on grief and loving and remembering. He was so fully and completely heartbroken as no one I've ever seen before, so close he and my mom were to each other, in every way. I remember his eyes, lost, like a child's, empty, hollow. I don't know how he made it through that initial period, for I know I still haven't, and wonder if I ever will. Yet, while he still misses my mom terribly, if you look at him now you see a man who's at peace with himself, happy for the love he had, not distraught over the love he lost. Love did not die in him when the love of his life died.

Grandpa read a few books on near-death experiences, on what it felt like to be momentarily on the other side. Though he already knew in his heart that he and my mom would be together again someday, he now accepted in his mind what his heart was telling him, that there was something more out there to come after this life.

I can't fully explain how I came to my belief, but I've always felt that those who have left us look down on us after, not just watching our lives, but living them with us, feeling our hearts, knowing our thoughts. I don't really think we can reach them, but I feel they touch us, are a part of us, deep within us.

I've never gone back to my mother's grave, or Christine's, since the day I stood beside them and threw dirt on their caskets. They're not there in the cemetery, under the sunken piece of sod, but with me, always, everywhere I go, in everything I do.

You have your mother now, and will have her always in the same way.

Brian

≈

November 13
Dear Brian,

So, what are your plans for Thanksgiving? I've decided I'm going to give my mother a day away from the home, a holiday from the gray food, and have her to my place for a full Thanksgiving dinner. I'm planning the whole works: bird and stuffing, sweet potatoes, cranberry sauce, pumpkin pie.

Help!!!

I've never cooked a turkey before, let alone put on a full dinner like this, even if it's only for two. But I so want it to be right for my mother this year, and I need some help.

Could you please send me some recipes, helpful hints, or words of encouragement. In lieu of this, a fully cooked meal that just needs warming in the microwave would be nice!

Love,
Colleen

≈

November 19
Colleen,

Throwing a successful dinner party has more to do with preparing your guests than it does with preparing their food. A good rule of thumb — once everyone has had two cocktails and seems about ready to eat, pretend you forgot to make something and go hide in the kitchen for a while. By the time you return your hungry guests will have had a third drink, and it won't matter what the food tastes like!

Cooking a turkey is easy. Put it in the oven, uncovered, at the start of the Macy's Thanksgiving Day parade on TV. Baste each time a new parade begins, on any channel. When the Packer game starts, cover the bird, basting each time the Packers score a touchdown. When the guests arrive, about an hour after you've told them to be there, take the turkey out of the oven. Once your guests have finished their second old-fashioned, carve the bird.

The only critical part of the meal, besides beating the lumps out of the gravy, is the stuffing. Everyone thinks their mother's stuffing is the best in the world, which of course can only be true. My mom, however, did make the best stuffing ever created. I've enclosed her recipe, a pork sausage and dried bread stuffing with a hint of powdered walnut flavoring. Make it the day before and keep it in a glass-covered casserole dish in the fridge overnight. You are, of course, allowed to sneak down the stairs in the middle of the night and snitch pieces of the butter and walnut flavored pork sausage.

We're going to have a fairly quiet Thanksgiving this year. Niall and Claudia are staying in California, celebrating at a friend's cabin in the mountains. Aileen and Ryan are taking their Maggie to Ryan's folks' house in North Carolina. That just leaves Ciaran and Patrick coming up from Chicago, toting Bailey and little

*Liam, to join the four of us. We decided to do it at Grandpa's this
year, now that he's finally moved from his cottage to my place
next door for the winter. I'll cook the bird again this year, but he
wanted to make Mom's stuffing.*

*Christmas promises to be more hectic. Everyone is coming to The
Door this year, so it'll be a full crowd, fourteen in all, counting
Grandma Corchran, to stay for about a week each, crammed into
any beds we can find between the two houses. It's funny, there are
bodies everywhere – the people I lived with every day for the first
eighteen years of my life, and now see only a few times a year –
but no one ever seems to really get on each other's nerves, so
comfortable we all are during the holidays when the whole family
is together again.*

Brian

~

*November 25
Dear Brian,*

*Holidays weren't much of a celebration when I was young. I can
count my Thanksgiving memories on one hand. Three, all in a
row. There was the year my dad took us out for a fancy dinner,
then picked a big fight with my mom and stormed off, leaving us
stranded at the restaurant. The next year, after my dad had left
us, my mom tried to make a turkey and forgot about it, burning it
as she drifted off out the window. She didn't attempt a bird the
next year, staying in her room instead, crying as Brenden made us
frozen turkey dinners, TV trays serving as our banquet table as
we sat in the living room watching* The Wizard of Oz.

*To be fair, I do have my share of happy holiday memories. There
was the Fourth of July the whole family went to the picnic at the*

town park, and my bike won the decorating contest. Or the Halloween Brenden and I collected a whole pillowcase full of candy, and lay on the living room floor together all night, sorting it. And I'll never forget the time the Easter Bunny hid candy eggs all over the yard, and it rained, and I got my white dress covered in chocolate and mud, and my parents laughed together on the porch.

More often, though, holidays were less eventful, less memorable. Yet I've come to realize that my mother always tried, in her own way, to do the little things she could to make the holidays special for me. Maybe not the stuff children's dreams are made of, but memories I will forever hold dear.

She always made angel-food cake on my birthday, and corned beef and cabbage on Brenden's. She always hung special towels in the bathroom for every holiday, and sent Valentine's Day cards in the mail. She always knitted me a new scarf each Christmas, and sang Irish songs every St. Patrick's Day. She always helped me decorate my bike on the 4th of July, and sewed my trick-or-treat costume herself. And she always hid a tiny gift in my Easter basket each year, tucked under the fake grass beneath the candy.

Maybe I invited my mother over for Thanksgiving to try to replace some bad Turkey-Day memories, or at least add to them. Or maybe I wanted to let her know I understand and appreciate all the little things she did to try to make the holidays special. Whatever the reason, I created new memories. I'm glad I did, before I lost the chance.

After my mother went to bed I sat on the couch and wondered what my life will be like once she's gone. I looked around my condo, at the bare white walls staring back at me, empty, hollow. The place seemed suddenly so lifeless, without warmth or charm, and I thought of your house, so friendly and inviting — the cozy antiques, the creaky floorboards, the feeling of peace, and the life your two girls breathe into the house.

I thought I might move, find a flat in an adobe house, a place with a little character that I could decorate in southwestern style. But I've never been a huge fan of that decor, even though I've lived in the middle of it all my life. After some time I realized that what I wanted to create in a new house was the feeling I got when I was in your home.

But it's probably taken you years to collect all the antiques you have, to say nothing of the cost. How did you ever get the house to look as nice as it does? How did you create the feeling of comfort I had when I was there?

Love,
Colleen

P.S. - Your mom's stuffing was a hit. Say hi to Grandpa, and tell the girls I'll write to them soon.

$\sim$

November 29
My Dear Christine,

I'm sitting here tonight in my little hideaway under the stairs, thinking about the difference between house and home.

Grandpa went back "home" this past weekend and visited his grandma's house, a place he lived in for a while during World War II, a place I used to picnic at on the Fourth of July when I was little. We got to talking about the nooks and crannies of that old farmhouse, then other places he lived as a child, then the house that was my home when I was young.

Now a friend has asked me about this house, and I realize that's all this place is to me.

When I was a child I always called the place I lived my "home." I always said, "I'm going home" or "Let's go home." I never said, "I'm going to my house" or "Let's go back to the house."

When we first got married I always thought of the places we lived as "our flat" or "our apartment," but never as "our home." Then we had a family and bought that old farmhouse, and I immediately thought of it as "our home."

And the place I live now? I refer to it as "my house."

My Love Always,
Brian

∼

November 30
Colleen,

The change is coming. Fall is ending, winter on its way. No snow on the ground yet, but the feel is in the air. The leftover turkey is nearly gone, the wreath is hung between the second-floor windows, and every car that passes by either has a deer or a Christmas tree tied on top. Soon we will all close our doors, add our five pounds, and hibernate the winter away inside.

I don't really mind winter — like it, actually. The childlike joy of the Christmas season, the fun of sledding and skating, of snowmen and snowball fights. Nights by the fire, snuggled deep in a chair, deeper still in a good book. The frantic pace of the summer outdoors slows down, and we all get a chance to withdraw within. We all lose a little something in winter, yet gain a little something back as well.

You said you were thinking of moving and asked how I put together the "feel" of my house, and I've been stalling. I've only lived in this house for about a year and a half, since I ran away from the home Christine and I had created for ourselves and the girls.

We lived in a different old farmhouse, about an hour from wherever we needed to go, about a century from where we wanted it to be. It was just outside of a dying little town that was once surrounded by farm fields, which now grow subdivisions. We had wanted to let the girls grow up and enjoy their childhood in a less hectic environment, removed from some of the trappings of modern life, but progress chased after us faster than we could run away from it.

While I loved that old house, the world around it changed, as did my world when Christine passed away. I stayed for a while, for as long as I could, through the full cycle of dates, enduring each special day at least once without her. Then I sold the house, complete with all its contents and the memories they held, and moved up here to The Door.

I guess my heart has always been in The Door, since I was very young. We vacationed here every year when I was a kid, first in a rental place just up the shoreline from Grandpa's, then in the family cottage my folks were fortunate enough to buy. Whichever place I was staying, The Door was always the place I'd just left when I got the day-after-vacation blues. I always longed to move up here, to try to capture and hold that feeling one gets on vacation. But Christine was never the dreamer I tend to be. She knew that the dream has to be one step removed, or it isn't a dream anymore.

Anyways, a little more than a year after Christine passed away I was visiting Grandpa for the weekend, the girls staying back home with Christine's folks. I was driving to Egg Harbor for groceries and saw the "For Sale by Owner" sign being put up in the front lawn of this house. I'd always liked the old place, driving past it as I had for twenty-five years, so I just stopped and bought it right then, paying the asking price, never telling the girls or Grandpa I'd bought it. I hired contractors to fix the place up a bit, in time for summer vacation. When we came up for our first visit after the school year was over, and the construction complete, I showed it to Grandpa and the girls. We slept in it that first night, and every night since.

Sometimes I feel guilty about uprooting the girls like that, only a year after their lives had been turned upside down by the loss of their mother, pulling them away from their friends, and Christine's family. But kids bounce, and the girls have adjusted now, and do so love The Door. I think it's good for the girls and Grandpa to be together, to share their losses and draw strength from each other. I know it helps me to be near him too. It helps keep my mom alive within me, and ties me to the childhood I've never outgrown. And looking back, I know now that I couldn't have stayed in the old house one night longer than I did.

Our old house was furnished one step at a time, with love. From the early years, when we had no money for projects, deceased relatives' couches and a borrowed coffee table our only furniture, through all the antiques we bought and the remodeling projects we worked on, together. That old house was furnished one step at a time, with memories.

I just couldn't stay in that house any longer after Christine passed away. She was everywhere, in every room, around every corner. I left every item we bought together in that house when I sold it, except for the things we bought on our honeymoon, and took only a few family heirlooms and an empty feeling with me when I left.

It's funny that you got such a feeling of warmth from my current house, for though I've loved the place since I was a child, I don't find the comfort inside that I thought I would. Sure, it looks nice, but it doesn't feel right. It feels like a house, not a home. It was not decorated with love, but with money, blood money.

What is a life worth? In Christine's case, it was $1,319,854.27, after expenses. That's how much money I got from the pensions, her share of her practice, and all the life insurance proceeds. That much money from Christine's hard work, so that I don't have to worry about a thing anymore, except missing her. It's nice the girls will be well taken care of. At least Christine could give them that, if not her time. But imagine the guilt I feel from time to time that the money is the reward I get for the sacrifice Christine made. I'd give all that damn money back in a minute, if only I could.

I furnished this house in a weekend, renting a large truck and driving to three big antique shows, filling every inch of the truck — and every space in the house — and I didn't even make a dent in the money. And of all the nice pieces I got, none of them speaks to me, none of them has the special meaning the pieces Christine and I bought together for the old home had.

The tiny shop in the tinier town, where we bought a butternut hutch on a crisp fall day. The little park, with the stream and the ducks, where we took the girls for a picnic after we bought their painted metal beds. The auction we happened upon one day, where we found the dressing table Christine had always wanted. And the giggles we hid behind the menu of a coffee shop, the hairdo on the waitress even uglier than the lamp we had laughed about at the store down the street.

The house may look nice, but the feel just isn't there for me. These pieces I bought are all hollow, the story they tell not speaking to me. Except, maybe, for the piano.

Brian

∾

December 5
Dear Shannon and Kerry,

I'm making out my Christmas shopping list and I have two nice little girls' names on it, but I can't think of a thing to get them. Could you please help me think of gift ideas for them? If you were two nice little girls, what would you want for Christmas?

I'm going to spend Christmas with my mother. They're having a fancy dinner at the home she lives in, and she wants me to come so she can introduce me to some of her friends. Your dad told me the whole family is coming to The Door for the week to stay with you and Grandpa. Sounds like such fun. I wish I could be there with you and meet all of them.

Write soon with your ideas, so I'll have time to shop and mail presents before Christmas. Say hi to your dad for me, and Grandpa too.

Love,
Colleen

~

Dear Colleen,

Thanks for your letter. It's really cool that you want to get us presents for Christmas. I didn't even think about getting anything for you.

What I really want for Christmas is a new pair of roller blades, but Dad says they're too expensive and that our hill is so steep I'd never make it to the top on them, and if I did I'd probably kill myself on the way down. I'm kind of thinking maybe Santa will bring the roller blades anyhow. Kerry wants everything on every commercial, but what she really wants the most is Baby Golden

Slumber. She poops and pees, and eats food and drinks a bottle and needs about a hundred batteries!

Dad says we can send you a box of cookies when we get a few more kinds made. We've already done five batches already. Tomorrow we're going to cut down a Christmas tree from the backyard and decorate it. We play Christmas music and eat pizza rolls and build a fire, and it takes all day to hang the ornaments, and it's one of the best days of the whole year, almost as fun as opening presents.

What do you want for Christmas? Kerry and I have a few ideas, but maybe we should see what you want. I think it's better to get what you want rather than what someone wants to give you, even if it's supposed to be the season of giving.

Love,
Shannon (and Kerry too)

~

December 12
Colleen,

Santa has to get that one special present each year, so the ideas the girls gave you in their letter yesterday have likely already been handled by the big guy. I'm afraid I'm not much help with alternate ideas. With all the relatives asking for suggestions I feel kind of like a saleslady at a store in a mall.

I think you got to know the girls well enough in the few days you were here. Kerry still talks about you all the time. I'll trust your judgment to get something appropriate. Please don't spend too much. You'll either spoil them (which is easy to do), or make me look cheap (which isn't hard to do).

Sorry I couldn't be more help, but I'm fresh out of ideas. You're on your own.

Brian

∿

December 16
Dear Brian,

Not to worry on the gift front. I've got a few ideas. Your little girls will become little women sooner than you think, and women know what women like.

I'll be brief as I'm so far behind schedule I wouldn't be ready for Christmas if it were at the end of July. Presents to buy, and wrap, cards to write, parties to go to.

I imagine you've got things organized well enough so you can enjoy the season, bake cookies, decorate the house and tree. I know you try to make it a special time for the girls. Where are you going to hang the ornament Shannon told me you keep around the house all year long, to remind you always of the joy of Christmas?

I'll send a note with the gifts.

Love,
Colleen

∿

December 18
Colleen,

Here's a dozen each of nine different types of cookies, or one really big cookie with nine different flavors if this didn't make it through the mail too well. The girls made most of the cookies with me, decorated them too, then picked out the ones to send, which probably means you get the ones with extra sugar and frosting.

One week to go and I'm in pretty good shape, Christmas-wise. Cards went out yesterday, cookies coming along well, shopping all done, most of the presents wrapped. I save some wrapping for the day before, either to create some excitement and anticipation for the girls, or to give them something to do if they're driving me nuts as they wait impatiently for the holiday to begin.

First of the guests scheduled to arrive on the 21st, with another set the next day and the third set the following day. I sure do miss my old cleaning lady, but I'm looking forward to seeing everyone, clean house or not.

Brian

P.S. – It snowed today, so now we'll have a white Christmas. I'm so happy for the girls, because there should be snow for Christmas.

∾

December 20
Dear Brian, Shannon and Kerry,

Enclosed are presents for all. You have to promise not to open them early. Merry Christmas.

Love,
Colleen

∾

December 21
Dear Colleen,

More presents are always better than less. Here's a bunch. Don't open early!

There's a letter for you at the bottom of the box, under all the packages. Merry Christmas, and may all your dreams come true in the New Year.

Love,
Brian, Shannon and Kerry

Part III

~

Chapter 11

~

Colleen sat on the couch, looking past the rerun of *It's a Wonderful Life*, at the few bright lights that twinkled at her from the small artificial tree in the corner of the room, put up more out of a sense of duty than desire. Christmas Eve, alone in her apartment. A large box that had come from The Door sat behind the tree, a tiny pile of packages in front of it. Two small boxes for her mother. One leftover package from work, for a friend who'd left a few days early to fly home and be with family. One big box, the new robe she'd bought herself, and had wrapped at the mall.

The Christmas card she'd received from The Door lay open in her hand as she focused on the large box he had sent. It was filled with at least eight smaller packages, each individually wrapped. She looked from the box to the card and read it once more. *"There's a letter for you at the bottom of the box..." "...and may all your dreams come true in the New Year." "Dear Colleen." "Love, Brian, Shannon and Kerry." "Dear." "Love."* Was that the first time he had addressed and signed a letter that way? It was probably just what he wrote on all his Christmas cards, she told herself.

Colleen had always been a Christmas Day person, not a

Christmas Eve person. Some people had family presents, and Santa presents, and relatives' houses to go to, the gift-opening spread out over a few events. But Colleen had never had extra parties to go to. For her, Christmas never lasted more than an hour, if that long, so she usually tried to save the few packages she received for one joyous moment, and as a rule never opened gifts until Christmas Day, fearful she'd have nothing left if she started early.

It wasn't that she didn't have happy memories of Christmas. She did. Just too few. She recalled the year her mother bought her a new kitchen play set, and she and her mother and Brenden sat together on the basement floor all day and assembled it. She recalled the year Santa brought her the prized doll she had wished for, complete with an extra outfit and carrying case. And she recalled the Christmas she played Mary in the kindergarten play, when the whole family came to watch her, and Dad took them out for ice cream after.

But she also recalled the Christmas her dad got her a kitten, and the frightened little thing ran up the tree and knocked it over, the ornaments smashing as the kitten was taken away. She recalled the year her dad left, on Christmas Eve, her mother crying in the bedroom all Christmas Day. And she recalled the year Brenden went out and got drunk for Christmas, and never gave her a present.

Setting the card on the coffee table, she sank deep into the cushions of the couch, her eyes off the big box behind the tree, her mind off The Door. She tried to watch the movie but nodded off soon after, the tree lights reflecting off her long shiny hair.

≈

As the parade of people trafficked by him, Brian wondered how it was that Niall and Claudia always ended up quietly over at Grandpa's while he was left with his two sisters and their families, complete with crying babies and mischievous toddlers. He didn't really mind, he knew, for it brought back happy Christmas memories of when he was a child, or when his girls were younger. Christmas was for kids, even big kids such as himself, and his girls did so love playing with their cousins. With all the activity, the house felt alive again, like a home.

His sisters had just taken their children upstairs for baths before the Christmas Eve party, their husbands watching football in the little sitting room off the kitchen pantry. The festivities would be starting soon, now that it was beginning to get dark outside, but for the moment, things were calm.

Brian had always enjoyed a special quiet time before the start of the holiday, a time he relished more than any other in the season. Early Christmas Eve was reserved for the immediate family. When he was a child the family had always sat together and opened their gifts to each other early Christmas Eve, before going off to Grandma and Grandpa Corchran's for dinner, and more gifts. Santa presents came the following morning, then Christmas dinner at Grandma and Grandpa Bailey's after mass. All of the events had been wonderful, but the time alone with the family at the start of the holiday was always the time Brian cherished most.

He had purposely tried to recreate that moment with his own family, the girls with their kiddie cocktails, he and Christine with old-fashioneds or a brandy and eggnog, a low fire in the fireplace, soft Christmas music in the background. He sought that special time now, with his girls, the three of them alone together by the tree in the living room.

Opening their presents from him, not finding the hoped-for special gifts, the girls' faces dropped slightly, then smiled knowingly as they thought of Santa presents in the morning. Santa always brought the big gift. Brian loved his Packer sweatshirt and tie, making a fuss over each girl as they proudly unwrapped the present they had bought him. He mentally thanked Grandpa for knowing it was as important for the girls to give him a gift as it was for them to receive gifts.

"Can we open the presents from Colleen now?" Kerry asked.

"Yeah, Dad," begged Shannon. "Can we?"

"Well, we usually save this time for the special gifts to each other," he replied.

"But Colleen is special," Kerry stated as she picked up the pile of boxes from under the tree.

Both girls had three packages from Colleen, a matched set for each, tied together with an elaborate bow, the way Christine had always wrapped gifts. The girls ripped into their packages, more than pleased with the presents they found. Small Claddagh rings, the Irish symbol of friendship, loyalty, and love. Thin necklaces, each girl's birthstone set in a heart. And tiny wooden jewelry boxes, "Arizona" hand carved on the top. Thoughtful gifts, all three, filled with symbolism Brian wasn't quite sure the girls fully understood.

Brian picked up the larger of his two boxes, which contained six or seven smaller parcels, each wrapped in red and green tissue paper, all Santas, southwestern motif, thoughtful additions to his collection. The second box, smaller, had a little Santa card attached, which read, "A little bird told me. I hope this is not inappropriate. Enjoy." Inside, two-dozen peanut butter cookies with chocolate kisses in the middle.

Brian drifted back to a stormy night in early June, so long ago it now seemed. He drifted further, to a chance meeting in a bookstore one warm summer day, then further back still, to a fraternity party in the late '50s, when a cute little nursing student met a really nice guy she'd probably never see again. Chance encounters, all three, yet each had changed, and set, the course of so many lives.

The girls huddled close on either side of him as he drifted off, the box of cookies on his lap. Remembering, he didn't hear the wail of babies coming down the steps, or feel the rush of wind coming in through the front door. When he looked up his entire family stood before him, each person staring down at him, save one. Grandpa stood slightly behind the rest, leaning against the doorframe, looking across at the piano as the others bombarded Brian with questions about exactly who this Colleen was.

~

Colleen woke to the sound of church bells chiming on TV. Christmas morning. Alone. Again. Rubbing her eyes, she turned off the TV and went to make herself a cup of coffee. Returning to the living room, she set her mug on the table, next to the book he had sent, and retrieved the large box from behind the tree. She already knew what the robe she bought herself looked like.

The large box was filled with a number of smaller packages, each wrapped in matching paper, no tags. Picking one, she wished herself a Merry Christmas and began opening. It was a photograph of a red barn with a black roof, the way he had said barns should look. The next, a lighthouse, whitecaps crashing against the rocky shoreline at its base. The third, a fawn, hidden amongst the budding spring trees, the tower in the park visible in the background. And so on, nine pictures of The Door in all, all taken by Brian, each framed in handmade, weathered barn-board frames. They would add life to the barren walls of her condo, the perfect reminder of what she could not forget.

In the bottom of the box, under the last package, another of his Christmas cards. A winter scene of an old farmhouse, smoke rising from the chimney, candles burning in the windows, a solitary figure hauling a fresh-cut tree through the lightly falling snow, children waiting in the open doorway.

~

Christmas
Dear Colleen,

You said you could use a little something to bring life to your empty walls. I hope these pictures bring back happy thoughts of your time in The Door.

I'm not sending you our annual Christmas letter, filled with funny descriptions of our exploits over the past year. You know so many of them already that it would probably just be old news. Anyway, you might be surprised to find that you're not mentioned in the letter, a letter that's supposed to describe the highlights of the year. Either I couldn't find the proper way to work you into the letter or I didn't want to let anyone into our private world of letters. Maybe I just can't seem to figure out exactly how you fit into the picture.

Enjoy Christmas with your mother. I hope it's as special for you as Thanksgiving was. Hope to see you in the New Year.

Brian

~

December 26
Colleen,

Well, the three days of fun have come to a close, with everyone off to bed for the night. I find myself in the kitchen, huddled close to the old Franklin, where you warmed yourself that first night, one of my mother's special hot toddies between your hands.

Niall's birthday celebration marks the close of Christmas for a few days, until I take the girls down to Milwaukee to visit Christine's folks. We had a nice Christmas here, though once the excitement and festivities are over a certain melancholy sets in as we realize we will all soon be returning to our separate lives. It always feels good to have the whole family together, life back in the house, though it makes the house feel all the more empty when they leave.

We'll be back from Milwaukee early New Year's Eve, in time for the girls and me to ring in the New Year with Grandpa. We'll probably play Yahtzee and drink warm sparkling grape juice from paper cups as we try to stay awake till midnight, though I imagine by ten o'clock we'll all be yawning, ready for bed. What a difference a few years makes.

Christine and I used to have a big New Year's Eve bash every year. Everyone would bring their kids, the place awash in diaper bags. We'd wear silly hats and blow antique noisemakers, then shoot fireworks off at midnight. Twenty or thirty people would sleep over, and we'd have bacon and Bloody Marys for breakfast to start the New Year off right. The party New Year's Day was always more fun than the one New Year's Eve, our closest friends staying all day, the house so full of life, just like it's been the past few days with the whole family here.

The house rarely feels that way anymore. The last time I remember it feeling that way was this past June.

Brian

∼

December 31
Dear Brenden,

Oh, how I wish I could talk to you tonight.

Oh, how I wish you could hold me tight, hear my dreams and worries, tell me what I'm doing is right.

Oh, how I wish I could talk to you tonight.

Leeny

∾

December 31
Dear Brian,

I'm glad to hear you had a nice Christmas with all of your family. My mother and I had a really nice time together as well. She introduced me to some of her friends at the home — paraded me around, if the truth be told — but it was nice to see her so proud to show me off. We exchanged gifts after dinner, then watched The Bells of St. Mary's *together in her room.*

I'm sorry I haven't written since the holiday, but my mother said something to me on Christmas that has given me pause to think, and reflect. I asked her about all the time she spent staring out the window, and she said that if you stare at your reflection long enough you can look back into yourself and see what's inside you, what's important to you.

I'm sitting at home on New Year's Eve, by myself, by choice. I've seen my face in the window, and I know what I see when I look inside myself, and what's important to me. I see you, Brian, and Shannon, and Kerry, and Grandpa. And I see Christine, in you, in the girls — there with you always, watching over you, and watching me.

The card you sent with the Christmas presents said, "May all your dreams come true in the New Year." *I've been keeping quiet about my dreams, waiting for some sign from you before I express my feelings. I'm not sure if you were sending one in your last letter, but it's New Year's Eve, and I've made my resolution.*

I've fallen in love with you, Brian. I want to be with you, always, for the rest of our lives. I want to love those precious girls of yours like they were my own, fill in the missing love of a woman in their lives, and yours. I want to give you a son, someone you can play football with in the yard after a Packer game, while I hold the chili an extra half hour. And I want to be friends with Christine, and have you be at peace with her.

I love you, Brian. Please let me.

Love,
Colleen

∼

The piercing wind that rushed in through the holes in the cab of The Bucket felt refreshingly spirited as Brian drove lazily home on a late Saturday afternoon. The light fluffy snow that had just begun to fall slid its way up and over the windshield, no need for wipers. The setting sun reached up from below the horizon, casting eerie pink shadows on the gray sky above, the sparkling glow of the rising moon reflecting across the newly frosted fields of white below.

He had just dropped the excited girls off at a friend's house, a last sleepover to mark the end of the holidays, and was enjoying the peaceful quiet of the ride back. The three of them had spent a nice day at home together, packing up the Christmas gifts, the tree now barren underneath for the first time since being put up. The girls' backpacks and new clothes were neatly piled by the door, ready for the start of school and the return to real life. The holidays were over, no longer a point of anticipation, but of memory, and he felt the usual melancholy at the end of the season, like the day before the last day of a vacation.

It was the anniversary of Christine's death. Brian had never made a big production out of the day. It was not a day to be remembered, like her birthday or their anniversary, but a day to be gotten through. He was happy for the sleepover invitation the girls had received. It would help keep their minds off the day, and give him some time to himself. He was looking forward to the chance to be alone, to reflect on his time with Christine, on the holidays just ending, and the feelings just beginning.

The realization had been slow in coming since it first settled upon him, but it came nonetheless. He had first pushed it aside, then denied it, then tried to run from it. But he was finding it more difficult to hide any longer.

It had first come over him Christmas Eve, as he sat in the living room, the Santas and cookies on his lap, the girls close by him, his family standing in the doorway, staring down at him. They had all asked, his brother and sisters, the people he felt closest to, the ones who knew little of what went on inside of him, "Who is Colleen?" He didn't quite know how to answer, how to explain her, or their relationship. He tried to casually dismiss her at first; she was just someone who had had car trouble in the summer, they had exchanged a few letters, she had sent the girls some Christmas presents. But his siblings noticed his fumbling manner when he tried to pass her off inconsequentially, and the questions persisted, through dinner, through the gift-opening, through the long sleepless nights since. "Who is Colleen?"

At first Brian told himself she was just a friend, a needed friend. He had felt so alone since his mother had died, and then Christine, since he'd moved to The Door and isolated himself, with no one close to him, save Grandpa. He thought back to Christmas Eve, to his siblings' probing questions, to his own uncertain answers, and to the silent distance with which Grandpa had regarded both. As the long sleepless nights wore on, Brian knew he was lying to himself, and that Colleen was becoming, had become, more than just a friend.

Over the course of the fall he had found himself checking the mailbox, searching for the postmark. As October turned to November, and November to December, he found himself thinking back to June. As the holidays approached he had tried to picture how she would spend them, had tried to imagine setting a place for her at his table. He had been, he finally admitted to himself, thinking of Colleen quite often, and of Christine even more.

It had been three years now since she'd gone, though the pain was no less than it had been that first day. The time since she passed away had not widened the distance between them. He loved her still and felt she was with him, still a part of him. But something had been changing.

The feeling he'd had over the holidays, when the whole family was back together, had reminded him of how his parents' house had felt when he was a child, of how his old house had felt when he and Christine and the girls were together, of how his current house had felt for a few days last June.

The realization of what had been taking place inside frightened him, made him restless. He hadn't sorted it all out yet, but he felt serenely at ease as he drove toward home, neither fearful of offending Christine nor anxious over his feelings for Colleen. He was content in that moment, having them both isolated from each other, and safely distanced from him, though at times both felt so near, so much a part of him.

～

Dashing from the frigid cold of The Bucket, Brian leapt up the steps of the porch and into the warmth of the house, hanging his coat on a hook in the back hallway as he made his way into the kitchen. Dumping the mail on the chopping block, he added a few logs to the Franklin, put the coffee water on to boil, and pulled a chair up close to the fire. The snow began to turn wet and heavy, drifting against the side of the house, crawling up underneath the windows. Brian loved hard winter nights like these, the feeling of security, safely removed from the storm outside, able to reflect on the storm within.

The kettle began to whistle. He made his coffee, planning to sit in the dark of the alcove under the stairs, alone with his thoughts. Delaying the soul-searching, he grabbed the mail off the chopping block and made his way into the office, dumping the mail on the desk as he sat. Glancing at the letters fanning out before him, his eyes came to rest on the one with the familiar handwriting on the envelope.

Panic overcame him as he read the letter, first once, then twice, then three times. *"I know what I see when I look inside myself, and what's important to me. I see you, Brian, and Shannon, and Kerry, and Grandpa. And I see Christine..." "I want to be with you, always, for the rest of our lives." "I want to love those precious girls like they were my own, fill in the missing love of a woman in their lives, and yours." "I want to be friends with Christine, and have you be at peace with her." "I want to give you a son, someone you can play football with in the yard after a Packer game, while I hold the chili an extra half hour."*

He reread the last words Colleen had written, nearly the exact words Christine had once spoken. He crumpled the letter, swinging his chair around as he turned and threw the paper at the wall filled with pictures. Rising, he made his way to the tiny desk in the alcove under the stairs. Before him sat the keyboard; to its side, pen and paper.

≈

January 5
My Dear Christine,

If one glass slipper falls, the other is surely to shatter.

I almost let myself believe there might be another like you, for me, when in truth there will only be you, can only be you. My heart, now yours, is no longer mine to give.

Today, three years since you left me, I am yours, still, and will be, always.

All My Love,
Brian

∾

January 5
Dear Colleen,

Oh, if I could return the sentiments of your letter, I would, for I feel I so want to. But I can't. For you see, I still wear a wedding ring, and always shall. I'm so terribly sorry. Forgive me.

Love,
Brian

∾

Brian sealed the envelope, put on his coat and boots, coaxed The Bucket to start, then drove through the mounting snow, to the post office. He dropped the letter in the mailbox, forcefully closing the lid shut.

Finding himself at the liquor store, he bought the largest bottle of brandy they had, then drove on through the blizzard, barely able to see where he was going, or know if he was on the right path. He turned in to Grandpa's, to the cottage he himself owned but had rarely been in since Christine passed away. Getting stuck in a snowdrift at the end of the drive, he walked the rest of the way, dragging himself through the deep snow, then up the long stairway to the second-floor entrance above the boathouse. Letting himself in, he slammed the bottle of brandy down on the table as he looked across the room at his startled father.

"Let's get drunk!"

Chapter 12

~

Grandpa sat, with his coffee and hangover, paying little attention to the game of solitaire he wasn't really playing, the night before still too much on his mind. He knew, in retrospect, that he and his son had shared one of those special times when two people talk openly, and listen thoughtfully — one of those rare scenes that occur mostly in the movies, too infrequently in real life. He knew, as well, how troubled and confused his son was, and wished he knew what he could do to help him.

Stacking up the cards, he poured himself another cup of coffee, and took two more aspirin. Peering out the window, at the frosted cedars and peaceful snowdrifts that blanketed the yard below, he marveled at the serene beauty that was born out of the raging violence of the night before. Across the driveway the little summer cottage sat buried in the loneliness of winter. He thought of Maggie, and the time they were supposed to spend there during retirement.

She would help him.

Putting away the half-empty bottle of brandy, he retrieved the tattered shoebox holding Maggie's old love letters from under the bed, then made his way into the living room, adding another log to the fire. He settled into the armchair by the fireplace, carefully removing the worn string from around the box before randomly choosing a letter.

~

Dear Sean,

I know you're upset with Brian after he dropped the bomb that he was dropping out of college, giving us little explanation or time to digest the news before he ran over to Christine's.

Don't be too harsh in your judgment of him tonight. Imagine for a moment how hard it must have been for him to tell us, when he knew how much the news might upset us.

Eighteen is a tough age. So are all the other ages with numbers in them. Like forty-two. You may have a better perspective on his age than he does, though you might not have the full perspective on your own age.

New love is a rare jewel. Think back to those first few days we met, and recall how nothing else mattered. Then remember how difficult it was to be apart, when all we wanted was to be together.

Let's try to keep in mind how we both felt when we were in his situation. (If I recall correctly, college diplomas and retirement funding were not the first things on your mind at the time!) I think we should be patient and give him his space, for if we try to pull him in too close we risk pushing him away.

There is a time for talking, and a time for listening. There is a time for teaching, and a time for letting one learn. There is a time for holding on, and a time for letting go.

This is a time to let him find his own way. There will come a time when he will need you to help show him the way.

My Love,
Maggie

～

Driving home from work, Colleen thought about the changes she witnessed taking place around her. The holiday decorations had already come down at the office, and discarded Christmas trees were beginning to line the road, children's dreams packed away in the attic for another year. The season was coming to an end, though the usual sadness at its passing did not come over her as it had in previous years. She was not looking backward, but forward.

She was looking forward to cleaning up the Christmas decorations, the memories of the past year, and was planning to hang the pictures of The Door, the hope of the year ahead. And hope she had.

She had been picking up subtle statements in Brian's recent letters, words that led her to believe her dreams might simply be a matter of when, not if. *The piano spoke to him. He was thinking about where she fit into the picture. The house seemed alive again, in June.*

The letter she had written on New Year's Eve brought the calm she had sought. She had read the signs, cautiously, but felt confident she had read them correctly. She was anxious, yes – not about what the response might be – but only for it to come. Maybe tonight, she thought as she arrived home and grabbed the mail.

～

January 5
Dear Colleen,

Oh, if I could return the sentiments of your letter, I would, for I feel I so want to. But I can't. For you see, I still wear a wedding ring, and always shall. I'm so terribly sorry. Forgive me.

Love,
Brian

~

Colleen stared across the room, at the spot where she had planned to hang the pictures of The Door. She did not cry, or shake, or feel ill. She felt nothing. Nothing at all. When she finally thought, it was of the solitary leaf that had floated to the ground in Maggie's poem.

She read Brian's short note once more, though she already had it memorized. Unchecked tears flowed down her cheeks. She cried for herself, for her loss of him, and she cried for the losses of others.

She cried for the girls, for the loss of their mother, and her loss of them. She cried for Grandpa, for his loss of Maggie, and his lost son. She cried for Christine, for the love she had lost, and the love he kept. And she cried for Brian. Not just for his loss of her, but for his loss of hope, for the loss of the love he had known, and the loss of the love he might never know.

He had said good-bye, and she would leave him to himself. But she loved him still, now more than ever. For if anything, his letters had told her how deeply he could feel love, if only he could feel it again.

~

January 6
Dear Colleen,

I hope you don't mind my taking the liberty of intruding in your personal life by writing you this letter, but I feel the time is at hand when a son needs the help of his father.

Brian came over last night — not the sure, confident Brian we all know from the public persona he displays, but the troubled, unsure Brian of more recent memory, the searching child that surfaces from within now and then. We got drunk together, talking late into the night, remembering and laughing, dreaming and crying. Emotions are stirring deep within him — feelings of heartbreak and loss, of denial and guilt, of fear, and of hope. He's lost, between what he had and wishes he hadn't lost, and what he's afraid could be.

He told me about the letter you sent, the letter that brought everything to the surface, the letter that scared him so, the letter he said he could never read again, the letter he answered with finality, closing you off behind him.

Save that letter, Colleen. File it away in your box of memories, but don't dwell on it too long. I have a feeling that one day, in the distant future, the girls will find that letter, safely tucked away in a box in the attic of the old farmhouse up on the hill, next to a box of Christine's.

I'm guessing that Brian's letters over the past few months have said little, if anything, about Christine, determined as he is to hold on to her and keep her for himself. I think maybe it's time for you to meet her, to know about her, and what they had together.

Everyone loved Christine, and I think the world knew she touched a special place in my heart, for what she gave to Brian reminded me so of what I got from my own Maggie. Christine was soft and warm, caring and understanding, gentle and peaceful, mild and humble. She was also strong and determined, subtle yet forceful, serious but playful. She gave Brian everything he ever knew he wanted, and all he was unaware he needed. He was whole when they were together, lost now that they're apart.

Brian was right when he knew, the instant they met, that she was the one, just as I knew with Maggie. It was that feeling one gets when something just seems so right. I recall I had that feeling again last June, when you walked into Brian's life. He's fighting the realization that he may be having that feeling again, scared that by finding you, he may lose Christine.

Hold on to your feelings, Colleen, until Brian can come to terms with his own. The waiting won't be easy, but if it's meant to be, as I think it is, it will happen. Don't give up hope. Brian's carrying a lot of baggage with him, still, and it weighs on him heavily, but the load will lighten someday for him, as it has for me, and he'll be able to move on, I hope. If he does, and you're still there waiting for him, I promise you the wait will have been worth it.

In the meantime, I think it's only fair for you to know what you're up against, and to be aware of why your letter hit him so hard.

Your letter, stating your feelings for Brian, arrived yesterday, on the anniversary of Christine's death, on a day when he likes to spend some time alone with the girls, then alone with himself and his memories of Christine.

Your letter would probably have been a jolt to him no matter when it arrived, for he still hasn't learned how to hold on while letting go. But of all the days of the year to be forced to think of another, none could have been worse. And it wasn't only the day your letter came, or that it came at all, but something it said that reminded him too closely of the loss of Christine. I know for you it was an expression of the love you hope you've found, but for Brian it was a painful reminder of the love he's lost.

You said that you wanted to give him a son, someone he could play football with in the yard after a Packer game. You couldn't have known when you wrote those words that Christine died carrying the son she thought Brian wished for.

Christine had always had troubled pregnancies, three ending in pain and disaster, two in the beautiful girls they both loved so much, the girls who were always enough for Brian. But Christine had mistakenly thought that deep down inside Brian wanted a son – someone to carry on the family name, someone to play football with in the yard after a Packer game – and she wanted to try to give that to him, against his fears for her own safety. She was glowing as she carried the son that was not meant to be, filled with joy that she would give Brian the one gift she thought he wanted. Then the troubles with the pregnancy began, and she was forced to stay home on bed-rest. He came home from work one afternoon to find her, lying on the bathroom floor in a pool of her own blood.

Gone was the love of his life, gone were the hopes and dreams that sustained him, gone were the visions of growing old together, of grandchildren sleeping over, of quiet walks in the woods, of peaceful nights sitting together by the fire.

He's tried hard at times to move past that day, though he's never quite made it, drifting back as he does to a time when his world was right. The girls keep him going, bittersweet reminders of what he cannot forget, their faces so similar to hers. Without them I fear he'd prefer nothing else than to join Christine tomorrow.

Yet I saw that spark of life within him again, faintly, when you were here in The Door. I see it as well when the girls tell me about a letter from you, and his face calms momentarily. I think he's slowly admitting to himself the feelings he has, though the happiness he could find brings with it a new round of emotions. He's so scared of losing Christine, of being unfaithful to her memory, of letting another replace her.

Too many things about you remind him of Christine — things you could never know, things he could never forget. From your long flowing hair, to the memory of a sundress; from the way you are with the girls, to your wish to give him a son; from the bond you two seem to have formed in your letters, to the way you've become friends before lovers — just like him and Christine, just like Maggie and me.

Even the pledge you gave in your letter, to love him for the rest of your life, does not assure him that it will be for the rest of his life as well. For even if he could someday come to grips with the loss of Christine, I worry if the fear of another loss might prevent him from taking a second chance.

In the end you can only hold on to your love, as he has to his, and hope that it will one day be returned. I hope for both of you that it will be, and I feel that Christine would want it for him. There's a place for both you and Christine, if he can find a way to let you reside side by side. Be patient. You will have to wait and let it come from within him, when the time is right.

While you wait, I've enclosed two undated letters I found that should help you understand what Brian is going through. The first is one he wrote to me about six months after my Maggie passed away; the second, his own response to the first, after I'd sent it back to him, six months or so after Christine died. They should give you an idea of what's troubling him, and why you will need to wait.

In closing, I'd like to relate a dream I had last night. I'm not much of a dreamer, and know not if this one came from within, or out of a bottle of brandy, but it's your dream as much as mine, and it can be Brian's dream too, if only he'll let it be.

In my dream I was walking you down the aisle of the old stone church here in town — you dressed in white, Brian waiting at the altar, the girls by his side. As I gave you away I looked up toward the choir loft, where I found Maggie and Christine looking down on us, smiling.

I hope that my little boy may one day be as happy again as Maggie and Christine looked in my dream, and I feel that you are the one who could bring him that happiness, if only he'll let you.

Fondly,
Grandpa

~

Dear Dad,

It's been six months now that Mom's been gone and I still can't believe it all happened, can't believe that I won't see her walking through the door any day now, to be here with us, where she belongs. I feel lost and alone in the world, even as I'm comforted by Christine and the girls. I can't begin to imagine what life must feel like for you without Mom there by your side.

I fear I've not been the son you've needed of late, able to talk with you about the emotions you feel, or listen when you need an ear. I've always wanted to be someone who could discuss my feelings openly, but I find that what I feel I feel alone, and can express only from the safe distance of a letter. I'm sorry I haven't been there for you when you've needed me. Like too many things in life,

I suppose the moment has passed me by, and I've only felt the feelings, and done nothing about them. It's humbling to find out you're not the person you thought you were, or wanted to be.

I wonder, is six months enough time to put the grieving that will never end behind you, and look forward again? You said once, in your fear of the future shortly after Mom passed away, that you couldn't imagine being alone for the rest of your life, just as you couldn't imagine ever being with anyone but her. Can we step back from the picture for a moment, remove ourselves from it, and try to look at things from a different perspective?

No one can ever replace Mom or take away what the two of you had together, what we all had. Her memory is too dear to us. She will never leave us, but will remain a part of our lives, always. She's watching over us now, I know, and as the cliché goes, she'd want us to get on with our lives, to move forward, to be happy again. Mom's secure with the memory we have of the love we all shared, and the special love between the two of you. Having that a second time, with another, does not tarnish the shine of the first.

There is a difference between being alone and being lonely. The first you control, the second controls you. No one should have to be lonely, or choose to be so — alone with only their memories of the past, and no one to share their dreams for the future with.

Contrary to the popular saying, time will not *heal the wound of Mom's loss, nor lessen the blow. The key to overcoming her loss is to move forward while looking backward, one eye on the road ahead, one eye on the rearview mirror. If you only live off old memories, and don't create new ones, Mom's loss will overcome you.*

I know it's far too soon after Mom's passing even to think about another. But in a few years you may find that you're at peace with Mom, and that another has entered your life, and filled the loneliness. If that should happen, let it, for Mom would want that for you. Mom would not want you to be lonely, alone with only your memories of her.

If something is meant to be, it will happen, not because you went looking for it, but because it is right.

Brian

~

Dear Dad,

Dirty move, throwing my own words back at me. They seemed so true when I wrote them to you after Mom passed away, so hollow now that Christine is gone.

Life's not as simple or straightforward as it seemed just six months or a year ago, when we both had our special friends, and the youthful feeling that our love would last forever. Will the memories last, or will they fade over time, until we can no longer recall them?

I know I tried to tell you that you would find peace in the memories, that you might one day find love again, and that if you did Mom would be happy for you. The words ring so hollow now that Christine's gone, and I'm embarrassed I tried to give you advice on something I knew nothing about back then, advice I now know I can't follow.

For how can one love again, give a second time what one has already given away in full to another, give what is no longer there to give?

And what if it is still a part of me, not already given away? Could I then place it with another? I think not, for I'd never be certain if Christine would approve, if she'd be happy for me as she watches over me, or if she'd feel betrayed. We never talked about whether we'd want the other to remarry if something should happen to one of us. We tried to once or twice, but we couldn't. It was something neither of us ever wanted to consider, something we didn't even want to think about, something we couldn't bring ourselves to talk about.

And what if Christine did approve, and wanted me to be happy again, to find love with another, as I'd found it with her? Who would be there to greet me in the hereafter, Christine, the first Mrs. Bailey, or the new, second Mrs. Bailey? Or would they both be there? Would they be friends, happily sharing my love between them?

There's a single empty plot next to Christine's grave, waiting for me to one day take my rightful place next to her. Would I still use it, and leave the second Mrs. Bailey to be buried alone? Would I lie next to the second Mrs. Bailey, leaving Christine forgotten? Or would I find a new location, and move Christine, placing myself between the two Mrs. Baileys?

And what of the girls? Do I give them the friendship of a new mother at the risk of losing the memory of their own? Or do I keep Christine alive in their hearts, denying them the love another could offer? It's not like when Mom died, all of her children adults, with a full set of memories to keep her alive within us. The girls were so young when Christine left them. They'll barely remember her to begin with, and lose her for certain if another should take her place.

More questions than answers. We had it all once, both of us, and we have it still. What we had did not die along with Mom and Christine. It lives on, still, within us.

I'm left with my memories. You're left with yours. We're left with each other, and need each other now more than ever. I love you, Dad.

Brian

∽

January 11
Dear Brenden,

I will be going back to The Door, again and again and again, in my mind.

Oh, how I long to return to The Door.

I long to know how you endured the distance of winter, separated from The Door. I long to see the blossoms on the cherry trees once more.

I long to go Booger Ball Bowling in the humid August heat. I long to glide across the frozen lake, ice skates on my feet.

I long to hear your grand piano play for me once more. I long to finish the cottage book, a novel of The Door.

I long to climb the fire tower with one who will not go. I long to walk the old golf course when it's layered deep in snow.

He longs for life to be the way it was before. I long to create new memories, that now may be no more.

I long for him, as he longs for her. I long for the married widower.

I long to know if there's spring beneath snow.

Leeny

Chapter 13

～

*T*he bitter arctic winds blew up the drive, through the tunnel of trees that lined the way, picking up the downy flakes that had become light and brittle in the freeze-dried temperatures. Cold gray clouds blanketed overhead, back-lit by the ever-present moon, night closely following day, offering little to distinguish the two. Soon the light, powdery snows of January would give way to the heavy, wet snows of February, when snowmen would guard front lawns, snowballs flying overhead.

Brian sat on his stoop on the porch, watching the snowflakes as they were carried by the wind. Some were carried high, rising up over the barn, into the night sky. Some were carried just over the crest of the hill, falling on the regal throne of a newly forming drift, others around them. Some just lay flat against the gravel, unable to be carried forward.

Returning inside, Brian walked through the darkened hallway, glancing at the timeless clock on the wall, its wooden gears meshing with unfailing perseverance. Three o'clock. In the morning. His favorite hour of the day, and the one hour he could count on being awake for with some regularity. He had long been a night owl, finding it hard to relax, to turn off his mind, or let it give him any peace. Sleep had come even harder since his mother passed away, and then Christine, harder still of late, as the questions before him persisted.

Three o'clock became four, four became five. Winter became spring, spring became summer. Children became adults, adults became aged. Life became death, death became...

Brian rounded the curve of the back stairs and quietly tip-toed down the hall to the girls' room. Their two tiny faces lay softly on the pillows, caught by the dim glow of a night-light. He thought back to happier times at the old house, when the four of them would lie in bed together and read books, the girls begging to stay with Christine as he went back down-stairs to work in the office. When he finally came back upstairs he would sit on the edge of the bed, looking at the three of them, watching them for a while as they slept together in peace. Carrying the girls off to their own beds, he would climb into his, beside Christine. He'd never had any trouble falling asleep on those nights.

He remembered, as well, a night last June, three faces in a row, the middle face different from the memory, the scene hauntingly familiar. He had not slept well that night, or since.

As he peered in on the girls it occurred to Brian that since Christine had passed away he hadn't been the father he'd always thought he would be, always hoped he would be. Lost in remembrance, he'd forgotten that it's the little things that seem so big to a child. Yes, he'd made the effort, now and then, to give the girls a special day, or mark the holidays with the childhood memories they would one day try to create for their own children. Yet life is not about those few cherished days, he thought to himself, but all the days between. It isn't the special events that are important, but the special feeling between events that matters, the sense of belonging, the feeling of being loved, every moment of the day, every day.

Brian wondered what the girls remembered of Christine, what they would carry with them. So many of his memories of the love they all shared as a family were of times when the girls were infants and toddlers, times they would not, could not, remember. *How often do they think of her?* he wondered. *How much do they miss her? How will they learn to become good mothers, with no one to teach them? And how will they feel if another is allowed to take her place?*

Leaving the girls, Brian climbed into his empty bed, pulling the covers tightly around him as the moon surrendered to the sun. Another new day to be gotten through was on its way, and he needed a few hours peace, away from himself, before the girls rose for school, with no one to help coordinate their outfits, or fix their hair.

∼

Colleen had buried herself at the office the past month, arriving early, staying late, purposely keeping her mind occupied, with little time for dreaming of what might have been. If she kept herself busy, one day would turn into the next, a few days into a week, a few weeks into a month, a few months into a season, until there would come a day when she would wake to find that enough time had passed.

It was already February, a month since she'd gotten his last letter. She had somehow managed far better than she thought she might, though the passage of time had done little to fill the emptiness. But she no longer checked her mailbox each night, no longer thought of taking the next plane to The Door, no longer expected him to call, saying he was sorry, and that he loved her.

It would have to come from him, and she knew that now, as surely as Grandpa had told her in his letter. He needed time, and she would give him all he needed. For she realized with each passing day, as she missed him more, that she loved him more.

∼

February 10
Dear Brenden,

I was cleaning out a closet tonight, creating a make-work project to keep my hands busy, and my mind occupied, and I came across an old shoe box filled with cards you gave me over the years.

I wonder if you ever knew that I saved all of them, or how much each one of those cards meant to me.

Left on my dresser or tucked under my pillow, stuffed in my backpack or slipped into my laundry basket, I could always count on a card from you, whenever I needed it most.

A few little words was all it would take to lift my spirits, or brighten my day. Just a simple little note from you let me know that you were there for me, and that you cared.

You always sent me a card.

I think I'll send a card.

Leeny

~

Grandpa kicked the snow off his boots and placed them on the mat in the back hall. Entering the kitchen, he crossed the room and stood in front of the old Franklin, warming his hands. Brian was drying the breakfast dishes, placing them in their appointed spots in the old pie safe next to the sink.

"Was it supposed to snow today?" Grandpa asked.

"It's winter, Dad."

"So, what are we going to do with ourselves?" Grandpa wondered. "First Sunday without football in months."

"The girls want to play Monopoly. You game?"

"Sure. Sounds fun. Where are the little devils?"

"Upstairs, in their room, working on some secret project. I'm supposed to knock before I enter," Brian laughed as they heard the sound of footsteps running across the hardwood floors overhead, then down the back steps.

"Are you ready yet, Dad?" they called ahead as they rounded the last curve of the stairs.

"Almost," he shouted over his shoulder. "Grandpa's here."

"Grandpa! Grandpa!" they exclaimed as they entered the kitchen, Kerry hopping up into his waiting arms.

"So, I hear you're both planning to lose to me at Monopoly," Grandpa teased, kissing each of them on the cheek. "What pieces are you planning to lose with?"

"I'm the thimble," said Shannon. "And the banker."

"I'm the race car," Kerry added. "And the property passer-outer."

"I think I'll be the flat iron," said Grandpa. "Now, what's this I hear about a super-secret project you've been working on? Your dad tells me he's not even allowed in your room."

"We're making Valentine's Day cards," Shannon informed him.

"Red hearts, out of construction paper," Kerry added.

"Kerry!" Shannon reprimanded. "You'll spoil the surprise."

"Well of course they're red hearts," Grandpa cut in before the argument could take place. "What else would they be, orange pumpkins? Are any of them for me?"

"Uh-huh," Shannon answered, "and Dad and Niall and Ciaran and Aileen, and our teachers."

"And Colleen, too," Kerry added.

Brian turned at the sound of her name.

Grandpa noticed the look on Brian's face and sent the girls off to get the Monopoly game. "It's nice of them to think of her, Brian," Grandpa said after the girls had gone. "They talk about her all the time when they're over at my place, especially

Kerry. How's Colleen doing?" he asked. "Have you heard from her lately?"

Wiping his hands on the dish-towel that hung over his shoulder, Brian turned his back to his father and stared out over the sink, at the driving wet snow that clung to the window.

"Brian?"

"I haven't written since that day we got drunk."

"And her?"

Brian shook his head.

"And how do you think it will look to Colleen," Grandpa asked, "if the girls send cards, and you send nothing?" Grandpa paused for a moment, remembering. "A single rose might be nice," he suggested. "Your mother liked yellow."

Brian turned to face Grandpa. "Christine preferred red."

Colleen fumbled through her desk in search of a dollar or two to tip the delivery boy who stood before her, a long, thin box in his hand. She had seen him in the office earlier, delivering large bouquets of roses to some of the other women on her floor, though she'd never expected him to stop at her desk. Locating a few crumpled bills in her drawer, she handed them over as she took the box, looking for a card.

"No card?" she asked.

"No, ma'am, order says no card."

"And does it say where it's from?"

"Let me see," he said, checking his slip. "Here it is. Door Floral, wherever that is."

"Thank you," she smiled as the delivery boy turned and walked off. She carefully undid the tape and opened the package. Inside lay a single white rose.

Brian trudged up the steep drive, the lightly falling snow landing in his open boots as he flipped through the stack of red envelopes. Two cards for the girls, from Grandpa. Two more from California, Niall and Claudia. Two from Chicago, Ciaran and Patrick. Two from North Carolina, Aileen and Ryan. Still more cards, for the girls, from Christine's folks, and the cousins in Milwaukee. Brian continued flipping through the sea of red until he found the single white envelope with the Arizona postmark.

Entering the house, he set the mail on the chopping block and retreated to his little alcove under the stairs, jacket still on, wet boots dripping, a single envelope in his hand. He held the envelope for a long time before opening it. The outside of the card was white, a single red heart in the middle. The inside was blank, except for the handwriting that had become so familiar. *"Colleen"* was all it said.

Colleen stumbled home from the office late that evening, nearly falling into the bushes as she tried to insert her key into the lock on the front door. Having gone out for margaritas with some of the other single women at work, she'd had a few too many as she sought answers to the questions her friends asked about the single white rose.

White, the color of the cherry blossoms that brought them together. White, the color of the snow that separated them. White, the color of his shirt she wore to bed nearly every night.

Flipping through the mail as she staggered through the doorway, she found two plain white envelopes, children's handwriting greeting her below the Door County postmark.

Opening the first, she unfolded a cut-out shape of a heart, the thick red construction paper sticking together from the white glitter glue that rimmed the border. *"Be My Valentine,"* it said on the outside, *"Shannon"* on the inside.

She opened the second envelope, from Kerry. The edges of the heart were not cut quite as cleanly as the first card, the glitter glue not quite as elaborate. No greeting adorned the outside, only a simple crayon drawing of two small hearts. *"Colleen, Happy Valentine's Day, Love, Kerry"* it said on the inside, above the note that asked, *"Why don't you write to my Dad anymore? I think he misses your letters."*

"I miss his too," Colleen slurred as she fell asleep on the couch, the crushed rose held tight against her chest.

∼

February 26
My Dear Christine,

Who have I been? Who am I now? Who will I be?

I have been a happy little boy, an uncertain teenager, a blissful newlywed, and a proud new parent. I am a lonely widower, a single parent, a reflective loner, a detached observer. Will I be a lonesome dreamer, a solitary lover, a nostalgic historian, or a memory creator?

Who have I been? Who am I now? Who will I be?

I can predict tomorrow about as easily as I can bring back yesterday.

My Love Always,
Brian

∼

February 27
Colleen,

Thank you for your recent card. It was an unexpected, though pleasant, surprise.

I know I didn't handle things very gracefully after Christmas, and I've felt bad about it since. I still haven't sorted everything out yet, and don't know when or if I will. All I know for certain is that at the very least I owe you an apology. Please know that I am sorry.

My reason for writing now is that I find myself in a bit of a "situation" and need to ask a favor of you, if I still may. I understand I might have lost the right to do so, and wouldn't blame you if you were less than thrilled by my asking, but as you'll see I'm kind of backed into a corner here, and I need some guidance.

I belong to a group of general miscreants whose annual meeting I've been attending for years. We always used it as an excuse to get away from reality for a few days, sneak away from the end of winter and relax together in a warm climate. After Christine passed away I continued the tradition with the girls, having found a few days in a foreign setting can give perspective to a few months at home.

My "situation" is that this year's meeting is in Phoenix. Colleen, the girls are all over me, especially Kerry, about how much and when we might see you, and I honestly don't know what to tell them, or you. Can you give me some guidance?

I don't want to be a schmuck and hide behind the girls on this. I'm all too aware there are other issues involved here besides just the girls, such as how you may feel about seeing us, me, again, after the way I shut you off. My own feeling is that it might be nice, and perhaps time, to see you again. Maybe it will give us the chance to talk, though I'm still not sure exactly what I'll have to say.

I'll leave things up to you, Colleen. While I don't know how you feel about this, I do understand the position my asking puts you in. Please know that I won't blame you if you decide you don't want to see me again, and that I'll be the fall guy in whatever I tell the girls. I just need to know what to tell them.

In closing, know that it was hard for me to write this letter, and that I did not take it lightly. I'm still trying to sort things out, Colleen. The only thing I know for certain is that I've missed your letters. Is it still possible to go back to the short pass while I try to sort things out?

Brian

~

March 4
Brian,

You aren't the only one who has some things to sort out.

I have to be honest with you, Brian. I was completely crushed by your short note of good-bye after Christmas. The only time I can recall feeling that hurt was when I had the lead in my high school play, and Brenden never came.

I was hurt as much by the answer your letter gave as by the questions it left. Was it me? Was it what I said? Was it how or when I said it? Was it the girls? Was it Christine? Was it you?

It has taken me a long time to come to terms with that short note, Brian, and I was getting closer to moving past it when your recent letter came. If it was hard for you to write that letter, it was harder still for me to read it. I've run the full spectrum of emotions the past few days, just as I had over the past few months, and haven't enjoyed the experience.

I've always believed in playing my cards face-up on the table, though I've recently learned at times it can be more prudent to hold them a bit tighter to the vest. While in hindsight I may have been guilty of tipping my hand too soon, it is still the hand I was dealt. While a lot of things have changed over the past few months, others remain unchanged. The idealization may have suffered, but the reality is still the same.

As for your trip, I'm sympathetic to your "situation" with the girls, for their sake. I've got plenty of vacation time saved up at work and can likely be free whenever you want. But if I'm going to see you again it has to be about more than the girls. As you said, you can't hide behind them.

Yes, I'd very much like to see you again, but if I'm just setting myself up for another fall, I could do without it.

When I returned from The Door last summer I wrote in my journal to Brenden that I'd met a really nice guy I'd probably never see again. I dreamt, all fall, of seeing you again, Brian, worried, all winter, that I might not. Now, as spring approaches, and I know that I might, I can't begin to envision it.

What do you see?

While the short pass might be nice, I wonder about the game plan. You've got the ball, Brian.

Colleen

∽

March 8
Colleen,

Once again, I'm sorry for what has been. The problem is, I don't yet know what may be.

I understand I've got the ball, though sometimes it's easier to play defense and react than to play offense and plan strategy. I still haven't got the game plan figured out yet, but it was clear from your letter that a team meeting might be in order while I'm in town.

We'll be coming down next Wednesday, a fairly quick trip through the weekend, heading back home Sunday afternoon. I've got morning meetings on Thursday and Friday and would like to spend some time alone with the girls, though they seem more interested in when we will see you. (Kerry already asked if you'll be picking us up at the airport, holding a chauffer sign with our name on it!)

I was thinking maybe we should get together a couple of times while we're in town. The girls will be all over me if they only see you once, and if we limit ourselves to a single encounter, expectations may be disappointed. Maybe we could get together for dinner once we're settled in, say Thursday night, then spend some time together on Saturday.

Since I've never been to Phoenix I'll let you play tour guide, if you don't mind, and leave the specifics to you. Southwest food would be nice for dinner, but Saturday is yours to plan. If it helps, I'll let you know that Shannon likes to shop and Kerry likes anything to do with nature. Of course, you should also know that Kerry hates to shop, and Shannon doesn't really like much to do with nature. We'll call you when we get into town to confirm plans.

Thanks, Colleen, for your understanding about the girls. I want you to know that I understood your letter all too clearly, and apologize again for the trouble I've caused you. I hope you can understand that I still don't have all the answers, but I'm searching for them.

Brian

∽

March 12
Dear Brenden,

I need you tonight.

I need you to hold me, tell me everything will be all right, like you did when Dad left us on that long ago night.

I'll see him tomorrow, but will he see me? I'll have him for the next four days, but what about the next forty years? I'll create more memories to recall, but can I compete with an idealized memory?

I need you to hold me, tell me everything will be all right, like you did when Dad left us on that long ago night.

I need you tonight.

Leeny

Chapter 14

≈

Brian breathed a sigh of relief as the wheels of the plane safely touched down. Although the flight had been the least of his concerns about the trip, he was still a nervous flyer, and never fully relaxed until after landing. It wasn't so much that he minded the plane going down, as long as they were all together. He had always hated the flights he and Christine had taken without the girls, fearful of leaving them alone should something happen. Better we all go together, he had selfishly thought, than to leave someone alone.

As they taxied toward the gate, he turned his attention toward his other concerns. He knew from her letter that Colleen was hoping their time together might provide her some answers, though he still had only questions. Some might be answered over the next few days, though others would likely arise. She deserved some direction, he knew, though he was looking for some of the same.

Collecting their carry-ons as the plane came to a final stop, Brian and the girls once again thanked the pilot for the tour of the cockpit, and the souvenir wings, then headed up the ramp. Entering the congested terminal, they moved through the crowd of people waiting to greet other passengers, then paused to search for directions to the baggage claim. Had it not been for the girls' habit of reading chauffeur signs, hoping just once to find their name, Brian might have walked right past her.

∼

Colleen stood near the back of the crowd, holding her sign, worrying suddenly if she was making a huge mistake. She'd been too forward with her New Year's Eve letter, she'd learned, forced his hand too soon, and wondered now if she was doing the same. He'd suggested Thursday night as a first get-together, a safe dinner out with the girls, she thought. Would finding her here at the airport catch him off guard?

She knew, as Grandpa had said in his letter, that she had to give Brian his time, and let things come from within. But she also knew how crucial the next few days could be in helping him along. Meeting them at the airport had seemed like such a good idea last night, a chance to take the edge off dinner tomorrow, though as she waited for them to come off the plane Colleen felt more anxious and uncertain than if she'd have waited for Thursday night.

They came up the ramp toward her, filtering their way through the crowd, then paused. Colleen watched them for a moment, surprised by how much the girls had changed, comforted by how little Brian had.

∼

"It says Bailey!" Kerry shouted excitedly when she saw their name on the sign. "See," she said to Shannon, "I told you Colleen would be at the airport."

Brian turned at the sound of her name. Seeing her, he wondered if he would have recognized her, wondered if he'd have walked right past her had she not been holding the sign.

She wore heels and a business suit, had cut her hair short, and looked like a hundred other women at the airport.

"Dad! Dad! It's Colleen!" Kerry called out, running to greet her.

"So I see," Brian laughed, picking up Kerry's discarded backpack as he joined them. "Colleen," he greeted her with a smile, "what a nice surprise."

"I was hoping it would be," she worried aloud.

"It is," he assured her. "A great surprise. Though I might not have recognized you without the sign," he commented, her appearance so different from the vision he carried with him.

"That's why I brought it," she said as she handed the sign to Kerry.

"I didn't think you were supposed to meet us at the airport," Shannon stated as they collected their things and began to weave their way through the terminal. "How did you know what plane we'd be on?"

"Only one flight a day from Green Bay," Colleen explained as she took Kerry by the hand and led the way.

"Dad said we weren't gonna see you till tomorrow," Kerry told her, asking, "Can you spend the rest of today with us too?"

"Sorry, no," Colleen answered. "I'm afraid I've got to get back to work for a meeting later this afternoon. Just time to come meet your plane and help you find your hotel. But I've got a fun spot picked out for dinner tomorrow night, and I'll see you again then."

Waiting for their luggage, the girls excitedly racing around the conveyer, Brian found himself alone with Colleen. In that moment of uncertainty he remembered how nervous he'd felt in high school, standing on some girl's front porch before a dance, waiting for her parents to answer the door. He'd never felt that with Christine.

"I hope you don't mind my just showing up like this," Colleen said.

"Not at all," he replied, his voice slightly hoarse, mouth dry.

"I just, well, I couldn't wait to see you again," Colleen offered. "All of you."

"It's fine," he reassured her, "don't worry about it." Brian paused, looking at her. "At least now," he continued, "I don't have to wonder what it will be like to see you again."

"Man, Dad, this one's really a lunker!" Kerry called out as she struggled to drag a large suitcase toward Brian and Colleen. Shannon sat on a cart next to the conveyor, watching the two of them as she waited for her suitcase.

∼

The girls rode to the hotel in Colleen's car, Brian following alone in the rental. Kerry noisily chattered in the front while Shannon sat quietly in the back, peering out the window at the desert plants and mountain landscapes, so different from what she was used to back home.

"It's really cool you don't have an airbag on this side," Kerry said, "so I can sit in the front. I never get to sit in the front at home, except in The Bucket. And I can't believe how different you look with your hair cut," she rambled on. "I'm thinking of getting mine cut short for the summer, but I don't know. What do you think?"

"I think it's up to you, Kerry. Anyways, it shouldn't really matter what others think, now should it?" Colleen schooled as she wondered what Brian thought of her hair. "And what about you, Shannon?" she asked into the back seat.

"I'm keeping mine long," Shannon shot back quickly.

"That's fine," Colleen smiled into the rear-view mirror. "Do you like long hair?"

"My dad does," Shannon told her as she studied Colleen's new haircut.

"So, what do you have planned for our trip?" Kerry asked, filling the void before Colleen could begin to worry. "Dad says he made you the tour guide."

"Well, doesn't he have anything planned?" Colleen inquired, moving from one concern to another.

"Nope," Kerry answered. "He didn't even bring his 'clipboard of fun'. He said he was leaving the whole trip up to you."

～

Colleen pulled up to the hotel, thankful the ride with the girls was over before any further insights could be revealed. Having hoped this surprise visit would take some of the tension off Thursday, she now found herself with even more to worry about.

She helped them check in, then took the girls on a quick tour of the pool area while Brian unloaded the car. They met back at the suite just as he brought in the last suitcase.

"Well," he chuckled, "I see you girls haven't lost your timing."

"Dad, you should see the pool," Kerry exclaimed. "It's got steps in the shallow end, and a deep end with a diving board, and two hot pools!"

"Gee, did we pack the suits?" he kidded as the girls ran off to check out the bedrooms.

Colleen made her way onto the balcony and peered out over the courtyard. Brian followed, the girls joining them soon after.

"Cool rooms, Dad," Shannon stated. "Can we have the one with the TV?"

"We'll settle it all after Colleen leaves," Brian told her, knowing the girls would end up in the room with the TV.

The four of them chatted on the balcony for a while, planning out the events of the next few days until it was time for Colleen to return to work. Relieved that her ideas had met with the girls' excited approval, she gave Brian directions to her place and set up a time to meet the next evening.

As she drove off into the Wednesday afternoon sun Colleen began to think about Thursday night.

～

Brian stood on the balcony after she'd gone, surveying the courtyard below. The foreign setting, so different from The Door, transfixed him. The air tasted dry, the shrubs looked plastic, the birds sounded strange.

Brian had always preferred the leisurely pace of driving trips, on two-lane highways through old towns the interstate had forgotten, when he could feel the changing landscapes and lifestyles he rode through. Looking out at the unfamiliar environs, he appreciated for once how nice it was to be able to hop on a plane and in a few short hours be a world away — away from the ghosts that haunted him by day, away from the visions that kept him awake at night.

"Dad, can we go swimming?"

～

Climbing the steps from the pool, they quickly scampered across the cool tiles of the patio, toward the hot tub. Brian jumped in first, letting out a gasp as the heat engulfed him, his head popping back up out of the water, shoulders resting just below the waterline. He stood, taking the girls in his arms, dipping them in slowly at first, a bit farther each time as they adjusted to the steaming heat, then pulling them all the way under before setting them on the ledge that ran around the whirlpool.

"Ah, this is the life," Shannon stated as she laid her head back over the side of the pool.

"Ah, this is the life," Kerry repeated, her head just reaching the edge.

Brian smiled to himself as he leaned back, looking out over

the sunset. The cool of night came quickly to the desert, the sun beginning to descend below the mountains. He'd always liked mountains — wished they had them back home — but these were different from the lush green forests and snow-capped peaks he'd long ago hiked, and longed to return to. The cacti were interesting, all the various types and shapes, some just beginning to flower, each finding a way to survive in the barren landscape. But these mountains looked lonely, with nothing but empty space to fill the void between the sparse cactus plants.

"Boy, Colleen's hair sure looks different than it did last summer," Kerry thought aloud.

"A lot of things look different than they did last summer," Brian said as the sun slipped below the mountains, no clouds to wave good-bye to its last rays. "A lot of things look different," he repeated, wondering what the next sunset would bring.

∼

"God, I hate these places," Brian complained to the girls as they drove aimlessly through the maze of asphalt, lost in the search for Colleen's condo. He pulled over and looked out at the twisting rows of identical buildings, unassociated lives packed so tightly together, yet so separated, and wondered how he was going to find his way.

Colleen answered the door in her bathrobe, a towel wrapped around her head. "Nice you're so punctual," she laughed as she invited them in. "As you can see, I'm all ready to go," she continued, one hand making a sweeping gesture to show off her outfit, the other reaching for the necklace she'd taken off in the shower. "It's new," she winked at the girls, holding the sleeve of her new robe out for them to feel. "I hear it's all the rage in Paris evening wear."

"The girls were a bit anxious to get here," Brian apologized as he ushered Shannon and Kerry in. "You're lucky we got lost in your condo complex or we might have gotten here even sooner. Sorry if we're early."

"Oh, you're on time," Colleen assured him, "I'm late. A few things came up this afternoon, but I'll be ready to go in a couple of minutes. My hair doesn't take quite so long to dry these days, you know," she smiled.

"So I noticed."

"Margarita mix on the counter, if you'd like," she said, motioning toward the kitchen. "I'm gonna run and get dressed. Make yourselves at home. I'll be ready in a few minutes."

Shannon and Kerry ran off to inspect the condo while Brian stayed back and took a look around. The living room was large and spacious, though it was filled with too much empty whiteness. There were too many silent pieces of laminated furniture bought at a discount store, and not enough friendly brown wood that spoke to him. There was too much thick carpeting that softened your steps, and not enough hardwood flooring that taught you to walk softly. There were too many flowery prints on the couches and curtains, and not enough fresh-cut flowers.

Brian surveyed the contents more closely, focusing on smaller details that drew his attention. The pictures of The Door he had framed for Christmas hung on the living room wall. The book he had sent sat on the coffee table. The pictures the girls had drawn covered the fridge. A margarita was definitely in order.

The girls came running into the kitchen at the sound of the blender. Colleen appeared soon after, wearing a long sheer skirt, southwestern print, and a light button-down sweater, the top two buttons undone, revealing the gold cross and chain that lay flat against her chest. Her long flowing hair was gone, though she still wore the familiar leather sandals he recalled from last summer. Brian handed Colleen her drink, then took a long sip of his.

She led them into the living room and sat on the couch, the girls sitting on either side of her as they flipped through the book on The Door, recalling her visit the previous summer. Brian leaned against the desk near the window, setting his drink beside the journal that sat atop, "Brenden" written on the cover.

"Nice place," he commented when Colleen and the girls had finished paging through the book.

"It'll do," she answered, "but I don't plan to live here forever."

Brian picked up his glass and finished his drink. "Anyone else for another?" he asked, then noticed her glass was still full.

                                       ~

They drove off toward Scottsdale, Kerry observing how one of the mountains looked like a camel, then made their way into Old Town, parking by the horse-sculpture fountain. They strolled through the shops that lined the curving brick streets, took a ride on the trolley, then toured more shops. Colleen bought Native American earrings for the girls, Brian a chili-pepper Christmas ornament for the vacation tree, Shannon a t-shirt. Kerry bought a grow-your-own cactus kit, and a bag of polished rocks, and a tiny Gila-monster stuffed animal, and a vial filled with Arizona "gold."

"I have to go to the bathroom," Kerry announced, struggling to carry all her souvenirs as they walked along the raised wooden sidewalk.

"The restaurant's just up ahead, if you can make it," Colleen encouraged as she lent a hand with the packages.

They ran the last block to Frank & Lupe's, Colleen leading Kerry past the front door to the restrooms out back while Brian and Shannon got a table and ordered drinks. Surveying the cantina, Brian was pleased with her choice, a colorful little local place, and not some chain restaurant they could have eaten at in any city.

Colleen and Kerry returned as the menus and drinks arrived. "Just made it," Colleen said, winking at Brian as she took her seat. "So, how do you like the place?"

"I was just thinking it looks like a great choice," Brian confided. "Food good?"

"Great," Colleen answered, relieved.

Brian scanned his menu, stopping part way through. "Carne Adavada!" he exclaimed as he closed the menu and licked his lips. "Why, I haven't had that since Christine and I took the girls to Santa Fe."

Colleen took a long sip of her margarita.

The girls kept the conversation moving through dinner; the waiter kept the margaritas coming. Summer memories were relived, Saturday plans discussed. Dessert finished, Kerry needed to wash up, her face and hands and elbows sticky from the sopapillas and honey. Shannon offered to take her to the bathroom out back, then asked if the two of them could go to the store next door to look at a souvenir she'd seen on the way in. With ample warnings about safety Brian allowed the girls to explore on their own for a bit, but only next door. They quickly ran off, leaving Brian and Colleen alone for the first time.

The comfort they'd once felt in quiet was gone, replaced by the unknown of silence.

"Another margarita?" Brian offered, feeling he could use one.

"Thanks, no," Colleen answered as she dipped her fingers in her nearly full water glass and dried them on her napkin. "Three's my limit, though I could probably use another after the day I've had."

"Trouble at work?"

"No, nothing like that. It's my mother, actually."

"Something wrong?"

"She had a bit of a dizzy spell or something this afternoon, fell over, blacked out for a minute."

"You should have called and canceled," Brian said, "stayed with her."

"I thought about it," Colleen told him, "suggested it actually. But she insisted I see you and the girls, said I could see her anytime."

"She's okay then?"

"Fine, I guess. She was already complaining about doctors and all the fuss by the time I left."

"I'm glad to hear it was nothing serious."

"I don't think it was. Oh, they'll run a few tests, but they told me they didn't think it was anything to worry about," Colleen explained. "Still, I do worry."

"About losing her?"

Colleen twirled the gold cross between her fingers, raising it from her chest to her chin, then back down again. "About being alone," she answered.

Brian ordered another margarita.

"I know a thing or two," he offered after some thought, "about being alone."

Colleen wished she had ordered another margarita.

"Christine always hated to be alone," he began. "Especially on weekends when she had to stay home and work, and I'd bring the girls up to the cottage without her. She'd have a million projects she wanted to get to when she had the house to herself, but she'd always call us on Saturday night with a lonely voice and a movie on in the background. When we'd get home the next day we'd always find her sitting in her chair with a book and an Afghan, waiting for us, projects untouched.

"I guess she doesn't have to worry anymore," he said as he took another sip of his margarita, "about being alone."

"It must be lonely for you," Colleen ventured, "without her."

"Oh, I won't pretend it isn't," he admitted. "But I'm starting to get used to it, as sad as that may sound."

"At least you have your memories."

"Idealized, I'm afraid."

"We all do that to a degree, I think."

"Well, I don't suppose it's real kosher to talk about the faults of the dead," Brian philosophized.

"Probably not," Colleen agreed. "Though I suppose in my memories Brenden has a few less fits and gives a few more hugs than he actually did when he was alive."

Brian took the final sip of his drink, running his finger around the rim of the wide glass, the few bits of salt that remained falling onto the table.

"Christine may not have been perfect," he offered after the last of the salt had fallen, "but I used to think I was.

"Man, I used to just ride her about some of her petty faults, which was one of my major ones. I suppose that says less about her, though, and more about me. And now I have to ask myself, did it really matter if she closed the cabinet door, or changed the toilet paper roll, or wrote a phone message on a piece of paper bigger than a postage stamp, and put it where I could find it?

"Oh, those minor things didn't really matter, I know, except that I didn't know it at the time. What mattered was whether the major things lined up, which they did, most of the time. Still..."

Colleen watched him struggle, watched his eyes not make contact with hers.

"... there were times when I asked myself why, out of all the millions of people in the world, I ended up with her. There were little things that bugged me, meaningless actions on her part that contradicted the very essence of what I wanted to stand for – like how she always tried to worm her way to the front of a line rather than waiting for others to have their turn, or how she always got her hair cut for a family picture, to be remembered as she wanted to appear, rather than as we saw her.

"And there were a few times when I really needed her to be more, more than she was capable of being." He paused, lifting his glass for another sip, realizing it was empty. "Of course," he continued, "there were also plenty of times when she was more than I knew, or could have asked for.

"In the end, looking back on it all as I do now, I think..."

"Dad! Dad! Look at this really cool dolphin wind chime I got!"

∿

Brian paid the bill as Colleen helped the girls collect their packages. They strolled around Old Town for a few blocks, window-shopping as they walked off their meal. Rounding a corner, they came to a stop in front of the Sugar Bowl. "Ice cream?" Colleen asked, recalling the stop at the Yum Yum Tree. They sat at the counter and ordered cones and sundaes, laughing at the puzzled look on the face of the young soda jerk when they asked for booger balls.

The girls reviewed the Saturday plans with Colleen as they drove her home, Brian wondering where the night had gone. They all walked Colleen to the door of her condo, Kerry giving her a long good-bye hug, Shannon a shorter one.

"I had a nice time," Colleen offered into the darkness.

"Me too," Brian answered. "Slipped by too quickly, though."

"It did just kind of breeze by, didn't it?"

"Like talking with an old friend," Brian said.

∿

She was ready when they arrived early Saturday morning, waiting by the front door in her sandals and cutoffs, and a baggy old sweatshirt. They'd picked up breakfast on the way, their laps filled with doughnut bags and juice boxes, Brian's with two cups of coffee. Colleen grabbed her hiking boots and the lunch she'd packed and climbed into the front seat.

"Gonna be a beautiful day," she greeted them as they handed her the doughnuts. "With a nice early start like this we should have plenty of time for all our plans."

"I can't wait to see the desert," Kerry blurted out, crumbs tumbling from her mouth. "Shopping was fun, and I got a lot of really neat stuff, but I spent all day yesterday looking forward to today."

"Me too," Colleen answered, "me too."

"Now I forget," Kerry continued, "where are we going first?"

"A National Monument, called Casa Grande," Brian reminded her. "You remember, old Indian ruins."

"Oh yeah, that's right," Kerry recalled. "Is it a fun place?"

"Fun might not be the right word," Brian informed her. "Just some faded memories about a forgotten people."

"Gee," Shannon said dryly, "it sounds like a real hoot, Dad."

They drove south out of Phoenix, toward Tucson, the city winding down behind them, the desert opening up ahead. Kerry stared out the window in wonder, calling out the newly learned names of the various cacti she saw. Shannon read a book, her back to the window as Colleen attempted to fold a map in the front, losing the struggle.

Brian drove along quietly, taking in the desert, each cactus different, the scene always the same. He could see the landscape with his eyes, but he couldn't feel it inside him, like he did back home. Cruising down the flat, straight highway, he focused on the distant mountains that seemed to stay on the horizon, never quite coming into clear view.

Reaching Casa Grande just as the first guided tour was starting, they listened to the ranger's talk and viewed the ruins, strolling through the small museum afterwards. Brian was mesmerized by the mystery surrounding the Indians who had once lived there, and the purpose of the place. The girls, less interested, grew restless, anxious to get on with the rest of the day.

"Just let me stop in the gift shop for a minute," Brian begged. "I want to see if they have a book on the Hohokam Indian's religion. Then I promise we'll go."

The girls groaned. "You're not going to read it out loud in the car, are you, Dad?" Shannon protested.

"I'll get them something to drink while you look," Colleen offered. "Don't be too long," she advised as she took the girls outside. They sat together on a ledge, sharing a bottle of water.

"So, your dad's into religion?" Colleen asked.

Both girls rolled their eyes. "Yeah," Shannon answered, "but he doesn't like going to church. He just likes to read about what other people believe. That's what his meeting is about. It's called 'Dead Religions,' or 'Religions of the Dead,' or something like that."

"He did have some opinions about religion in one of his letters," Colleen recalled.

"My mom used to joke that he studied alien religions in college," Shannon said.

"I like watching the TV shows about how people in other religions get married," Kerry said. "They have some really cool outfits the girls wear." Kerry kicked at the dirt for a minute before looking up at Colleen.

"Are you gonna marry my dad?" she asked.

Shannon choked on her water, spitting it out as she turned toward Kerry. "Dad would *never* do that to Mom!" she scolded her sister as she jumped down from the ledge and walked off toward the car.

"Ready to go," Brian called out as he emerged from the gift shop, book in hand.

～

They drove off toward Saguaro National Park, Brian aware of the tension in the car, though not of its cause. His attempts at drawing them out drew little response, his passengers reflective and stoic.

They entered Saguaro, stopping to take a quick picture by the sign – Colleen with the girls, Shannon slightly off to the side – then continued down a bumpy gravel path that led to a much-needed rest stop.

"Not a pitter," Kerry cried out as they pulled over.

"Care to wait?" Brian laughed as they got out of the car.

"Want me to take you?" Colleen offered, recalling the outhouse at Brenden's.

"Nah, I'm bigger now," Kerry answered as she headed off with Shannon.

Brian and Colleen stretched their legs for a moment then leaned back against the car, sharing a water bottle as they waited for the girls. Wondering about the altered mood of the group since they'd left Casa Grande, he turned toward Colleen. "Has something happened that I should know about?" he asked.

"Maybe you should ask the girls," she answered.

"About what?"

"It seems they have some questions," she said, "about us."

Brian kicked at the dirt for a moment before looking up at Colleen. "They're not the only ones," he said as the girls returned from the outhouse.

~

Winding their way through the park, they stopped at the ranger station, picking up a map of hiking trails, staying to watch a movie depicting native beliefs about the saguaro and the desert. Deciding on a route, they hiked for a while, Colleen bounding ahead on the trail with Kerry, Brian falling behind with Shannon.

"So, how did you like Casa Grande?" he asked.

"About as much as the dentist," Shannon answered curtly.

"Did something happen I should know about?" he inquired.

"Has something happened *we* should know about?" she shot back quickly.

Brian wished he were walking with Kerry instead. They walked a bit farther in silence before he tried another approach.

"This is a really nice trail, don't you think?"

"I like the one we took in New Mexico with Mom better," Shannon replied as she picked up the pace and caught up to Kerry and Colleen.

Reunited, the four of them stopped atop a peak to eat the lunch Colleen had packed. Kerry read aloud from a brochure during the meal, marveling at the life of a saguaro. Brian was more interested in the cacti's skeletal remains after death, Shannon on when they could leave.

The girls ran off to play on the outcroppings of rocks that adorned the peak, timing their exit perfectly, escaping the clean-up chores. Colleen leaned over the picnic blanket on all fours, raking the items into a single pile beneath her, then re-sorting them into smaller piles again before placing them in the backpack.

"How's your mother doing?" Brian asked.

"Much better, thanks. When I saw her yesterday she looked fine," Colleen informed him. "The doctor said all of her tests came back normal."

"Today was my mother's birthday," he stated. "You reminded me of her just now, how you leaned over the picnic blanket and collected up the stuff, the same way she used to. Funny," he continued, "how she just pops into my head like that from time to time, like she's trying to reach me, trying to tell me something."

Colleen set the backpack aside and sat down on the blanket. "And what do you think she's trying to tell you today?" she asked.

He paused for a moment before answering.

"Not to be afraid."

"Of what?"

He looked at her as she leaned back on her elbows, her long tan legs stretching out on the blanket before her, and wondered what her long hair would have looked like just then, blowing in the breeze.

"Of myself," he said. "Of repeating past mistakes. Of making new ones. Of losing old perspectives. Of gaining new ones. Of forgetting old memories. Of not creating new ones. Of growing selfish. Of remaining alone.

"Sometimes," he continued, "I sit in the diner back home and look at the people at the counter, eating by themselves. Some days they look like the loneliest people in the world, other days the least troubled."

Brian paused, leaning back against the rocks that rimmed the picnic area, looking out at the desert, at the tall green saguaros waving back at him, and the light brown skeletons of past saguaros that waved no more. He sat quietly, drifting away as Colleen chewed on the end of her necklace.

"Look! Look!" Kerry exclaimed. "I caught a lizard!"

"Can we go now?" Shannon begged.

Leaving Saguaro, they drove to the Desert Museum, where they looked at the javelinas and roadrunners and coyotes, viewed the various cacti and native plants, and learned about the desert environment. Kerry ran excitedly from one exhibit to the next as Brian tried to keep up. Shannon and Colleen trailed behind.

Since leaving Casa Grande earlier that morning, Colleen had felt a need to reach out to Shannon — both to address the child's concerns, and to relate her own experiences — though she hadn't been able to find a quiet time alone. As the two of them leisurely strolled along the winding pathways of the outdoor museum, falling farther behind Brian and Kerry, Colleen decided to take advantage of the opportunity, stopping to sit on a bench in the shade. Shannon walked on a few steps, then returned and sat down next to her.

"I'd like to talk to you for a minute, Shannon, if I may," Colleen began.

"Are you gonna marry my dad?"

"I have no idea, Shannon," Colleen answered slowly. "No idea."

"He still loves my mom, you know."

"I know. Boy, do I know!"

Colleen paused, allowing the child the chance to continue, to express her feelings. Shannon turned and looked away from Colleen, the same empty look on her face that her father sometimes slipped into.

"You know, you and I have something in common," Colleen told Shannon. "I lost my dad when I was about the same age you were when you lost your mom."

Shannon turned on the bench to face Colleen.

"Different situations, of course, but the same result. So, I know a little bit about being a child and losing one parent, worrying about the other.

"My mom never got over the loss of my dad," Colleen continued, "and she's been lonely ever since.

"Your dad will always love your mom, Shannon, whether he finds someone else or not, and he'll always miss her, whether he's lonely or not. But he doesn't always have to be lonely.

"I don't want you, or Kerry, or your dad, to ever forget your mom," Colleen said as she rose from the bench and took Shannon's hand. "But I also don't want you to only remember her, and not know me."

∼

When the museum closed they headed back north, on the two-lane highways that Brian preferred, through the tiny weathered towns visited only by residents. The tired girls fidgeted noisily in the back seat, the scenery outside, so new only that morning, now old. Brian drove silently, lost in the view, and the contrast this place held to The Door. Colleen wondered how the day was slipping away, and when she would see him again.

They stopped at a lively little place in Florence, filled with locals just in from the town softball game. Brian had a couple of margaritas with dinner, to help loosen the tongue; Colleen iced tea, to keep the mind clear. Kerry fell asleep at the table, her head resting in her hands, elbows beside her plate. Shannon sat across the table from Brian, next to Colleen.

They bought souvenir t-shirts on their way out, stopping to join the crowd as they sang "Happy Birthday" to the softball coach. Kerry nodded off quickly again in the car, Shannon fighting off sleep, Brian hoping she'd let go, just this once. They arrived back in Phoenix too soon, the reflection of darkness shattered by the lights of the city. As they pulled up to Colleen's condo, Shannon leaned forward, poking her head between the two front seats.

"Will we see you tomorrow?" she asked.

"I'm not sure," Colleen answered. "I don't think it was in the plans."

"Well, you have to say good-bye to Kerry."

"I'll try," Colleen said, giving Shannon's hand a tight squeeze before opening the car door. "We'll see."

Brian and Colleen walked toward her front door in silence, each of them knowing this was good-bye.

"It's been nice to see you."

"Very nice."

"I'll miss you."

"I'll miss you, too."

"I'll write."

"So will I."

Colleen grabbed the key out of her backpack and unlocked the door, leaning against the frame, her hand drifting toward her necklace.

"About tomorrow..." they both said at the same time, then laughed.

"I really should say good-bye to Kerry before you leave," Colleen offered.

"The airport?" Brian suggested.

"That might be a scene I could skip," she confided. "Anyway, I have to visit my mother in the afternoon."

"How about a morning swim? We usually pack up and check out, then sneak in for one last trip to the pool before leaving."

"I usually like to go to church on Sunday mornings," she said. "Any chance you'd like to meet me there?"

"Not much of a churchgoer back home," Brian informed her, "though I do enjoy going when we're on vacation. I like to visit little old churches when we travel, see things from a different perspective. I think God looks different when He's on vacation."

"What?" Colleen asked, confused. "Like Bermuda shorts and a Hawaiian shirt?"

Brian laughed at the image. "No," he said, "I mean, sometimes you have to go away and look at things differently to see them more clearly when you get back home. Vacation church lets you look at God a little differently, that's all."

"So, care to join me then?"

"Uh, thanks, but no," Brian declined. "In addition to the fear of lightning striking if I actually do show up, I think we've got too much packing to do in the morning. But feel free to mention my name while you're there."

"Well, it looks like tomorrow might not work out..." Colleen said, her voice trailing off as she tilted her head back against the doorframe. "I guess this is good-bye then...."

Brian stared at her for a moment, wondering if he'd ever see her again. "Brunch!" he blurted out suddenly. "We were planning to have Sunday brunch at the hotel before heading off to the airport. You could meet us by the pool after church, then we could all go to brunch together before you go visit your mother."

"It's a date," Colleen smiled back at him. "I'll meet you there."

$\approx$

Brian drove off into the stillness of an Arizona spring, recalling a Wisconsin summer, and a fall filled with letters, a winter with none.

Shannon leaned forward from the back seat and tapped him on the shoulder. "Dad," she asked, "are you gonna marry Colleen?"

"I have no idea, Shannon," he answered slowly, "no idea."

He drove silently for a while, then turned toward the child who looked so much like her mother. "How do you think Mom would feel if I did?" he asked.

"I don't know," Shannon replied, shrugging her shoulders.

"Would you like to talk about it?"

"I think you should talk to Colleen."

$\approx$

Colleen leisurely strolled across the parking lot toward the pool area. As she approached, she could hear their voices rising toward her, shouting out as they splashed each other in the water. Pausing for a moment as she reached the gate, she watched them as the girls chased Brian into the hot tub.

"Colleen! Colleen!" Kerry called out, waving her hands over her head when she saw Colleen coming through the gate.

"Well good morning, sleepy," Colleen kidded as she reached

the hot tub. "You were really zonked out in the car last night. Did you have fun yesterday?"

"It was PK!"

"PK?"

"Pretty Kool."

"Family joke," Brian explained as he got out of the hot tub, offering Colleen a chair as he dried off.

"I thought maybe it was just a bad spelling teacher," Colleen replied, winking at the girls as she sat. "So," she asked, turning to Brian, "did you get packed up OK?"

"Well, OK might not be the right description," he chuckled, "but there's nothing left in the room and the suitcases managed to close, so we'll call it packed and sort it out later." Brian wrapped himself in a towel and took a seat next to Colleen. "We're almost done here," he informed her. "We were just taking one last dip in the hot tub before getting dressed for brunch."

"Take your time," she said. "I'm in no hurry."

"Five minutes, girls," he told them. "Don't want to miss those strawberry crepes with the whipped crème."

"Colleen!" Kerry shouted, jumping up in the pool. "They have about twenty of those cans of that whipped crème at the brunch, and Dad said I can have as much as I want, and...." Kerry paused at the sound, a look of confusion coming across her face as she tried to locate the source of the noise. "...and I think your purse is ringing."

Laughing at Kerry's expression, Colleen retrieved the phone from her purse, moving a few steps away from the gurgle of the hot tub as she answered.

"What?"..."When?"...she asked, her face turning ashen. "I see."..."Yes, yes. Right away. I'll be there as soon as I can," she said, closing up the phone.

"Oh my God," Colleen whispered quietly as she looked across at Brian and the girls.

"What's wrong?" Brian asked, rising from his chair.

"It's my mother," Colleen explained. "She's had some kind of a stroke or something. They're taking her to the hospital right now. I've got to go."

Brian stood motionless for a moment, remembering a similar phone call. He explained things to the girls, who quickly dried off and hugged Colleen good-bye, thanking her for the fun times, wishing her good luck with her mother, asking when they would see her again.

"I'm not sure," she replied uncertainly as she rummaged through her purse in search of her keys. "But I'll be looking forward to it," she smiled at them.

She turned to Brian. "I'm sorry to run out like this, but I've got to…"

"Go. Go!" he instructed as he gave her a quick hug, the smell of her hair reminding him of the scent that had filled the cab of The Bucket the morning after they'd slept at Grandpa's. "Go," he repeated. "And make sure you let us know about your mother."

"I'll send you a letter."

Chapter 15

〜

*T*he Door had changed greatly in the few short days they'd been gone. The snow had melted away, revealing the matted brown grass that would soon spring to life. The ice was beginning to break up on the lake, and buds were starting to appear on the hardiest trees. Brian was certain the snows were not yet done, that the cold blanket of winter would again cover all, snuffing out the feeling of hope. Yet he could sense, as they drove toward home, that things were beginning to change. Everything was changing.

The sound of the tires as they rode over the steel section of the big bridge in Sturgeon Bay roused the girls, who had fallen asleep on the drive back from the airport in Green Bay. Passing the abandoned outdoor movie theater and turning at the fork in the road, they began to make their way up the quiet side, the long day of travel nearly over. Stirring awake, Shannon asked if they could stop by Grandpa's on the way home and tell him all about their trip with Colleen. Brian agreed, feeling in need of his father's timeless familiarity, some children never really leaving home.

He felt at ease when they arrived at Grandpa's and found everything just as it should be, the safety of routine more comfortable than the uncertainty of change. Grandpa was sitting at the table eating scrambled eggs and tomato soup, the usual Sunday night dinner. The paper lay neatly stacked alongside the La-Z-Boy, shoes on the other side of the chair, small fire in the fireplace, news on TV, purse hanging on the coat rack by the door. *Purse hanging on the coat rack by the door?* Brian paused, staring at the purse, then closed the door behind him, making his way toward the kitchen table where Grandpa sat, a granddaughter perched on each knee.

"Welcome home," Grandpa said after receiving a kiss on the cheek from each girl. Returning it in kind, he looked up at Brian. "Have a good trip?"

"It was nice," Brian nodded.

"Tell me all about it," Grandpa ordered, his attention turned back to the girls.

"We went to a really neat nature museum in the desert," Shannon informed him.

"And we went shopping, and I got a ton of really cool stuff!" Kerry added.

"Whoa, wait a minute," Grandpa interrupted. "*You* went shopping? And *you* went to a nature museum? Now that's a change."

"A lot of things," Brian said as he looked over at the purse, "seem to be changing."

Grandpa looked up at Brian, following his son's gaze. He finished listening to the girls' description of their trip, then sent them off to the living room to play with a new gadget he'd bought at the wood store in Fish Creek.

"So," Brian said, looking at the purse once more, "I see you've started cross-dressing, Dad."

Grandpa laughed. "Just a friend," he replied.

"How'd you meet?"

"Known her for years," Grandpa told him. "She works at the hardware store in town. Her husband made that hand-carved Santa I gave you a few years ago. Your mother and I used to go out for a fish fry with them now and then. He died a few years ago, shortly after your mother."

"How long have you been seeing her?"

"I'm not seeing her."

"She left her purse here."

"You've never left anything anywhere?"

"You two serious?"

"Would that bother you?"

"No, of course not," Brian said as he pulled out a chair. "I'd be happy for you. Tell me about her."

"Tell me about Colleen."

They sat across the table from each other, worlds apart. The girls sat quietly by the fire in the living room, the TV holding their attention, the new toy now old. Grandpa rose, poured two small glasses of Cream Sherry from the bottle in the fridge door, then sat back down, looking thoughtfully across the table at his son.

"It's nice," Grandpa began slowly, "to have someone to talk to once in a while. Just a companion to chat with, someone to fill the daily void. Being alone is bad enough, but the loneliness is even worse.

"I remember when I used to go on business trips, hectic days filled with seminars, busy nights filled with dinner meetings and banquets. I was never alone on those trips, never five minutes to myself the whole time, yet I remember how alone I used to feel, away from your mother. Then I'd get home, and the two of us would just sit together, not talking, just being with each other, and the loneliness would melt away."

Grandpa took a long, slow drink from his glass, then continued. "Now I sit here sometimes, listening to the damned clock tick on the wall, feeling like I used to on those business trips, wishing to God I had someone to talk to.

"Your mom and I never really talked about what we would do if we found ourselves alone one day, or what we wanted the other to do. We tried to talk about it once or twice, but it wasn't something we could ever bring ourselves to imagine, so we avoided the subject. But I think your mom wouldn't want me to be alone, to feel so lonely without her. No one could ever take your mother's place. I don't think she'd feel threatened by my being happy again." Grandpa paused. "It's an empty life," he added, "without someone special to share it with."

Finishing his drink, Grandpa headed off toward the living room to sit with the girls. Pausing in the doorway, he looked back over his shoulder at Brian, who sat staring into his untouched glass. "Colleen's a keeper, Brian," he said. "Christine would like her."

∼

Kerry sat on the edge of her bed, sorting her souvenirs from the trip. "Man, Colleen really bought me a lot of stuff that night we went shopping," she said. "How come you only just got a t-shirt from her?"

"I don't know," Shannon answered, shrugging her shoulders. "I guess I just didn't feel like shopping."

"You weren't sick, were you?" Kerry asked. "You *always* feel like shopping."

"I wasn't sick."

"It seemed like you were mad at her or something."

"Not mad."

"Well, something."

Shannon set her hairbrush down on the dresser and crossed the room, sitting on the edge of Kerry's bed. She looked at the keepsakes from their trip, the reminders of Arizona, and Colleen.

"What do you think about Colleen?" she asked her sister.

"I think she's really neat."

"I know, I know. I mean, what do you think about her and Dad?"

Kerry set down the bottle of Arizona 'gold' she was investigating and looked across at Shannon. "I wonder if she'll make Dad forget about Mom," she said. "What do you think?"

"I think she'll help him remember," Shannon replied.

∾

March 17
Dear Christine,

Everything is changing — around me, within me — and it scares me. You know I don't do real well with change, unless it's two quarters, a dime, and a couple of nickels.

Change scares me, like I'm falling from a tall tower, with a large kitchen knife in my hand.

Sometimes change is sudden, and we recognize it immediately. Other times it's gradual, and we come to realize it more slowly. Either way, change alters our perspective — in the way we look at others, and the way we look at ourselves.

I've experienced a change in perspective with all the people I've been close to in my life, that point in the relationship when I see them differently, and see myself differently for it. And once that moment occurs I can never fully go back and see that person, or myself, from the same perspective I had before.

My perspective is changing.

Everything is changing — around me, within me — and it scares me. You know I don't do real well with change, unless it's diapers.

My Love Always,
Brian

∾

March 17
Dear Brenden,

Take good care of Mom.

Watch over her, as the two of you watch over me.

Leeny

∼

March 18
Dear Brian,

My mother passed away shortly after I left you on Sunday, dying as quietly as she lived, living as alone as I found myself at that moment.

I thought of trying to reach you, but knew you'd be on your way to the airport. Instead, I went to the cemetery, to sit with Brenden as I watched the planes fly overhead.

I thought about a lot of things yesterday afternoon — about my mother, about Brenden, about how some people touch so many lives, others so few. And I thought about the girls, and you.

I learned from losing Brenden that it will take time for me to sort through all the memories and feelings I have about my mother, but I think I'll be at peace with her. I don't think I'll dwell on the past, and what might have been. I think, instead, I'll recall fondly all that I've recently found.

Love,
Colleen

∼

March 21
Dear Colleen,

I'm so sorry to hear about your mother. I wish I could have been there for you when you needed someone.

There is much I could say about death and remembrance, though little that would really help. There is more I could write about mothers, though less that I understand about losing them.

I'm glad you found your mother before the chance slipped by.

Brian

P.S. — The big news around here is that it seems Grandpa has got himself a girlfriend! He sure seems to be making a lot of trips to the hardware store she works at to pick up things he doesn't really need. As if I didn't already have enough to worry about.

~

April 1
Dear Brian,

I'm sorry I haven't written in a while, but I've been busy making arrangements and attending to details, to the trivial matters you are all too aware we must deal with exactly when we'd rather not. And then, of course, there was the funeral.

Though the loss of Brenden was more of a shock, I think my mother's funeral was sadder still. A Mass was held at the home, attended by myself and four wheelchair-bound patients who drifted in from the hall. The scene at the cemetery was even worse, the funeral director and the priest the only ones there to keep me from being alone. After they left I stood over my mother's grave for a long time, wondering what it means to be alone, then realized I have the rest of my life to wonder.

I no longer have my mother, or Brenden. I have memories of them, times I will always cherish, though these memories will remain forever in the past.

I have memories, as well, of a few days in The Door, of a fall filled with letters, of a trip just completed. Do those memories have a future, or will they too remain in the past?

I was so nervous about seeing you again, Brian, so relieved when it felt like last summer, so sad when it came to an end.

I had so many questions before you came, questions that seemed to matter little when you were here, questions that have come back since you've gone.

I know you still have questions you need to answer, things you need to think through, resolve, with the girls, with Christine, with yourself. But I have questions too.

While you question the girls' memory of their mother, I wonder about their acceptance of me. While you question how Christine might feel, I wonder if she is watching me. While you question my feelings for you, I wonder about your feelings for me.

You question, I wonder.

I wonder why your trip to Arizona made me homesick for The Door.

I wonder, will I ever learn to water-ski behind Grandpa's boat? I wonder, will I ever go pick cherries in the orchard down the lane? I wonder, will I ever hear a piano being played inside your home?

I wonder, will I ever have my picture taken on the deck of a ferry? I wonder, will I ever climb the old fire tower, holding hands with you?

I wonder if Christine and I would have been friends? I wonder if she and I can share you? I wonder if you can find a place for both of us? I wonder if I'll always be compared to her memory?

I wonder, am I making the same mistake with this letter that I made on New Year's Eve?

I wonder, am I just an April Fool?

I wonder, Brian, what I have to look forward to.

Love,
Colleen

∾

As he reached in and took the letter from the mailbox, a sudden, chilling snow began to fall upon him, beating against his face, covering his hair with a white cap as he climbed the hill back up the driveway and ran into the kitchen. It was a heavy spring snow, the kind that sticks to the branches of the trees, snapping them under its weight, cutting short the new life of the leaves just beginning to form. By midnight the snow would be clinging to the panes of the windows, obscuring the view. It would melt and be gone in a few days, he knew, but tonight, as he sat at the tiny desk in the alcove under the stairs, the storm raged.

He sat there, her letter in hand, and knew the weather made sense. It was time to look inside, to face the storm within.

He wondered, was it eighty and sunny in Phoenix?

∾

April 5
Dear Colleen,

What you have to look forward to are the teenage years of two young girls who already love you, and barely remember their mother. What you have to look forward to is the good-natured interrogation and loving acceptance of my brother and sisters. What you have to look forward to is the eventual funeral of my father, though I hope it is still a long way off.

What you have to look forward to is the memory of a mother barely known. What you have to look forward to is the memory of a wife who is still deeply loved. What you have to look forward to is the memory of a past you never knew.

What you have to look forward to are crabby outbursts when I am tired. What you have to look forward to is the nit-picking anal retention of someone who will restack the dishwasher after you've loaded it. What you have to look forward to is someone who is hard on the people he loves most, yet harder still on himself.

What you have to look forward to are quiet nights curled up by the fire. What you have to look forward to are Sunday walks in the woods. What you have to look forward to is laughter, and tears.

What you have to look forward to is life with a dreamer. What you have to look forward to is life with a child at heart. What you have to look forward to is life with a lover who loves love.

What you have to look forward to is a broken heart still on the mend.

What you have to look forward to is time, time to wait, until I'm ready.

Love,
Brian

Brian trudged down the driveway, through the mounting drifts, and placed the letter inside the mailbox, flipping up the red flag that would soon be covered in white. Back inside, he brushed the snow off his clothes, made himself a strong cup of coffee, and returned to the alcove under the stairs.

One letter down, one to go. If the first letter had been difficult to write, the second would be impossible. But he knew it was time to answer all his questions, to learn what he already knew.

He turned on the computer. "My Dear Christine," he began to type, continuing into the night, through a second and then third cup of coffee, until the winds outside began to die down just as the light of day was beginning to break. Finishing as he heard the footsteps of the rising girls overhead, he saved the letter in the file with the others, unsent, first printing a copy and sealing it in an envelope. He wrote a large "C" on the envelope, then tucked it away on the back corner of the tiny desk, on top of a book about antique flatirons.

Colleen sat in the corner of her couch, Brian's letter in hand. She had read it repeatedly, not counting the number of times she had read it, but the number of hours she had spent reading it. She had smiled. She had frowned. She had cried. She had laughed. She had made herself an old-fashioned.

She had fallen hopelessly in love with a man she had spent less than a week with but knew better than some people know their mate of a lifetime. She had once thought the whole thing so crazy, now knew it to be so right.

April 8
Dear Brenden,

How is it that you first went to The Door? How is it that you kept going back to The Door, year after year? How is it that I never went to The Door when you were there? How is it that I went to The Door when I did?

How is it that I ended up at a particular old farmhouse?

I've asked you how, not why.

I will be returning to The Door someday, though I know not when. But I know that, when I do return, I will never leave. Thank you.

Leeny

～

Brian hadn't slept well the first few nights after the storm, but in the weeks that followed he had grown more relaxed, now falling asleep easily as he lay in bed at night, reading to the girls. He told himself it must be all the fresh air he was getting, grooming the trails, turning over the garden, mucking out the barn.

But he knew that was not the reason.

Throwing another shovel full of manure into the back of The Bucket, he heard a car coming up the drive. Poking his head out of the barn, he saw Grandpa taking the steps onto the porch, heading toward the back door. "Dad, over here," Brian called out, waving.

Grandpa turned, descended the steps, and crossed the barnyard toward Brian. "Knee deep in shit again, I see."

"Story of my life. What's up?"

"I wanted to pick up that book I lent you about antique

Chapter 15 / 283

flatirons. We're going to an auction over in Egg Harbor, and I want to use it to check prices."

"We?"

"We," Grandpa replied.

Brian looked over at his father. Freshly showered, he was wearing a new plaid shirt, and had the camera case looped through his belt. Through the stench of the manure Brian could smell Grandpa's aftershave wafting toward him. "Book's somewhere on top of the desk in the alcove," Brian said. "You'll excuse me if I don't go get it for you," he added, raising his boot out of the muck.

"No problem," Grandpa laughed. "Short on time myself. I'll just grab it and be off."

Grandpa ducked into the tiny alcove under the stairs and found the sought-after book, sitting under an envelope with a big "C" written across it. Grabbing the book, he pushed back through the swinging door into the kitchen, then through the adjacent swinging door into the old dining room, where he paused to admire the pictures of Maggie and Christine that graced the wall. Through the window he caught site of Brian, standing alone in the barnyard, his gloved hands resting under his chin atop the pitchfork. Grandpa looked back at the pictures of Maggie and Christine, then out again at Brian. Leaving the room, he returned to the alcove under the stairs and picked up the envelope, placing it inside the book.

～

Grandpa sat in the rocker in his tiny cottage later that night, wondering what he had done, and what he should do. The box of Maggie's old love letters sat in his lap, the sealed envelope he'd taken from Brian's on top of it. Setting the envelope aside, he removed the string from the box.

～

Sean,

Oh, how I feel for Brian and Christine tonight.

I'll never forget the looks on their faces at the hospital. Can you even begin to imagine losing your first baby, before it is born? I grieved at the thought of it when I looked at Brian, our firstborn.

It will be so difficult for them to go back home tomorrow. For while I was so looking forward to becoming a grandmother for the first time, I can put away the baby blanket I've already bought and remove the terrible memory fairly easily. They have the nursery you and Brian just fixed up to remind them, daily, of the memories they will never recall.

We have to do whatever we can to help them in their loss, and show them how to move on.

My Love,
Maggie

~

May 9
Dear Colleen,

Now that spring has finally arrived — late again — I've moved across the driveway, back into my favored little cottage. I don't know exactly what it is, but there's something special about this place, something extra I feel inside when I'm here.

I'm sitting by the fireplace tonight, a new flatiron on the coffee table, a box of Maggie's old love letters on my lap.

I'm staring at an envelope, considering where the duties of a parent end and those of a friend begin. I'm staring at an envelope, considering the difference between recovering from a loss and moving forward. I'm staring at an envelope, considering the fine line between the little things one does to help and the major mistakes that cause harm.

I'm staring at an envelope, considering why Brian is alone. I'm staring at an envelope, considering why Christine and Colleen both start with a "C." I'm staring at an envelope, considering what I'm about to do.

I found the enclosed envelope when I stopped over at Brian's earlier today. Judging by the amount of dust there was on top of it, I'm guessing it's been sitting around for a few weeks.

I'm going to make myself an old-fashioned now, and suggest you do the same.

Grandpa

~

Colleen made herself an old-fashioned and settled into the corner of the couch, running her fingers back and forth across her necklace. She sat staring at an envelope, considering.

She considered why Grandpa had sent it. She considered why Brian had not. She considered why it had been collecting dust. She considered why she hadn't yet opened it.

She considered how she'd savored his letters all fall. She considered how she'd missed them all winter. She considered how thick the envelope was. She considered how thin it could have been.

She considered how much longer she might have to wait, until enough time had passed for him. She considered how much longer she could wait, before too much time would pass for her.

And she considered that both Colleen and Christine started with a "C."

Colleen let the necklace fall to her chest, took a long sip of her old-fashioned, and picked up the envelope.

~

April 5
My Dear Christine,

Life hasn't turned out the way it was supposed to.

Do you remember when we first started dating, when I dreamt out loud about us growing old together, shuffling our feet across the kitchen floor as we forgot what it was we were looking for? You said you never wanted to get that way – that I should shoot you first. Well, I never got the chance.

I was at the hardware store the other day, standing in line behind an old woman who was slowly counting out change from the bottom of her purse, a penny at a time, complaining about the high cost of everything as she paid for an $0.89 part for the back of the toilet. When I was done checking out and returned to my car, the old woman had just finished making her way across the tiny parking lot. She bent gingerly as she got into the car, throwing the package across the front seat to her husband. He sat on the passenger side, the cane on the floor riding up between his legs. He fumbled with the package she threw him, trying to figure out how to open it, and I wondered how he was going to attach the part to the toilet once he got home – if he made it home, if his wife's driving didn't kill him before then. She pulled the seat all the way up to the windshield and hit the gas, snapping her husband's head back as the car lurched forward into traffic. I sat in my car for a long time after they left, crying.

That old couple was supposed to be my parents one day, then us. Fifty-plus years of marriage, a cardigan sweater over a flannel shirt in the summer heat, teeth absent-mindedly left in a glass above the bathroom sink as we take our coupon from the newspaper and head off to the coffee shop for our $1.79 breakfast special, eaten for dinner at four-thirty in the afternoon amidst complaints that the mailman came at 10:15 rather than 10:00.

Why didn't my folks get the chance to be that old couple? Why didn't we? Why did my mom have to leave us? Why did you have to die?

Why can't my mom and dad be enjoying retirement together at the cottage, holding hands as they walk in the woods, sitting quietly together as they read by the fireplace, smiling back at each other as they ride the boat across the lake into the setting sun?

Why does my dad have to be alone? Why didn't my folks get the next twenty years they thought they had before them? Why did my mom have to die?

I think maybe I finally grew up the day she died. You're no longer a child once you don't have a mother. I had planned on trying to be a better person in her honor. I was going to be a better son to my dad, a better father to my children, a better husband to my wife. I was going to try to live on the outside what I felt on the inside. I was going to rededicate my life to life, to the gift we all rent but don't own. Then suddenly you were gone, and the already shaky ground I was standing on began to crumble beneath me. I fell faster and farther than I could ever have imagined possible.

Why did you have to die? Why can't we be growing old together, sharing the years my folks had stolen from them, sharing the years we too were robbed of? Why can't we be lying in bed right now, reading a book to the girls? Why can't we be looking forward to having our grandchildren sleep over one day? Why can't we be planning out our retirement years together, when we would once again have time for each other? Why can't I be vacationing in Arizona, with you?

We had that once-in-a-lifetime feeling together, Christine, you and I. Now that feeling is only a memory. Now all I feel is that Sunday-night feeling you used to get in college, when I'd have to get on the bus and go back to school, and you'd feel all empty and hollow, fearing the lonely week that lay ahead. I've lived with that Sunday-night feeling every day of my life since you've gone.

Do you remember the old morning routine, when I'd sit sideways on the closed toilet seat, coffee mug between my hands, feet up on the little stool the girls used to reach the sink, and we'd talk? You'd be getting ready for work, just out of the shower, standing naked in front of the sink. I used to look at you, knew every inch of your body, every curve, every blemish. Yet, as well as we knew each other, as close as we'd grown, there were times when I'd look at you and wonder to myself who you were, wonder exactly what went on inside you, what made you tick. You could always tell when I was thinking that. You knew me so well, in an unquestioning way; knew me better than I knew myself. You were more than the love of my life. You were my friend.

Do you know I've been making a new friend?

She's different from you, in her own unique ways. Little things I didn't notice at first, then noticed in comparison. Like the way she quietly sits back and plays with her necklace when she's nervous, while you leaned forward and confronted your fears; like the way she can't read a map, while you always gave me directions; like the way she dips her hand in her nearly full water glass after a meal, while you always drank your glass dry; like the way she bounds down a trail on a hike, while you always walked slowly and peacefully; like the way she cut her hair short, while you kept yours long.

Will these cute little mannerism's continue to delight, or will some of them become an annoyance over time, as a few did with you? And what of the things I don't yet know, but want to find out?

There are differences, yes, but similarities as well, and she reminds me of you in so many ways. I'm certain the two of you would have been friends, if only you'd had the chance.

Maybe I'm getting that feeling again because she reminds me of you, and I worry about that. I worry she'll wonder, when I look into her eyes, if I'm seeing her clearly, or still seeing you. And I worry she'll always have a hint of doubt when she looks into my eyes – a slight bit of wonder about my love for her, and my love for you. She deserves better than that, deserves to know my love is complete, just as you knew my love for you was, just as I knew your love for me was.

You know how faithful I was to you when we were together. It was never a conscious decision, as if there were one to make. It was simply a fact that my heart and desires were reserved for you, and could never be given to another. I could never have cheated on you, in mind or body. With all that we shared, with all that we'd been through together, with all that we meant to each other, to be unfaithful to you would have been to be unfaithful to myself. Besides, you know if I'd ever strayed I would never have been able to look you in the eyes again.

I've remained faithful to you since you've gone, as I did when we were together. I've not thought of another, nor wanted to, since I've been without you. Until I met her.

She's one of the most beautiful women I've ever met, yet strangely enough I've never fantasized about her in the way you'd think a man who's been alone for three years might. I only desire to have her near me, to see her smiling face, to smell her hair, to hear her laughter, to hold her hand. Do you remember how we used to say that we never had sex, but only made love?

She mentioned once, in a letter, that she wanted to give me a son, someone to carry on the family name, someone to play football with in the yard after Packer games. The same words you said to me before you got pregnant, for the last time.

I wonder if she knows, wonder if I can ever tell her, how deeply her declaration affected me, too close to home for comfort. It would be selfish of me, and not fair to her, to deny her the chance to have children of her own, to experience the joy and the special love that only a mother can know. That feeling you had for the girls as you held them in your arms for the first time, the new life that came from you, from us. I don't know if I could live through another pregnancy, so hard I've tried to bury the unhappy memories of the last one, so difficult it is for me to watch the three-year-old boys I see all around me, playing in the dirt with their trucks, swinging on the playground in the park, standing next to their fathers in the men's room. She'll be such a wonderful mother, I'm sure, just as you were, just as my mom was, and I'm afraid I'll be left with no choice but to live through my fear, because I can't deny her her dreams.

She's so good with our girls, and they're so taken with her, and I truly believe she genuinely loves them. If the truth be told, the girls could probably use the love of a woman in their lives again. I've tried so hard, since you've gone, to be both father and mother, but know I can never replace all that only you could give them. I can't do their hair like you did, or shop for nice dresses. I can't pick out earrings, or accessorize outfits. I can't hold them the same way when they cry, or laugh with them the same way about boyfriends gone by. I can't explain womanhood to them, or how to deal with their father. And the coming of puberty has me scared to death! The girls need a mother, Christine, and I wish every day that it could be you, but it can't.

The girls really like her, love her, I think, and likely did long before I could admit the same. I'm happy for them, for they've found a new friend, though I'm worried as well, for I fear that in finding her, they may lose you.

They were so young when you left them, too young, I fear, to have the lasting memories of you that they should, for their sake, and yours. When my mom died the loss was so deep, though at least I had a trunk full of memories to keep her alive in my heart. The girls have not the same filled trunk, but only a tiny box, and I worry they'll forget you. Yet I sense that she won't let that happen, that she'll be comfortable with you and honor your memory, make sure that you live on in the girls' minds, and in their hearts.

She'll do the same for me, I think, and be at peace with my memories of you, of us. She'll find some excuse to be gone for the day, each year, on our wedding anniversary, to leave me alone with you. She'll let the girls and me celebrate your birthday, alone, without her, without you. For she'll know she can never replace you in my heart, only share it with you. She'll be content with the portion she has, not resentful of the portion she doesn't.

But I'm making excuses, using others to mask my own feelings. I can't hide behind the girls and the way they feel about her. I can't hide behind her and the way she'll honor your memory. I can't hide behind you and my worries over how you might feel. I have to be honest – with you, and with myself. I have to face up to my own feelings, face up to the way I feel about her, face up to the fact that I can't imagine living my life without her, just as I couldn't have imagined living my life without you.

Do you read my letters, Christine? Are you really out there, like I believe, watching over me, still a part of me? Do you know how much I miss you? Do you know how much I love you, still? Do you know how lonely I've been? Do you know how alive Colleen has made me feel? Do you see her too, as you look down on us all? Do you like her? Are you happy for me?

Or was I right when I thought you'd be jealous, or hurt, if someone else worked her way into my heart, next to you?

I worried for the longest time about how you'd feel if I ever felt this way about another, worried that I'd lose you if I ever loved again. I know now that what we had can never be taken away, nor diminished in any way. You'd no more be unhappy about what's happened than I could ever forget you. I believe you're smiling as you look down on me now, just as certainly as I know we'll be together again one day, reunited in our love. We'll all be together someday, the three of us, old friends.

In the end, the old softy with the glass heart got a happy ending to the romance novel he couldn't see he was living. I'll not ask for your blessing, for I know that I have it. Watch over us all, and be happy for us, as happy as we were together, as happy as I now hope to be, as happy as when we'll be together again.

I love you, Christine.

My Love Always,
Brian

~

Colleen looked up from the letter. She was completely alone in the world, her mother having just left, her dear brother already gone. Yet for the first time in her life she felt whole, completely whole.

She called work, telling them she wouldn't be in tomorrow, or next week, or maybe ever. She changed her clothes, putting on her sandals and cutoffs, and Brian's white shirt. She took the pictures of The Door off the wall and put them in her duffel bag, along with the book he had sent, and the girls' fridge drawings. She wrote a short note in her journal, then picked up Brian's letter, got in her car, and drove off.

~

May 12
Dear Brenden,

Good-bye from Arizona.

I'll see you when I get to The Door!

Leeny

~

It was a warm spring afternoon in The Door. The ice had long since melted off the lake, the buds had all opened to leaves, and the once brown grass was now a lush green. White blossoms filled the cherry trees, their scent riding across the warm gentle breeze that blew in the open window, filling the room with the hope of things to come. Shannon and Kerry sat at the piano, playing a recently learned duet for Grandpa and Brian.

The tune complete, the applause subsided, they took their old-fashioneds and kiddie cocktails and returned to the front porch to sit and chat as they waited for the grill to heat up. The cold darkness of winter a thing of the past, they looked out before them, down the hill, over the marsh, and across the shimmering waters of the lake, at the breath of life that is spring. They were too busy enjoying the view to notice the car that drove over the causeway and came to a stop at the base of the hill.

~

Colleen pulled over to the side of the road and turned off the car. Resting her hands on the wheel, she looked out the window at the old farmhouse perched atop the hill. They were all there, sitting on the porch together as if waiting for her, the four people who would be her life from now on.

Grandpa, the father figure she never knew, who even through his own loss and pain had never stopped being a father to his son, watching over him. Shannon and Kerry, the two little girls she already thought of as her own, who wanted only for their father to be happy again. And Brian, her Brian, who could love so deeply, and had had his love returned, only to lose it. Had he found it again, with her?

Colleen got out of the car and closed the door behind her. She walked up the hill toward the tree-lined gravel driveway, the path that led the way into the lives of the people on the porch.

~

They sat on the steps of the front porch, the girls on Grandpa's lap, Brian off to the side, poking a stick into the grill, stirring the coals. They each noticed someone turn off the road and walk up the long driveway toward them.

"I wonder who that could be," Grandpa said as they focused on the approaching visitor.

"It's Colleen! It's Colleen!" the girls shouted together, struggling to free themselves from Grandpa's tightening grip.

Brian stepped away from the grill, his face a mix of delight and bewilderment as he looked out at Colleen, then turned toward Grandpa.

"I wonder if she got that letter that was sitting on top of the flatiron book," Grandpa winked, restraining the girls as Brian stepped down off the porch and walked toward her.

They met at the corner of the porch, in the spot where he had first seen her nearly a year before. He opened his arms and she flew into them, throwing hers around his neck.

"I've come for my piano," she said, looking up at him.

"It's not leaving, and neither are you," he answered as he bent to kiss her.

～

The girls bounced excitedly on Grandpa's lap as he looked on approvingly.

"Do you think my dad will be happy now?" Kerry asked.

"And Colleen, too?" Shannon added.

"And Grandma, and your mom," Grandpa answered. "I think we'll all be happy again."

The End

Epilogue

~

*T*hey were married a few weeks later, on the anniversary of the day they first met, in a simple ceremony on the stage in the park, the lilting sound of an Irish folk song rising from the piano beside them. Colleen wore her sandals and cutoffs, and Brian's white shirt. The girls, her bridesmaids, wore the t-shirts she'd sent them from Arizona. Grandpa served as best man, standing beside his son. Brian wore his boots and jeans, and the fancy shirt with the thin gray stripes – the one Christine had bought, and Colleen suggested – a single white rose pinned over the pocket, matching the bouquet she held.

They took pictures on top of the old fire tower after the ceremony, then had nachos and root beer at Wilson's, taking an order of fries to go, for the gulls. They finished off the festivities with a round of Booger Ball Bowling at the ice cream store in Baileys Harbor, Grandpa getting a northbound boat trailer doubler. The girls slept at Grandpa's that night, in the loft above him as he lay in bed writing in the cottage book, the box of Maggie's letters by his side.

Mary Brigid Bailey was born the following March, on Maggie's birthday. Grandpa served as godfather for his new granddaughter, the girls as co-godmothers to their new sister. Michael Brenden Bailey was born at the end of the following football season, on the day the Green Bay Packers won another Super Bowl.

~